D0831191

THE MELTING MAN

THE
MELTING MAN

*

VICTOR CANNING

THE
COMPANION BOOK CLUB
LONDON

This edition is published by
The Hamlyn Publishing Group Ltd.
and is issued by arrangement with
William Heinemann Ltd.

Made and printed in Great Britain
for the Companion Book Club
by Odhams (Watford) Ltd.
S.1169.UBN.
600773108

CHAPTER ONE

'O, how that glittering taketh me!'
ROBERT HERRICK

I HAD MY FEET UP on the window sill, watching the pageantry of life outside. It didn't amount to much. The cab driver at the head of the rank was reading the morning edition of the *Evening Standard* and smoking a cheroot. A handful of early fallen leaves from the plane trees did a little dervish dance in the wind. A coloured gent went by in a big, blue bedspread. He had a beaming 250-watt smile on his large face that could only have come from transcendental meditation or a new and satisfactory addition to his harem. A traffic warden was booking a Mini-Austin for parking on a yellow kerb line. Two girls went by on the far pavement; one had blonde hair and a face that would have made Botticelli's eyes pop, the other carried a transistor set and sucked at an ice-lolly. A porter polished a brass plate. A pigeon bullied a couple of sparrows in the gutter. Two businessmen hurried towards Trafalgar Square, bowlers set, brief-cases and umbrellas at the ready.

I got tired of the pageant and looked at my feet. The suède shoes wanted a good going over with a wire brush. My green socks didn't look good with a dark suit. I didn't care much. At this time of the year lethargy and sloppiness always seemed to set in. In another five days I would be off on holiday. The battery wanted recharging. Pretty soon, I thought, I must decide where I was going.

The office door opened behind me. I didn't turn. I knew it was Wilkins: Hilda Wilkins, thirty-five, spinster, rusty red hair, honest blue eyes (too honest), thick tweed skirt, plain white blouse, sloppy grey cardigan—no oil painting, my partner, and the bond between us unshakable. There was little about me

5

that she approved of. I sometimes wondered why she stayed. Certainly not for the salary.

She said, 'I'm going to the bank.'

I turned.

'Put or take?'

'Take,' she said. 'I've switched the office phone through here.'

I said, 'I didn't think there was any to take.'

'A little. Have you decided where you're going?'

'No. Nor who I'm going with. Or should it be whom?'

She sniffed, and backed for the door. She had no opinion of my morals or my grammar.

I said, 'I thought about the Gritti Palace in Venice.'

She said, 'Why not—if you're only staying one night? You'd do better with your sister in Honiton. You'd eat free.'

'It's a point. Devonshire cream and cider, great rashers of bacon, fried eggs, chitterlings, black puddings, roast pork, boiled beef and dumplings. . . . Yes, I need feeding up.'

She looked pointedly at my lowest waistcoat button and said, 'That's not the impression I get.'

She went, and I looked down. Maybe she was right. Life had been sedentary lately. I looked at the calendar on the wall opposite and because I had nothing else to do I wondered how many more shopping days there were to Christmas. I couldn't bother to work it out.

The telephone rang. I let it ring a while and then picked it up.

I said, 'Carver and Wilkins. Can I help you?'

A man's voice said primly, 'I wish to speak to Mr. Rex Carver.'

I said, 'Hold on a moment, I'll see if he's in.'

I put the phone down and lit a cigarette. It was a small office, just Wilkins and myself and a little outside help when we were pressed. It didn't hurt, though, to give the impression of a big organization. And, anyway, years of experience had given me a sixth sense that could always pick a new client on the line. I was going on holiday, somewhere, and I didn't want to be tied up just then with some crumby recovery job or an insurance fiddle or wearing my feet out looking for some man or woman who didn't want to be found.

I picked up the phone.

'I'm sorry, Mr. Carver is not available at the moment.'

'You mean he's not there?' He sounded as though he weren't used to people not being there when he wanted them.

'I'm afraid not. He's out.'

'Then would you take a message?'

'Certainly.'

'Tell him it's from Mr. Cavan O'Dowda's secretary. Mr. O'Dowda's car will call for him at three today. I think it would be advisable if he brought an overnight bag.'

I said, 'Does Mr. Carver know about this appointment?'

A little irritated, the voice said, 'Of course he knows. I wouldn't be phoning to confirm it otherwise. The car will be there at three o'clock. Thank you.'

There was a click and he was gone.

Interesting. But not enough to make me get up and check the O'Dowda's in the London telephone directory. I needed a holiday, not work. Mind you, I needed money too. I always needed it, and sometimes when the need was great I wasn't too fussy how I got it. But just now—so long as there was a little in the bank—I needed complete rest and relaxation. I sat there and thought of all the places I could go to. I had a friend who'd retired to Malta to beat the tax game—but that would mean sailing and I hated pulling away at sheets, the kind you find on yachts, anyway. The Costa Brava? Fish and chips, ghastly *gazpacho*, and even ghastlier flamenco singing. Biarritz? Quiet, Edwardian—only it wasn't any longer. Just big, bustling and noisy, the streets full of Citroens and the Atlantic filling your face full of wind-blown spume and sand the moment you went over the dunes. Somewhere quiet, way up at the back of Cannes? Well, I might find that; peace, solitude and relaxation under some grape-festooned arbour, swigging *vin rosé* in the morning to taper off from the previous night's Pernod. Fine, all except the solitude. I'd have to have company to beat that.

7

I'd almost worked up enough energy to reach for my address book in the desk drawer when the phone rang. I changed my hand direction and picked it up.

Wilkins said, 'I'm back.'

'Good. The office wasn't the same without you.' When she didn't reply, I said, 'Did you make an appointment for me with a Mr. O'Dowda?'

'No.'

'That's good then.'

I put the receiver down and forgot about my address book. They'd all have some excuse anyway. I could break fresh ground, of course. Perhaps a cruise, if I could get a booking. No, they were all so damned hearty, betting on the day's run, deck quoits, table-tennis and that bloody fancy dress thing, and, anyway, all the unattached girls were too soon swiped by the officers. You can't compete with a uniform and that deep sea-tan.

My private outside line rang. I got the receiver to my ear with an effort.

'Carver here.'

Migg's breezy, booming ploughman's voice made me wince.

'How are we, me old cock? Haven't had you here for a work-out in a month. I'll bet you can't see your Poupart's ligament for fat and if there's a depression over your great trochanter I'm a Dutchman.'

'Go away and carry on with your drinking.'

'Stone sober. Have to be in this job. But come round and we'll have a couple. Also, I've got something for you.'

'Anything you've got you can keep. But I'll come for the drink—that's if my rectus muscles can make it.'

In the outer office Wilkins was knitting something in a bilious yellow wool and doing the *Daily Telegraph* crossword.

'Going to see Miggs,' I said.

She gave me a look and said, 'Don't forget to have some lunch. And why did you ask me about Cavan O'Dowda?'

'I didn't say his name was Cavan.'

She nodded to the equipment panel on her desk. 'I left the recorder on.'

'Know him?'

'I've heard of him. He's—'

'Don't bother to tell me. I've only one problem at the moment. Where to go for a holiday.'

I flexed my legs and went out.

I went down the stairs and stood in the doorway, looking out into Northumberland Avenue. Away up to my left Nelson was standing on his column turning a blind eye to the assault of pigeons and starlings. To my right the brass plate which said *Carver and Wilkins* wanted polishing. It had just been *Carver*, until in a more than usually bad year Wilkins had insisted on emptying the old tea-caddy on the mantelshelf at home (where she lived with her father, a retired ship's steward and an indefatigable but not very successful player of the horses) and coming to the rescue—with a look in her eyes which dared me to show even a two-second flash of gratitude. Without saying anything to her I had had the plate changed. From its present state I knew that somebody soon was going to get hell about it.

I went down to Miggs's place. It was hard work for a man in my lackadaisical state but I stuck to it, the whole of four hundred yards.

Behind his garage Miggs had a gymnasium. His charges were salty, but his appointment book was always full. Miggs had once been a sergeant in the Commandos. After a work-out with him, a really fit man would discover he was aching in about a dozen muscles he never knew he had. For special clients—and he had quite a few of them—he ran a course in unarmed combat which comprised some very fancy ways of killing a man swiftly and silently.

He was finishing a session when I got there, so I went and sat quietly in his office. He came in, his red face shining from a shower, took one look at me and said, 'My God—a young man in an old man's body. You'd better let me book you in for a dozen sessions. Special price for you.'

'I'm happy the way I am. I like to put it on around

9

September. Live off my fat during the winter. Bears do it. What about a drink?'

He opened a cupboard and brought out the whisky.

We sat and drank and he shook his head sadly at me, his eyes running disappointedly over me as though he were a sculptor and I his first clay mock-up for a Greek athlete which had gone wrong everywhere it possibly could.

'A job is just what you need. But before you get stuck into it, you report here for a few days.'

'A holiday is what I need—and what I'm having.'

'A holiday can wait—but good money can't. You take the job. There could be a lot to make on the side, too. That's what you like, isn't it? Anyway, the cropped-headed bastard has got more than he knows what to do with—not that he throws it around without being sure of a return. These millionaires never do.'

'What I like,' I said, 'is someone who doesn't talk in riddles, and a higher percentage of whisky to my soda.' I pushed my glass towards him and he obliged.

'Didn't you get my message?'

'No.'

'I phoned your Mrs. Meld last night and gave it to her.'

'Today is Monday. I spent the weekend at Brighton and came straight into the office this morning off the train. Do I gather you've been trying to fix me up with a job?'

'Have done. He said he'd send a car for you at three today.'

'Presumptuous.'

'Not when it's a millionaire. His son was killed alongside me in Italy. He's always had a soft spot for me and gives me all his car business. Makes Jack Barclay and those types mad because it's all Rolls and Bentley stuff and he changes on whim four or five times a year sometimes. I delivered a Facel Vega to him yesterday—he's giving it to his daughter as a birthday present.'

'I always wanted a millionaire daddy. What do you think of Ireland for a holiday?'

'Nothing. All those bars they call Select which turn out to be a table and three chairs in half a grocer's shop. And then their screwy attitude to the weather. You step out of your hotel into driving rain and wind and the doorman says 'It's a grand day, sor." In addition I don't like Guinness or John Jameson.'

'Ireland's out then.'

'So take the job. I gave you a good write-up. Honest, reliable, intrepid and the soul of discretion. Quick in a tight corner, resourceful, and a contempt for all hazards.'

'Nice. Add a pair of wings and I'd be Batman. I presume you're talking about Mr. Cavan O'Dowda?'

'Didn't I say?'

'No. But don't bother. I don't want any job. I'm going on holiday.'

'You take the job.'

'Which is?'

'Somebody stole one of his cars.'

I laughed. Anyone at Scotland Yard would have done, too. By now it would have been cannibalized—number filed off the engine block and restamped, gear-box changed, number on the chassis plate changed—resprayed and up for auction with a phoney log-book in some car mart, or sitting abandoned around Hackney after a couple of villains had used it for a job.

I said, 'Let the police worry. Not that they will.'

'There's more to it than that. It wasn't stolen in England.'

'Where?'

'Abroad somewhere. He didn't say. And I don't think it's the car he's really worried about, though he pretended it was.'

'I don't want a job. September I always take a holiday.'

'Just go and see him. After all, I said you would, and if I let him down he might take his business from me.'

'I'd weep if I didn't know you were lying.'

'Just see him. If you turn him down, that's okay. But I gave you the build-up of all time. The daughter was there, the Facel Vega one—you should have seen her eyes shining as I painted your picture. Though I must say, I thought you were in better shape than you are. Still . . .'

'Thanks for the drink.' I reached for the door.

'You're going?'

'To have lunch. I've been instructed not to miss it.'

'You disappoint me.'

'I disappoint me, sometimes. But I need a holiday. Sometimes a man has got to get away.'

'What for?'

'I'll send you a postcard and let you know.'

I went.

And there it was. A man should always know what he wants to do and, if he can, why he wants to do it. And what I didn't want to do was to chase some stolen car. Let O'Dowda buy another car. And if there was more to it than just a stolen car, well, let someone else worry about it. That's what Scotland Yard, Interpol, the Deuxième Bureau, and the Garda Civile were for. Yes, eleven months of the year I worked, if it was there to work at, but come September, season of mists and mellow fruitfulness, I took a holiday.

But not this September.

At four o'clock that afternoon I was sitting in a Rolls-Royce going like a hot knife through butter along the A 21, heading down into Sussex.

The explanation was very simple and touchingly human. Herrick had the lines for it of course, not only because he had her name right, but because he was a Devonshire man like me and, contrary to the ploughboy school of thought, Devonshire men are great romantics, particularly when as in silks a woman goes and all that about how sweetly flows the liquefaction of her clothes to finish with the real punch line—'O, how that glittering taketh me!'

It took me, in twenty seconds dead.

At two minutes to three I had my heels up on the desk and was reading for light relief the August copy of *The Criminologist* —for some reason the Forensic Publishing Co. Ltd. always sent me complimentary copies. I was well into an article on 'The Forensic Aspects of Dust' when the intercom buzzed like a tired hornet and Wilkins came on.

'Mr. Cavan O'Dowda's car has arrived for you.'

'Send it away.' I switched off.

Analyses of ordinary household dusts, I read, show a fine line-up of materials like silica, oxides of aluminium and iron, magnesia, lime, titanium oxide, alkalis—

The buzz came again.

Wilkins said, 'Mr. O'Dowda's driver would like to see you.'

'Tell Mr. O'Dowda's driver,' I said, 'that I made no appointment to go to his employer. Tell him—if he's interested in personal details—that I don't want a job. I want a holiday. Tell him—'

Wilkins cut me off, fearing no doubt some more telling expression.

Three seconds later the door of my office opened. I looked up, and of course that was fatal. I was hit straight between the eyes.

She looked at me for a moment or two in silence while I blinked to get the glittering out of my eyes. Then she closed the door and came slowly across to the desk. It was pure lique-faction with even a little sweet disorder in the dress. Not much, just a hint of it. It was a grey silk dress shot with tiny gold and silver threads that helped to roll the light over each moving swing and curve and stretch. If you can imagine a dress that might have been made out of water with gold and silver sun-ripples on it then I needn't say more. There was a jaunty little bow at the lowish vee of the neck, like some butterfly poised for flight. If it took off, I thought, it would kindle in her clothes a wantonness.

She said, 'What is all this? I've come all the way up to London for you.'

With an effort I said, 'If you're Mr. O'Dowda's chauffeur, that's a wonderful uniform you're wearing.'

'Don't be an ass. I'm his daughter, Julia.'

I stood up. I wouldn't have done it for a chauffeur, but a millionaire's daughter was different. And even if she hadn't been a millionaire's daughter I would have done it. She was in her early twenties and her hair was as dark as a raven's wings and her lips cherry bright. Her face was tanned, her dark eyes had a what-the-hell look, and there was a suggestion of stubbornness about the nicely pointed chin. Her face was beautiful, a bit gipsyish, but full of self-confident sparkle. Angry or excited, I decided, she would be hard to handle.

She was taller than I, but I didn't mind. You can't have too much of a good thing. I just stood there, quivering finely like a pointer, waiting for the command to flush game.

She said, 'It's a nice dress, isn't it? Jacques Fath,'

I said, 'I can't keep my eyes off it. I'm Rex Carver.'

With a little lift of her eyes for my persisting stupidity, she said, 'I know you are. But you don't quite come up to the description Miggs gave of you. Sort of blurred around the edges somewhere.'

'Come autumn,' I said, 'I begin to disintegrate a little. My best month is May.'

She looked at her watch—I caught the faint sparkle of a diamond setting—and said, 'I can't wait until then, neither can my father. Are you coming or not?'

'I was thinking,' I mumbled, 'of taking a holiday.'

'You look,' she said, 'as though you could do with one. I'll tell my father you're not available.' She turned for the door.

I went across the room and picked up my weekend case.

'You're bullying me,' I said. 'But I don't mind. For you I would go anywhere.' I gave her a big smile. It was an effort, but I thought it worth it. 'Julia O'Dowda. It's a wonderful name. Wild Irish, a strong Connemara wind whistling through your hair and—'

She moved to the door, saying, 'I'm his stepdaughter. The name's Julia Yunge-Brown. And on the way down you'll sit in the back. I don't like a hand on my knee as I drive. Okay?' The dark eyes, faintly smiling, fixed me.

'Okay,' I said.

Obediently I followed her through into the office. Wilkins looked up at me woodenly.

I said, 'The next time you use the word "driver" over the phone, qualify the sex. I'm being led into captivity.'

Julia, ahead of me, giggled. It was a nice sound, like a fast brook tumbling over stones.

Wilkins said, 'I'll phone Mrs. Meld to say you won't be back tonight.'

It wasn't the Facel Vega, but a big black Rolls, looking a bit like a hearse and as quiet in the back as a funeral parlour. Clipped into a silver holder alongside me was a speaking horn.

Going over Westminster Bridge, I whistled down it and then said, 'What happened to the regular chauffeur?'

Horn to my ear, I got the reply: 'Tich? He's gone fishing with my father. Stepfather.'

I said, 'What's all this about a stolen car?'

'Something to do with Zelia. She's always messing things up.'

'Zelia?'

You had to be quick with the trumpet thing, but it was fun for a long journey.

'My sister. You'll get all the details.'

'Where are we going?'

'Sussex. Near Sedlescombe. You'll be just in time for the evening rise.'

'Evening what?'

She nipped between a bus and a petrol tanker, and then said, 'Stop talking. There are magazines in the rack in front of you.'

I fiddled for a bit and got the rack down. It held the latest numbers of *Vogue*, *The Field*, *Illustrated London News*, *Playboy* and *Reveille*. And also a half-empty box of cigars, Bolivar Petit Coronas. I lit one and settled back with *Playboy*.

Once we were clear of London she drove the car as though she wished to God it had wings, half-hoping, maybe, that if she did go fast enough it would take off. Anyone riding in it might not have been able to hear the clock ticking in the silence, but they would have heard my heart going *bump*, *bump* against the roof of my mouth. I began to regret my hasty impulse. A good-looking gipsy girl walks into your office, wearing a Fath number that would cost more than your cigarette bill for a year, gives you a what-the-hell look and there you are—every good resolution gone, back at work again when you should be on holiday.

I didn't try to keep track of where we were going, but it took us an hour and a half. Finally we turned in through lodge gates, the pillars ornamented with stone greyhounds, each holding a shield. I couldn't see the device on the shields because we went by too quickly. We then did a half a mile of drive through parkland. Up ahead I saw the big bulk of a country mansion, but I didn't get a long look at it because we turned off, away from the drive and down a long slope through beech and fir trees with dirty, dank-looking rhododendron growths under them.

We came through the trees and the side drive ended in a wide circular turning space below a high grass bank. Julia swung the car round and stopped. She sat in the driving seat while I got out and went up to her.

'Stimulating drive,' I said. 'Tonic for the nerves. When you get her back in the stables, give her a good rub down and a handful of oats. But don't let her drink for a while. Sometime you can take me out in the Facel Vega and we'll really enjoy ourselves.'

She looked at me thoughtfully, up and down and then down and up, as though I were a piece of antique furniture, a tallboy or something she fancied she might fancy, and then she said, 'You've got something. Just something—but I suspect you're trying too hard with it.'

'Or just out of practice. All I need is a few days' country air. Where's Daddy?'

'Daddy is someone you want to be bloody polite with.'

I knew then what it was that had boosted me off my office cushion. She was a border-line girl. Somebody you could go either way with. Get her wrong, rub the knap the reverse way, and you had, not an enemy for life (there's always hope there), but someone who just obliterated you from her memory. But get her right, handle her with the capable, finessing touch of a master, and you had a star-spangled carnival stretching ahead of you. But there wasn't any hope of that unless you were at the top of your form.

I winked at her. 'I've dealt with millionaires before. They handle easily so long as you let them know it's their money you're after. Where is he?'

'Up over the bank. Just ring for him. You can leave your bag. I'll take it up to the house.'

She started the engine.

Before she could move off, I said, 'What is it about step-daddy that you don't like?'

I got it then, full and square for the first time; a cold, dark stare that came from surprise she was not quite able to hide. She put her foot down and the Rolls swung away from me and back into the beech trees.

I lit a cigarette and climbed a flight of stone steps to the top of the grass bank. It was a dam, grassed on this side and faced with concrete slabs on the other. Along the top of it ran a grass walk, mowed tight. Stretching away from it was an artificial lake of about thirty acres. It was fringed with pine woods and backed at the far end by a hill studded with great oaks. On the far bank, away to my left at the end of the dam, was a boat-house and a landing pier that projected twenty yards into the water. Way out in the centre of the lake I could see a rowing boat with two men in it.

I walked along the dam towards the landing pier. A couple of pigeons came over the pines, a pheasant called from some-where back in the beeches and a flight of duck got up from shallows at the far side of the lake. It was a good spot and, from the state of the damworks, the boat-house and pier, I guessed that it hadn't long been constructed. It must have cost O'Dowda a packet. Nice, I thought, when you couldn't get away to Ireland or Scotland, to have your own fishing on the doorstep.

I made my way past the boat-house on to the pier. A fibre-glass hull with an outboard was tied up alongside. At the end of the pier was a vertical wooden post, rather like a small gallows, with a big brass bell hanging from it. I gave the tongue of the bell a whang or two. The noise rolled out across the water and I sat down, legs dangling over the edge of the pier, to wait for the rowing boat to come in.

The men in the boat took no notice of me, though they must have heard the bell. I sat where I was, content to finish my cigarette. They'd heard. They would come when they were ready. One thing you can't do is to hurry a millionaire. If I took the job, I decided, I'd add 5 per cent for being kept waiting. A water-rat swam leisurely out from under the pier and headed for the iris beds up the bank. A swallow dipped near the dam and made a ring like a trout rising. A hundred feet up a heron went over the pines, legs trailing, unhurried, a real dowager of a bird. There was sun and some cloud, a little ripple on the water from a faint breeze, a perfect day. Out on the lake I caught the sudden shine of sun on wet lines as one of the men false-casted. I didn't mind waiting. It suited my mood. I was almost at peace with the world.

The next moment I was almost right out of it.

Two things happened, simultaneously it seemed to me. First the crack of a rifle, and then the thud of a bullet smacking into the bell-post three inches above my head. A chip of wood flipped by me and curved out over the water. Before it hit the surface I was on my feet, running for the shelter of the boathouse.

CHAPTER TWO

'A bright torch, and a casement ope at night,
To let the warm Love in.'

JOHN KEATS

WHOEVER IT WAS took another shot at me just before I reached
the boat-house. The bullet whined overhead, too close for
comfort. Angry, frightened and short of breath, I reached the
shelter of the side of the boat-house.

I looked back along the pier. The two men were fishing on
the lake, not even looking in my direction. There's nothing
like a fisherman for being truly absorbed in his sport.

I poked my head round the far side of the boat-house and
eyed the near pines. To my surprise a man in jeans and a
Windbreaker came out of the cover of the trees and began to
run up the side of them. In his hand he carried a rifle.

Sportingly, I gave him fifty yards' start and then went after
him, doing a zig-zag along the outer row of pines so that I had
cover most of the way. The ground sloped gently upwards and
where the pines finished was a five-barred gate.

The man with the rifle vaulted it and stooped to pick
something out of the grass near the hedge on the other side.
It was a motor scooter. He slung the rifle over his back by the
sling. Seeing this, I sprinted. I saw the movement of his right
leg as he kicked the engine start.

I reached the gate just as he drove away fast down a rough
lane. I leaned on the gate and watched him, making a mental
note of the number of the scooter. JN 4839. Twenty yards
from me, he twisted his head back over his shoulder to look at
me. I gave him a wave and the bastard briefly waved back.
His face was coal-black.

I went slowly back to the pier wondering what I had done
to incur the wrath of the coloured races. Nothing as far as I

19

knew, recently. As I reached the end of the pier the boat was just pulling in.

It was being rowed by a little jockey of a man with a face like a shrivelled lemon. Round his neck was a pair of field-glasses. This, I guessed, was Tich, the chauffeur. He was in shirt and trousers and had a big cigar clamped into the corner of his mouth and on his head was an old cloth cap stuck about with trout-flies. Sitting in the stern, on a comfortable chair-arrangement which had been fitted, was Cavan O'Dowda.

While they made the last twenty yards I had time to get a good look at him. Standing, I reckoned he would go about six feet six, and he had more than the girth to go with it. He would have had trouble packing himself into any overnight sleeper. When he'd been made there must have been a lot of spare material lying around which they'd decided to get rid of. I put him at somewhere around sixty. He was wearing a light blue siren-suit and gum-boots. His head was pumpkin-shaped and large enough, if it had been one, to take a prize anywhere. So far as I could see he had no neck and his hair was so close-cropped that it looked like a faint powdering of red-brown dust. He was wearing dark Polaroid glasses and had a cigar clamped into the corner of his mouth. His hands were huge, backed with a faint down of ginger hair—but they were good hands, capable and sensitive, as I saw when he began to fish later.

As the boat steadied at the bottom of the pier steps, O'Dowda said, 'You Mr. Carver?'

'Just.'

He gave no sign of being aware of the irony.

'Get in,' he said.

As I went down the steps, he took off his glasses to rub his eyes and I saw that they were light blue, much too small for his face, and embedded in a puffy setting of fat wrinkles. He was not only the most unwholesome-looking millionaire I'd ever seen, he was the biggest as well.

I settled myself in the bow.

'Take her out again, Kermode.'

Tich began to pull away from the pier and I watched O'Dowda over the back of his head.

'Nice of you to come,' said O'Dowda. 'Good of Miggs to recommend you. He must make a couple of thousand every year out of me. Welcome, of course. Real character, Miggs. Thought we heard a shot back there just now.'

'Two,' I said. 'Somebody using your bell-post or me for target practice. I followed him up to the edge of the wood and he rode away on a scooter.'

The big face showed no surprise.

He just said, 'Kermode,' and nodded at a basket at the chauffeur's feet. Tich stopped rowing, dug in the basket and handed a flask over his shoulder to me. I unscrewed and swallowed. It could have been Courvoisier V.S.O.P. I handed the flask back. Tich took it with one hand and held the other out to me with a cigar in it. I lit up as he began rowing.

'Ever fished?' Irish his name might be but I couldn't hear a spot of accent. It was a big, resonant voice. If anything there was a transatlantic touch to it—Canadian, maybe.

'My father, rest his soul,' I said, 'taught me how to tie a turle knot when I was five.'

'And damn right he was. More fish have been lost from a boshed-up half-blood than most people know. Take Kermode's rod.'

The rod was at my side, half over the bows. It was a Hardy job and Tich had got a Bloody Butcher on the point and a couple of Invictas as droppers.

I said, 'What have you got in here?'

O'Dowda, beginning to fish, said, 'Rainbow and brown. And a few gillaroo. Know them?'

'No.'

'Irish. Find 'em in Lough Melvin and Erne. They don't do so well.'

I worked out some line, false-casted once or twice to get the feel of the rod—it was a beauty—and then made a cast of about twenty yards. It wasn't bad, considering I hadn't touched a rod for a year. I knew O'Dowda was watching me. O'Dowda, I reckoned, was a man who watched everything and everybody around him.

Tich held us in the wind-drift and we wet-fly-fished down the length of the lake. Halfway down I saw the quick water-bulge out by my flies and the sharp knock of a take. I struck, the line sang, and the rod-tip bowed. I played him for about five minutes and then he came in, tired, flashing his flanks, and Tich put the net under him. It was a rainbow on one of the Invicta droppers. A nice fish, just over two pounds, I guessed. I unhooked him and tapped his nose with the priest. He lay on the boards, the sunlight bringing up boldly the broad carmine band down his side, the bright colour that fades so soon with death. I looked at the bordering pine woods. The black bastard could easily come back.

'Not bad,' said O'Dowda. 'You can have him for dinner. The chef has a way of grilling 'em with a Parmesan cheese flavouring that's out of this world. Not enough to kill the flavour of the fish. Just enough to bring it up. Did you get any kind of look at the man who shot at you?'

'No. Not really. He was away before I was close enough. It has occurred to me, though, that he might come back.'

'He won't.'

'I'm glad to hear it.'

'Anyway, he wasn't after you. He was after me. Just made a target mistake. Badly briefed.'

We were in close to the tree-lined bank now. O'Dowda did a neat switch-cast and dropped his flies just off a clump of lily-pads. A moment later he was into a fish and Tich finally netted a big brown trout for him. Watching O'Dowda, I was wondering how badly briefed a man had to be to mistake me for him. If I took this job, I was thinking, there would have to be substantial danger money.

We fished for an hour. O'Dowda got three brace of brown trout. I got a brown and then hooked something that finally smashed my trace and got away.

'Must have been a big one,' I said.

'You rushed him a bit,' said Kermode.

'Out of practice,' said O'Dowda. Then he slewed his head at me and gave me a Polaroid look. 'Little fish land easy. Big fish . . . well, the time element is in geometric not arithmetic proportion. For big fish, you need time and patience. That's why I'm a millionaire.' He laughed and it was a sound like flood water rising rapidly in a underground tunnel. I didn't like the sound and—I had a strong feeling—I didn't like him.

O'Dowda looked at his watch and gave Kermode a nod. Kermode reached into the hamper at his feet and pulled out a hand microphone on a flex. He spoke into it.

'Mr. O'Dowda's car. Five minutes.'

He replaced the microphone and we began to row back to the landing stage.

O'Dowda saw me looking at the hamper, and said, 'Time and patience, Mr. Carver. And always keep in contact with the outside world. Life is full of sudden emergencies.'

I said nothing. I had no real quarrel with his philosophy. But you had to be a millionaire to be able to afford it.

There was a big navy blue Ford Zephyr station wagon waiting for us in the turning space when we arrived. In the driving seat was a small, neat-looking man of about forty. He had a bristly little toothbrush moustache, large teeth and hard agate-coloured eyes which he kept moist by constant blinking. I wasn't introduced to him but from the conversation I gathered that he was called Durnford and was O'Dowda's secretary.

The only item of conversational interest on the way to the house was O'Dowda saying, 'I want a full report on how that fellow got in, Durnford.'

'It's the public bridle path, sir.' His voice, even to O'Dowda, was clipped, sharp, just as he had been to me on the phone. 'We've got not legal right to close it.'

'Then find some other way.'

That was all. The millionaire's solution. No legal right—then find some other way.

The house was a great square construction of rag stone. You went through a small archway into an inner courtyard that was flagged with great paving stones and lined with a small raised walk, the balustrade of which was marked every few yards by nude classical statues, mostly of women with expressionless faces and large thighs. The entrance hall was small and one entered through mahogany doors which, I later learned, were steel-lined. O'Dowda and I got into a lift, went up two floors and stepped out into a long picture gallery. A manservant was waiting and O'Dowda instructed him to take me to my room. O'Dowda then gave me a nod and disappeared in one direction while I followed the manservant in the other, walking gingerly on the highly polished floor-boards to avoid slipping.

'Dinner,' said the servant as he left me, 'will be in one hour.'

'You'd better leave me a map of the place. Otherwise I'll get lost.'

'It won't be necessary, sir.' He went.

I had a bedroom and a bathroom. From the bedroom window I could see the park. Outside the window was a small balcony, big enough to take a deck-chair. Standing on it. I could see that all the other rooms on this side of the wing had similar balconies.

My Brighton pyjamas and dressing gown had been laid out on the downturned bed. There were cigarettes and a glass, siphon, water-jug, ice and four bottles on a silver tray on top of a low dressing table. The carpet gave little wheezy gasps as I trod on it. There were two water-colours of the fishing lake, and there wasn't a piece of furniture which didn't have the shining, well-kept patina of age. The bathroom was chrome and marble and the toilet flushed with just the hint of a faint sigh. The bath-towel was so big it really needed two men to handle it. I finished my inspection of the luxuries and went back to the silver tray to fix myself a whisky and soda. Underneath the soda siphon was a little piece of pasteboard with a message in ink on it.

I want to come and talk to you late tonight.
So don't scream when I arrive.

Julia.

I sipped my drink, staring out at the now darkening parkland. Titch Kermode wore field-glasses. He could have seen
the man run out of the woods. They would be good glasses
and they could have seen as much as I saw. And clearly, from
O'Dowda's remark to Durnford, the incident had been
reported over the radio to the house. If the two bullets had
been meant for O'Dowda then he was being remarkably calm
about it. If they were meant for me, then he was being
remarkably cavalier about his concern for a guest. But, as he
was a millionaire, I suppose he'd long ago given up having a
normal person's reaction to abnormal events. Not that that
made me any happier. And what the hell did Julia want?

I finished my drink and picked up the telephone by the
bed. It was a house-phone and somewhere, probably in some
basement office, a girl asked if she could help me. I gave her
Miggs's number. She said she'd call me, and I went and got
another drink.

Miggs came through in about three minutes. He started his
usual jossing act, but I cut through it and he knew at once
that it wasn't the time or place. I was willing to bet that every
phone call that went out of the house was monitored, or would
be for a guest of my standing.

I said, 'See if you can get me a line on a motor scooter,
don't know the make, number JN 4839. Gubby at the Yard
will do it for you, and you can let Wilkins know.'

'Okay. Will do.'

I put the phone down, and went through for a bath. The
cabinet held a wide range of bath essences. I chose Floris,
No. 89, and soaked for half an hour.

He was wearing a green smoking jacket, a loose white silk
shirt open at the neck, tartan trousers and black patent-leather
slippers. He had a glass of brandy in one hand and a cigar in

25

the other. I sat opposite him, similarly armoured, except that my cigar wasn't as big as his—my choice—and I hadn't been poured—his doing—so much brandy as he had given himself.

The manservant had come for me and escorted me to the dining room, a small private one off his study, where we had dined alone; a clear soup and sherry, the trout, lightly flavoured with Parmesan cheese and a good Mersault, and then fillet of beef, spinach *en branche*, roast potatoes and a claret that was nameless to me, out of the decanter, but which was so good that we had finished it between us. Overall he ate and drank twice as much as me, but I suppose given his size it was reasonable. Apart from that it was evident that he enjoyed the delights of the board for their own sake. In fact, I was sure that he was a man who enjoyed most of the world's delights for their own sake, which, of course, would make him dangerous if anyone got in the way of his getting what he wanted. Through dinner he had talked of fishing and his various houses. I didn't have to say anything. I just listened, and wondered when he would get around to business. Okay, he had this house, a London house, another in Cannes, a château just outside Evian, a flat in Paris, the fishing rights on an Irish river, the shooting over a few thousand acres of Scotland—oh, and an estate in the Bahamas where he went for the golf and big-game fishing—and, boy, wasn't it good to be alive and have all that. Not that he said that, but it was there. Naturally, as the claret mellowed me, I felt jealous. Why not? I've got nothing against wealth. I would have settled for a third of what he had and been happy for life. Not that I wasn't happy as I was, but a little more cash to go with it would have taken the greyness out of Monday mornings. I should add that somewhere in the catalogue he mentioned that he had six cars in the garage at this place, and quite a few in other places—so why was he concerned about the loss of a Mercedes 250SL? To him that was like losing a bicycle.

He fixed me now with his tiny, fat-set blue eyes, all comfortable in his chair, his tartan trews wrinkled up a little to show two inches of big, pale leg above his wrinkled black silk socks, and said, 'You don't seem to be in any hurry to talk business?'

I said, 'I haven't got any business with you. You have business with me. If it's urgent you'd have got it off your chest on the lake.'

He considered this to see whether he liked it then decided he had no feeling either way, and said, 'Miggs gave you a good write-up.'

I said, 'That's what friends are for. But sometimes they exaggerate.'

'How much do you make a year?'

It's funny. They can't keep away from it.

'Less than you spend on fishing and shooting—but if you're going to be a client, I'm hoping this is going to be a big year.'

He considered that, too, fractionally, before he laughed. Then, rather surprisingly, he said in a friendly voice, 'You've got the usual conventional idea about millionaires, haven't you? And you've picked one of the two conventional responses. Truculent, to-hell-with-you. The other is an anxious subservience. I get tired of both. Why not just be natural?'

'You're asking for the impossible. But I apologize if I sound truculent. Why not just tell me what the job is and let me get on with it—if I take it.'

'You'll take it—otherwise you wouldn't be here. Anyway, the job is simple. I've lost a motor car. To be exact a Mercedes-Benz 250SL. The registration is 828 Z-9626. It's red, hard-top, 1966 model . . .'

As he was talking I was thinking that I wouldn't have minded one myself. They sold in England at around three thousand pounds . . . elegant, distinctive lines, a car designed for zestful driving, modern without being tied to short-lived fashion, bold design and technical perfection . . . I could hear Miggs giving that patter if he were trying to sell one.

'It was lost, somewhere between Evian and Cannes. My stepdaughter Zelia was driving it. This was two weeks ago.'

He paused and blew a cloud of cigar smoke.

'You notified the police?'

'Yes. But I have no faith in them. They have their hands full of other stuff. They'll be content to wait until it turns up —or if it doesn't, well . . .'

He shrugged his shoulders.

'If it doesn't, will it break your heart? You're insured against theft, I presume?'

'Yes.'

'Then why do you particularly want this car back?'

'Let's say I do. I don't like losing things. I want it back and I want to know who's had it and where it has been. Every detail.'

We faced one another across almost immobile layers of cigar smoke.

I said, 'You want more than that.'

He smiled at me, cradling the brandy-glass in his big palms. 'Could be.'

'You want something that was in it.'

'Obviously.'

'Hidden in it?'

'Yes. Miggs was right about you.'

'Forget Miggs. A child could read the message. Did your daughter know that something was hidden in it?'

'No.'

'Does she now?'

'No.'

'Or your other daughter?'

'No. And I don't wish it to be known to either of them. Not that it concerns them in any way.'

'And am I to know what is hidden in it?'

'Not unless it becomes absolutely essential for the recovery of the car. Now ask the other question, Mr. Carver.'

'Which is?'

'Is whatever is in it something illegal, something prohibited by law, say, drugs, gold bullion, diamonds and so on.'

'Well?'

'It is nothing that would interest the police at all. Something purely private. Let's just say papers.'

28

'Did you inform the police of these hidden papers?'

'No.'

'Why not?'

'Because, admirable though police organizations are, if they knew I wanted the car because of the hidden papers in it, then the fact might leak out in their enquiries—and I don't want it to be known that I don't care a damn about the car, but only what is in it. The fewer people who know, the better. More brandy?'

I shook my head. He refilled his glass.

'Where,' I asked, 'did all this happen?'

'Some place on the way down to Cannes. Durnford will give you what details he has. But to get the full facts you will have to see Zelia. I'm hoping that you will get more out of her than I have been able to.'

'Why do you say that?'

'Although I'm very fond of her, she is very unsympathetic towards me. But the fact is that she stayed at a hotel on the way to Cannes. Next day she drove off. . . . Forty-eight hours later she turned up at Cannes without the car.'

'And what was her story?'

'She hasn't got one.'

'She's got a tongue. She's got to have a story.'

'Not Zelia. Her memory is a complete blank for those forty-eight hours.'

'You believe this?'

'I've had her examined by two of the best amnesia specialists in France. They confirm that she is suffering from loss of memory.'

'People sometimes forget because the truth is too unpleasant to remember.'

'Exactly.'

'And why would you think she'd open up for me?'

'I don't know that she will. In that case your job is so much harder. But if she hasn't lost her memory, then she might let something slip that will help. I want the car back. I want you to get it. I think you're the man to do it.'

29

'Because Miggs recommended me?'

'Originally, yes. Since then I've made other enquiries. They confirm Miggs entirely. You have weaknesses—some of which I share, I may say—but if you take a job you don't go back on it. Correct?'

'If the money is right.'

'You can write your own terms. See Durnford about that. You have *carte blanche* for all expenses while you work for me. Everything. That includes any temporary relaxation or pleasure calculated to keep you going in full trim on this job. Over and above all, I'll add a bonus of one thousand pounds you find the car and the papers.'

'Even though they may not now be in the car?'

'Quite so. But I think they are. No one could find them accidentally.'

I said, 'Why travel important papers in a car driven by your daughter who knew nothing about them?'

He smiled. 'Because they were important.'

'You could have mailed them from Evian to Cannes, registered.'

His smile broadened. 'Come, Mr. Carver. Don't tell me you've never heard of mail being lost in transit?'

'And a car can be stolen.'

'Life is full of uncertainties. Can you think of a foolproof way of moving a valuable object from one point to another?'

'No. Not if somebody else wants that valuable object or bunch of papers.'

'Exactly.'

I stood up.

'How many people knew that you were going to ask me down here?'

He stood up too.

'Myself, Julia, Tich Kermode, Durnford, some of the household staff, and Miggs, of course. And the two or three people from whom I made enquiries about you. Why?'

'Because I have a feeling that those two bullets today were meant for me.'

30

'I assure you they weren't.'

'Why are you so sure?'

'Because in the last month. I have had three telephone calls, threatening my life. And this evening, just after we got back, there was another. It was a man. If I remember the phrasing correctly it went: *You were lucky today. But I'll get you, you bastard.*'

He gave me a fat smile. He could have been lying, of course.

'You don't seem worried.'

'I may not show it, Mr. Carver, but I am. I like living. But anyway, the attempt on my life has nothing to do with this business. Do you want to see Durnford now, or in the morning?'

I looked at my watch. It was past twelve.

'He'll be in bed.'

'I can always get him up.'

Sure, if you're a millionaire what does another man's sleep mean? But I didn't feel like dealing with those blinking agate eyes tonight.

'The morning will do.'

'All right. And before you leave, get a list from Durnford of my movements during the next week or so. I want you to report progress to me as often as you can.' He drained his brandy-glass and winked at me. 'I'm a big man, Mr. Carver. I've got big appetites. I like life and I'm prepared to like people. But I'm a millionaire. Nobody really likes me.'

'I shouldn't think that thought keeps you awake at night.'

For the first time using a thick Irish accent, he said, 'You're bloody right, boyo.'

The moment my head hit the pillow I was away. It was two hours later when I woke. I lay there for a while trying to place myself and wondering what had wakened me. Then there came a flicker of torchlight on the balcony outside my open window. It flicked off and, against the pale night sky, I saw a shape move to the window and into the room. Almost

31

immediately I heard the quick scrape of a chair. A woman's voice said, 'Damn the blasted thing.'

I remembered Julia's note, sat up in bed and switched on the bedside light.

She was standing just in the room, one hand on the back of a chair, the other stretched down to rub her left ankle. She was in a short evening dress and her dark hair was ruffled.

She looked at me crossly and said, 'You knew I was coming. Why did you leave that damned chair there?'

'It was there when I came. What was the balcony crossing like tonight, rough?'

'Keep your voice down.'

She turned and pulled the curtains across the window. Then she came and sat on the end of the bed. Even with my eyes still full of sleep she looked good. She curled up her left leg and went on rubbing her ankle. It was a nice leg.

I said, 'Can I do that for you?'

'You stay where you are.'

I said, ' "A bright torch, and a casement open at night, to let the warm Love in".'

'What the hell's that?'

'Keats. I've got a weakness for him and quite a few others. And when I'm embarrassed I always fall back on poetry.'

'Just fall back on your pillow and don't move.'

I did, and lit a cigarette, then tossed the packet and lighter down to her.

It was a pleasure just to look at her. The thing she had which had hit me in the office was still there, and I knew there was no fighting against it. She was in the *grand luxe* class compared with most other girls I had known—ones who had merited a detour only; but this one, if I could find the energy, was well worth a special journey.

As she lit up I said, "Why this secret, nocturnal visit?"

'You don't know this house. It's like a prison. Modern. Every security device. Walk down a corridor and a television eye or whatever picks you up. Open a door and a red light flicks on in the basement ops room. Nobody can get above the ground floor at night without a special lift key.'

'Millionaires have feudal habits. You wouldn't be a damsel in distress, would you?'

'I want to talk to you—sensibly.'

'Go ahead.'

'Why did you ask what it was about step-daddy that I didn't like?'

'I was just making conversation.'

'Liar.'

'What have you got against him?'

'Nothing. He's generous and kind.'

'Well, that's that. Can I go back to sleep now?'

She went over to the dresser and got herself an ashtray and then settled on the end of the bed, legs curled up underneath her.

'Why,' she asked, 'is he so keen to get his Mercedes back? He's insured—and God knows, we've got enough cars.'

'He wants it back. That's enough for me—so long as he pays the rate for the job.'

She stretched one leg out, and wiggled her toes inside the nylon.

'Meaning you don't intend to discuss the matter in detail?'

'Yes.'

'Because he asked you not to?'

To change the subject, and still far from sure why she had made this visit, I said, 'Tell me about Zelia.'

'Why?'

'I'm going to see her. I want to get details of how and where and, maybe, why she lost the car. So far, I'm told, she hasn't come across with much. Loss of memory, she says.'

'That's right. She's had treatment for it, but it hasn't helped.'

'It never does if people don't want to remember.'

'Why the devil do you say that?' There was a high-voltage flash of anger in her eyes.

'It was just a kind of general observation. Is she younger than you?'

'Almost two years.'

'What about your mother—can't she get anything out of her?'

'Mother died a few years ago.'

'I see. You're fond of Zelia, aren't you?'

'Of course I am. She's my sister.' There was no doubting her sincerity. On the other hand, there was no doubting the fierce, almost passionate, protective feeling that was coming from her as she talked about her sister.

I said, 'Before we get to the real reason for your coming here, do you think you could answer a few questions about Zelia and so on without biting my head off if I touch you on a sore spot?'

She gave me an obstinate little look, then softened it and said, 'I'll try.'

'Good. You know Zelia well, you're very close to her?'

'Yes.'

'She lost this car and her memory. Do you think she really knows what happened but is clamming up just to annoy O'Dowda . . . say, to get back at him for something?'

I wasn't there, but I was near it. I could tell from the movement of her body, the lift of her chin, as she considered it.

'Neither of us get on too well with our stepfather, but I'm sure that's not the reason. She really has lost her memory and . . . All right, I'll admit it—I don't think she wants to remember.'

I could have gone in straight away from there but I didn't think it was wise because I knew that once I did I might not get any more from her—and there was a lot more I wanted if eventually I was going to get my hands on O'Dowda's thousand-pound bonus. Mercenary, but there it is. I was in business for money.

I said, 'How many times has O'Dowda been married?'

'Twice. He married his first wife in 1926. They had a son. She died ten years later.'

34

'The son was the one killed alongside Miggs?'

She nodded. 'He was nineteen. He got into the army early by faking his age. I think he was the only person that O'Dowda really loved.'

I made no open comment that she, too, had now called him O'Dowda.

'After that?'

'He married my mother in 1955. She was a widow. Zelia was twelve and I was fourteen at the time.'

She looked at me, waiting for my next question. I didn't put it. I just contented myself with looking. She sat there, her dark hair a little disordered, gipsy eyes deep and large, and posed in a way that would have made a Goya want to strip and paint her, and I knew that she was reluctant to come to the real point of her visit.

I said, 'What kind of social life does Zelia have? I mean, is she a friendly, out-putting type? Does she get on well with men? Lots of friends?'

She shook her head. 'She keeps herself to herself. She's very lovely, but men don't interest her.'

I said, 'Then what's the problem? What are you doing here?'

She frowned. 'I don't get you.'

'Oh, yes you do—you've been making the signals for a long time. Maybe you don't want to put it in words. You'd like it to come from me, perhaps. Look, she's mislaid a car. It could have been stolen from her. She could have sold it. . . . Oh, there are lots of things that could have happened. But none of them would have inhibited her from telling O'Dowda about it—except one. And that one thing would have to be something to do with Zelia, something that happened to *her* that she doesn't want anyone to know about. Not even you—though I've an idea you can guess at it. Right?'

'How can you possibly know that?'

I shrugged. 'I've been digging dirt professionally for a long time. I know the form. Millionaires' daughters don't have anything to worry about. Money can fix anything. Except one—their personal pride, shame, anguish, or whatever. So what is it you want to ask me to do?'

She was silent for a while, and then she said, 'I think, maybe, I was wrong about you. I don't see how you could have known all this, but you do. Yes, there is something I want you to do. That's why I'm here and why I came this way. I wouldn't want him to know. For Zelia's sake, I just want you to say you can't do this job. I just want her left alone. This job doesn't matter to you. You can get another. But I don't want Zelia hurt——'

'And particularly you don't want me to find out what happened and hand the information on to O'Dowda.'

'Of course I don't. It would kill Zelia.'

I lit myself another cigarette.

'You'd even pay me something for chucking the job in?'

'Of course. That's what you're interested in, isn't it? Money?'

'Show me someone who isn't. But I'm also interested in logic.'

'What do you mean?'

'If I kick this job in, then O'Dowda will hire someone else. When he wants something he gets it, doesn't he?'

'If money could buy it, he'd organize the weather the way he wants it, and the crops could go to hell.'

She slid off the bed with an angry movement, and began to grope for her shoes.

'Then you'd have someone else to deal with. O'Dowda wants that car. You might find yourself landed with someone who lacked my sense of discretion. Someone who wouldn't care a damn about Zelia. Might even get a big laugh from it all.'

'You're just saying that you're not going to give up a good job.'

'Could be. And it's no good you being indignant about it. I'm going to find his car for him. That means I may have to find out about Zelia's missing forty-eight hours. But it doesn't mean I have to tell anyone else about it. Not you, not

O'Dowda. My contract is to find the car. The small print at the bottom of the form has a clause which says that I don't have to supply details of all my operations or betray any confidential information or sources. That suit you?'

She looked down at me, worked up, not sure whether to let it all slide and ignore me, or give me a blasting. Not because she had so much against me, but because she was worrying about Zelia, as maybe she had always worried about her, fighting for her, as maybe she had always fought her battles, and yet wanting to clear the load of her emotions with a first-class row with someone so that she would feel better afterwards.

'I don't have much choice, do I?'

'As a matter of fact, you do. I pointed it out to you just now—and you can make it. Either you settle for me, or for the next chap that comes along to take my place. Well?'

From somewhere outside a little owl screeched, and I kept an Indian expression of graven nothingness on my face while the night breeze flapped the curtains and this gorgeous wind-on-the-heath girl looked down at me as though she couldn't make up her mind which dagger to stick in my heart.

Then she said, 'You do anything to hurt Zelia, and I'll make it my business to find some way of hurting you.'

I gave her a big, boyish grin. 'Fair enough. And thanks for the vote of confidence.'

She moved to the window, picking up her torch. I liked the way she moved. In fact, I liked the way she did everything, even when she got angry with me, but from a personal point of view I couldn't kid myself that I had made a good start with her. Which was a pity, because not for a long time had I met anyone with whom I would have preferred to make a good start.

From the window, she said, 'Do you mind switching off the light?' Her hand was on the curtain, ready to draw it.

'Why?'

'Because there are two men who take it in turns to patrol the grounds at night. I don't want an audience for my balcony scramble.'

37

switched off the bedside light, heard the curtain sing back, felt the fresh night air billow into the room, and saw her shape slide across the long rectangle of pale night sky. I lay back then and thought about millionaires, about how ready O'Dowda had been to haul Durnford out of bed after midnight, how he had poured himself a bigger brandy than the one he had given me, about the dozen or so cars and almost as many houses, about the purple grouse moors and the peaty Irish loughs and the public right of way to the lake which had to be stopped up somehow . . . and I thought how wholesome it would be to be a millionaire and not to have to go digging around in other people's dirt but to have minions ready at hand to clear up your own. And then I thought of Zelia who didn't have any time for men. That hadn't pleased old Mother Nature and I was prepared to bet that, as usual, she had chosen an awkward moment to do something about it. And then I went to sleep and dreamt of walking over MacGillicuddy's Reeks with Julia, wind and rain in our faces, and the same song in both our hearts. At least my dreams never let me down.

Breakfast was brought to me in bed by the manservant. I rolled over and sat up to find tomato juice, two poached eggs on toast, a pot of coffee, marmalade and all the trimmings under my bleary eyes.

The manservant said, 'Good morning, sir.'

I said, 'I don't think so.'

He just looked at me, puzzled.

I said, 'I've never known a good morning which began at six-thirty.'

Pompously, as though he were reading out a club rule which every member should have had at heart, he said, 'Mr. O'Dowda, sir, believes in early rising. Breakfast is always served between half-past six and seven.'

I lay back and nodded at the tray. 'Take that away and bring it back at a quarter to eight. And I'd like boiled eggs, not poached. Two and a half minutes. And if Mr. O'Dowda is checking the breakfast programme tell him that because of a professional ulcer I'm under doctor's orders not to rise or eat before seven-forty-five.'

I rolled over and went into a light sleep filled with unpleasant dreams about millionaires.

I got my boiled eggs on the dot.

And I was in the secretary's office just after nine. Durnford looked bad-tempered. He had probably already done a full day's work. I did my best not to look at him much because it was still too early in the morning for me to face those blinking cold agate eyes, the big teeth and the nicotine-stained wisp of moustache. If I did my best not to look at him, he did a much better best of not wasting time on me. I didn't know it then, of course, though he might have done, but time wasn't going to improve our relationship. We both knew quite instinctively that we were never going to like one another, which in many ways was a good thing. We knew exactly how we stood with one another, and weren't going to waste time over any damned nonsense about brotherly love.

He quibbled over my terms and I stuck fast. He gave way.

He gave me a list of O'Dowda's movements, addresses, and so on for the next two weeks and against two of them he had made a red asterisk. They were the names of hotels, and at these, if I wanted him, I was to make personal or telephone contact before eight at night. After that hour on no account was he to be disturbed.

I said, 'Why?'

Durnford just ignored the question.

He gave me an itinerary of Zelia's movements with the Mercedes from Evian, so far as they knew it, and her present location which was on O'Dowda's yacht at Cannes.

I said, 'Do you really think she has lost her memory?'

Stiffly, he said, 'If Miss Zelia says she has, then she has. I have never had occasion to doubt her word.'

'That's good to hear. By the way—how does she get on with her stepfather?'

He considered this, then said curtly, 'Not well.'

I said, 'How did her mother get on with him?'

Something moved in him, briefly but violently, and I couldn't miss the quick tremor of control as he held it back.

'I don't see the relevance of that question. You're being hired to find a car.'

'Which includes finding a reason for Miss Zelia's loss of memory, which might arise from a lot of things. However, let's stick to the car if you don't care to discuss O'Dowda's marital relationships.'

'I don't,' he said.

He then gave me details of the Mercedes and a colour photograph of it, and a list of banks abroad which were being informed of my credentials and on whom I could call for cash. He then stood up to indicate that he was finished with me. Although I had been going to ask him some questions about O'Dowda, about his business interests and so on, I decided not to. I could get them elsewhere. So I stood up and made for the door which he showed no signs of opening for me.

From the door I said, 'What are you going to do about that public footpath?'

For the first time, and not because he was warming to me I'm sure, he showed signs of being human.

'If you think, Mr. Carver, that working for a man like Mr. O'Dowda is a picnic, get it out of your mind. He expects results.'

'No matter how?'

He blinked his eyes rapidly as though I had suddenly let in too much light, and said, 'Usually, yes.' He looked at his watch. 'Kermode is waiting to take you to the station. You should get the ten-ten easily.'

I half-opened the door.

'Kermode,' I said, 'will run me up to London. Otherwise the job's off. Yes, or no?'

It took him some time, and I was damned sure that the station ploy had been his idea. When you work for a millionaire it's therapeutic sometimes to pass a few of the bitchinesses off on to somebody else.

He said, 'In that case, yes.'

Kermode drove me to London in the Ford station wagon. I sat alongside him and he talked fishing, horses, shooting, women and politics all the way. Of the lot he talked fishing most, and never once said a word about O'Dowda which was other than respectful and admiring. Tich Kermode was O'Dowda's man right down to the tip of the O'Dowda cigar he smoked.

I got into the office just before twelve. I had to use my key because Wilkins was out. I didn't know where. The note in her typewriter said, *Back after lunch*.

On my desk was a quarter-sheet of paper with a type-written message from her.

1. Message from Miggs, nine-thirty. Following informa-tion received by him from Guffy (Yard). Owner motor scooter JN 4839. Joseph Bavana. West African. Flat Two, Marshcroft Villa, Fentiman Road, S.W.8.
2. Message from Miggs, ten-thirty. Guffy reports Sussex Constabulary report. Joseph Bavana, driving motor scooter JN 4839, hit by unknown car, Uckfield-Forest Row road, 1800 hrs yesterday. No witnesses. Bavana dead when found.
3. Message from Guffy, eleven-thirty. Please call him.

I sat back and stared at the sheet. Joseph Bavana, West African. To block a public footpath could take time, even for a millionaire. But to wipe out a human being, that was easy— if you were an O'Dowda, and had two or three private guards around the estate. You just sat working a mallard and claret along the edge of the weeds for a brown trout while Kermode passed your instructions over the radio-telephone. Durnford's eye-blinking rate must have gone up as he listened to them.

The telephone rang on the outside line.

'Carver here.'

'And it's Guffy here, dear boy. Don't bother to come round here. I'll be with you in five minutes.'

He rang off, and I stared into space. It was a thing I frequently did. You just stare into it and after a little while you find yourself thinking about absolutely nothing at all, which is, while it lasts, comforting.

CHAPTER THREE

'Youk'n hide de fier, but w'at you gwine
do wid de smoke?'

JOEL CHANDLER HARRIS

GUFFY WAS FOR Gerald Ulster Foley. As far as anyone at the
Yard could be called a near friend of mine, he was the nearest,
and even that did not put us too close. However, he was—no
matter how hard pressed or frustrated by any dealings with
me—always pleasant and well mannered. It's nice to know
someone who would put you under the lights and grill you,
smiling, and murmuring apologies all the time.

Officially he was a Detective Chief Superintendent in 'C'
Department, earning around two thousand five hundred
pounds a year. With his qualifications and abilities he could
have got ten times that in industry—but not half the excitement
and fun, I imagine. And Guffy liked excitement and variety.
Just the thought of it narrowed his greeny-yellow tabby-cat
eyes and made him purr. He had a lean, alley-cat look, and if
his ears weren't torn and his face scarred from fights with other
toms, it was because he knew how to look after himself in a
scrap as well as almost any man I knew. No one that I knew
at the Yard ever had cared to outline what his specific duties
were. But I did know that he had done a two-year stint at No.
26, Rue Arnengaud, Saint Cloud, Paris, France, and, for all I
knew, still did work for Interpol.

He sat across the desk from me, smoking one of his usual
Dutch Schimmelpennincks, smiling, and looking as though he
was going to believe every word I said, and in return would
be equally trusting with me.

Very carefully I was outlining my interest in the defunct
Joseph Bavana. I told him the whole story of my visit to
O'Dowda, except that I did not mention the nature of the

43

assignment which my client had given me, nor anything about Julia's midnight heart-to-heart talk. Also, I omitted to mention the field-glasses or the two-way radio in the row-boat on the lake. O'Dowda might have had Bavana killed, or it might have been an accident. If it hadn't been an accident, then O'Dowda was doing his warm-hearted best either to protect me or himself. Either way ethics and common sense dictated that I shouldn't indulge in speculation with a man like Guffy until my arm was forced.

When I had finished, he said affably, 'A good synopsis of the whole affair. Taut, dear chap, crisp, omitting all the relevant facts. Such as, for example, the nature of your commission for O'Dowda.'

'He wants me to find something for him. A straightforward recovery job. You feel inclined to press me on that?'

'Not immediately. Perhaps never at all. Why would you think Bavana would want to shoot you or O'Dowda?'

'No idea. Tell me about Bavana.'

'Willingly. The rifle he used was found, dismantled and packed away in one of the carriers of the scooter. He was a student over here. Not London University, but a business college. Prior to that he'd done a course in computer management. None of it meant anything. Just a cover for political activities. Any idea how many African political groups operate from London at the moment?'

'No.'

'Far more than there ever were of *émigré* Poles, Russians and all the other run-of-the-mill Europeans. Every time you move you trip over them. Fifty per cent of them are as innocuous as a Band of Hope society. Of the rest, some are intelligence organizations for African states and some are exile organizations wanting to get back into the great wind-of-change game that's going on. Some of them are operated by idealists, but most of them by chisellers. Some of their activities would make you laugh and some would make you cry—and some would curdle your blood. Overall they're a nuisance, but we have to keep an eye on them. I was naturally curious about your interest in Joseph Bavana. He was one of the blood-curdlers, a paid killer.'

'Paid by whom?'

'I don't know. That's why I'm talking to you, old boy.' He stood up. 'Logically—and I've no doubt you've got there before me—if it were you he had wanted to kill, then it must have been because someone didn't want you to carry out O'Dowda's commission for the recovery of whatever it is.'

'O'Dowda says it was a mistake. They wanted him.'

'Could be, could be. And between ourselves, old boy, I wouldn't have shed a tear. But that's off the record.'

'So what,' I said, 'are you doing here?'

He looked genuinely surprised. 'Why, just having a chat. Haven't seen you for ages. Always enjoy talking to you.'

I stood up, too, as he moved to the door.

'It hasn't occurred to you, of course, that O'Dowda might have had Bavana bumped off?'

'I'm sure he did.' He gave me a charming, disarming smile. 'And just as we can never finger the big boys behind the gold-smuggling rackets through London, Beirut and Calcutta, say, though we know them—the same applies to O'Dowda. They give orders, but the chain of command downwards is as thin and elusive as a thread of the finest gossamer.'

'Poetic.'

'Not at all, old chap. Gossamer comes from goose-summer, that's early November, when spider's webs are most seen, and when geese are eaten. And it's always the foolish geese that get eaten. Nice parable there, somewhere.'

'In a minute you'll have me off *pâté de foie gras* for life.'

'Not you.'

I opened the door for him.

I said, 'Has O'Dowda got a record at the Yard or with Interpol?'

I saw the cat's eyes narrow, and I knew damned well that he had not come here for nothing, certainly not for a cosy chat.

'None at all. He's a respectable millionaire. All we know about him, you could read in *Who's Who*—well, almost all.'

'And you want nothing from me?'

'You sound like a guilty bloke that's been called in for questioning and is surprised to find that he's being let go, old boy.'

'I am. You don't waste your time like this normally.'

'Wish I could oblige you. But we don't want anything from you. Of course, that's not to say that if in the run of your work you came across anything which you felt was a serious police matter, well you might let me know. Or, since you will be abroad chasing this car, give Commissaire Maziol a ring at Interpol.'

'How did you know it was a car?'

'My dear old chap, Miggs said so. Just let us know if you come across anything interesting.'

'Like what?'

'Anything that strikes you. We can always do with outside help from the public. Even if it's only an anonymous letter.'

'You've had one about O'Dowda?'

'A little while ago, yes. Can't reveal the contents, naturally.'

'What was the handwriting? Male or female?'

'Couldn't say, old chap. It was typed. Unsigned. Well, keep your eyes open.'

He went.

Sometimes I thought I went a bit too far in keeping things to myself. But I was a novice compared to them. I didn't like the look of this commission at all. Right from the start it had begun to breed complications. Bavana shooting at me, Julia wanting me to chuck it, and now Guffy going away up Northumberland Avenue, laughing his head off and already knowing that he had me where he wanted me but in no hurry to let me know exactly where that was. I should have been firm and have taken my holiday. But it was too late for that.

I went over to the reference bookcase and pulled out a three-year-old copy of *Who's Who*—well, who's going to renew it each year at six quid a time? For wrist exercise I carried it back one-handed, all five pounds of it.

O'Dowda was there, Just. And it was clear that he hadn't cared a damn whether he was there or not.

The entry read:

O'DOWDA, Cavan: Chairman of Athena Holdings Ltd.; *b*. 24 Feb. 1903. *Educ*.: Dublin. Is also Director of number of public companies engaged in commercial and industrial enterprises. *Address:* Athena House, Park Street, Park Lane, W.1. *T.:* Grosvenor 21835.

There was a lot to fill in between the brief lines. And, I was sure, a lot that could never be filled in, otherwise Guffy would never have been round to see me.

I pulled out the almost as brief account, which Durnford had given me, of Zelia's trip from the château near Evian to Cannes.

On Day One she had left the château at two in the afternoon, driving by herself in the red Mercedes. On her own account she had driven south, through Geneva, Frangy and Seyssel, to a hotel on the west side of Lac Le Bourget.

I took the *Who's Who* back and found a Michelin map, 'Routes de France'. It was clear at once that a more normal route would have been to have come down through Annecy, Aix-les-Bains and Chambéry. But she had explained that. She had plenty of time and wanted to vary her route. She had stayed the night at a hotel called the Ombremont at Le Bourget-du-Lac. From here, around nine at night, she had put in a call to her father at his Sussex country house. O'Dowda hadn't been there and Durnford had taken the call. She had told Durnford that the next day instead of going straight down to Cannes she might break her journey to stay a couple of days with some friends on the way. She hadn't said who the friends were, or where they lived, and Durnford, the perfect secretary, had not asked for information which had not been proffered.

On Day Two she had left the hotel in the morning, before nine-thirty. This had been established because Durnford, like a perfect secretary, had got in touch with O'Dowda who was in London (probably a do-not-disturb-after-eight night somewhere) and O'Dowda had instructed him to phone the hotel and tell Zelia she was to make the trip straight to Cannes without any delays. Durnford made the call at nine-thirty and Zelia had already left. From then on, through Day Two, Day Three, until the morning of Day Four (when Zelia, on her own account, had found herself at Gap, a town on the Route Napoleon, some 160-odd kilometres south from Le Bourget-du-Lac) her life was a blank. In Gap she had been minus the Mercedes, minus her luggage and minus any memory of what had happened to her since she had left the hotel. Life, since leaving the hotel, had become a void. She had the clothes she stood up in, and her handbag with money. She had hired a car and driven to Cannes and the yacht, where O'Dowda had been impatiently waiting for her. No details of the scene on her arrival, or what had happened after, had been given me— except that no one, including Zelia, could think of any friends of hers or the family who lived in the area between Le Bourget-du-Lac and Gap. Betting on probabilities: for my money, Zelia was a liar. For my money, if she wanted to she could give a blow by blow account of every minute of every missing hour. And with O'Dowda's money I'd been engaged to prove it and find the missing car.

I had trouble with Wilkins after lunch. She'd been to the dentist to have a filling renewed. It was a bit difficult to understand her when she spoke because one half of her jaw was still frozen with novocaine.

Following my usual practice, I dictated to her a simple, straightforward account of what had happened so far for my confidential files, and I could see that she was taking against the whole affair. She sat there as though I were dictating the operation order for the extermination of some mid-European ghetto.

At one stage she said, 'I don't think you should have any more to do with O'Dowda. This Bavana man obviously was trying to kill you.'

'For big money risks must be taken. Life is full of hazards. Anyway, that one's been eliminated.'

I finished the dictating. She closed her notebook and got up to go. I stopped her.

'What do you think?' I asked.

'About what?'

'Various things. Zelia first.'

'She obviously had some emotional or disturbing experience and her subconscious mind has decided to force her to forget it. I wonder it doesn't happen to women more often.'

'Then, if you think Zelia's an innocent maid in traumatic shock—why shouldn't I go on with the job?'

'Because men like O'Dowda clearly aren't innocent—not when it comes to things that matter, like business interests and rivalries. Often there's no way of getting what they want legally. That's the moment when men like O'Dowda begin to use people. That's why—almost before you were on his payroll —somebody tried to kill you. Just write and tell him you have thought the matter over and regretfully, etcetera, etcetera. There's plenty of straightforward work waiting for you if you take the trouble to look for it.'

It was about the longest harangue I'd ever had from her. And I should have taken her advice. Two things stopped me. First, there was Julia, and her anxiety over Zelia. I'd more or less promised to handle that for her. And then there was O'Dowda. Something about his character rubbed me the wrong way. He'd got well and truly under my skin. I knew that most of it was pure envy. But, at least, it was pure. I just wanted to show him that here was someone he couldn't play around with and make dance his way at the flap of a cheque book. Whatever was in that red car he wanted it badly. Okay, it was my commission to find that car, and it stopped there. When I knew what was in the car, and perhaps had it in my hands, it would be fun to have him dancing for a while as I dangled it in front of him. Not nice perhaps, but then we all have to have our moments of power. Also, power meant cash, and that was something I could always use.

I said, 'I'd like you to book me on a plane to Geneva tomorrow morning and have a self-drive car waiting for me.

49

And then get me a reservation tomorrow night at the Ombremont Hotel, Le Bourget-du-Lac. If you have any trouble about it, use O'Dowda's name hard. It'll work.'

She just looked at me, nodded, and made for the door. As she reached it I said, and God knows what quirk of self-indulgence made me, 'About the hire car. I want a red Mercedes 250SL.'

Hand on the door knob, she jerked her head back at me. 'Why?'

'Because I've never driven one. And red is my favourite colour. Tell them I've got to have it, no matter what it costs.'

'Well, in that case, we must do our best for you, mustn't we?' She went out. It was a long time since I'd known her so icy.

By the time I went home that evening Wilkins had fixed my air travel and had an assurance that there would be a car waiting for me at Geneva and that, if it were at all possible, it would be a red Mercedes.

Home was a small flat—bedroom, sitting room, bathroom and kitchen—in a side street near the Tate Gallery. From the sitting-room window, by risking a crick in the neck, I could get a fair glimpse of the river. Mrs. Meld, who lived next door and did for me, had cheerfully been fighting a losing battle against my untidiness for years. She'd put some rust-coloured chrysanthemums in a vase on the window table and propped a note against them, saying, *Left a little something for you in the oven. We're almost out of whisky.*

The little something was a cottage pie. That meant she was in a good mood. I lit the gas oven to warm up the pie and then went back and fixed myself a whisky. She was right. There was only three-quarters of a bottle left. I sat down, put my feet up and stared out of the window at the London dusk. Life ought to be good, I thought; a cottage pie—plenty of onion in it—warming in the oven, a glass of whisky and my feet up, and tomorrow I would be off to foreign parts chasing a stolen motor car. Other chaps my age would be home now, cuffing their kids away from the telly to get on with their homework, hunting for a screwdriver to fix a busted plug lead on the vacuum cleaner, wifey would be in the kitchen opening cans of instant steak-and-kidney pie and rice pudding, and tomorrow would be the same old day for them. Variety is the spice of life. That was for me. Each day different. Never knowing what was coming. Never knowing when you were going to be shot at, or when a beautiful girl would come sliding into your bedroom appealing for help, never knowing when you were being used, lied to, conned or secretly laughed at and despised. A great life. The trouble was that just at that moment I didn't feel up to it. I suddenly felt moody and sour and I wondered what it was a reaction to. Something. I considered digging deep to see if I could find out, then decided against it and had another whisky.

I'd just settled with it when the flat bell rang. I let it ring two or three times hoping whoever it was would go away. It went on ringing so I got up and went to the door.

Outside was a man in a dark blue suit and bowler hat, umbrella crooked over one arm. He had a fat cheerful face with high arched eyebrows, a squat lump of putty for a nose, lips that somehow reminded me of a duck-billed platypus, and he was wearing a big floral-pattern tie against a pink shirt. Just to top the bizarre appearance his face was coal-black with a sort of underlying purple sheen, and to bottom it he was wearing ginger-coloured suède shoes. The distance between his shoes and the top of his bowler was all of fifty-four inches. With a flash of white from teeth and eyes, he held out a slip of card to me and I could feel the cheerfulness radiating from him like a convector heater.

'Mr. Carver, yes?' It was a cheerful singing voice.

I nodded and squinted at the card in the bad hall light. It wasn't easy to read because the whole thing had been done in Gothic type. He must have been used to people having trouble with it because, chuckling as a preamble, he recited to me—

'Mr. Jimbo Alakwe, Esquire, Cardew Mansions, Flat Three, Tottenham Court Road, London, West One. Representations. Specialities. Accredited Courier. Imports and Exports.' He paused, and then added, 'A willing heart goes all the way, your sad tires in a mile-o.'

'Where does it say that?'

He reached up and politely turned the card over for me, and there it was printed on the back.

'A splendid sentiment, Mr. Alakwe, but I don't want any representations, specialities, imports or exports, and certainly not a courier with a willing heart. Okay?'

He nodded affably. 'Okay.'

I made to shut the door and he moved in and shut it for me.

I said, 'Look, I've got a cottage pie in the oven, and I want a quiet evening. There isn't a speciality in the world you could provide that would shake me from a quiet night at home.'

He nodded, took off his bowler politely, pulled a handkerchief from inside it and gently tapped his face with it, looked at it—to see if any of the black had come off, perhaps—put it back in the bowler and put the bowler on.

'Ten minutes of your time. No more, Mr. Carver. And a splendid proposition to put. You will, I think, find it to your advantage. Did I say "think"? No, I know. You need me to help you. Splendid prospects and, believe me, absolutely nothing to pay, man. The contrary.'

'You should sell insurance,' I said to his back as he went into the sitting room.

He looked around the room curiously and said, 'Did that for two years once. In Ghana. Accra, you know. It is considered a U-thing there, you know. But I prefer now more variety. Lovely flowers, dahlias, no? Ah, your autumn is a prolific time for dahlias. I have seen some once, purple with a little white zebra stripe. Most splendid.'

He sat down in my chair and looked, his face wreathed in a rapturous smile, at the whisky bottle.

I gave up. I could have thrown him out, but it would have been an effort. And against all that *bonhomie* and cheerfulness any resentment would have been churlish. Churlishness and effort, I decided, could be postponed for ten minutes by which time my pie would be ready.

52

I tipped some whisky into a glass for him.

'Water or soda, Mr. Alakwe?'

'With many thanks, neither.' He took the glass from me, sipped, nodded approval, and said, 'A very nice place you have here. My own flat I share with three others. They are most uncongenial types but useful for business contacts. You have any idea how much I am authorized to offer you?' Big smile, another sip of whisky, and a fat hand momentarily adjusting and smoothing down the floral tie. It should have had dahlias and chrysanthemums on it, but it didn't.

I sat in the other armchair and just studied him, in silence. The silence puzzled him.

He said, 'I say, Mr. Carver, have you any idea how much I am authorized to offer you?'

'And I say, Mr. Alakwe, Esquire, that you'd better begin at the beginning. As a suggestion, in what role are you here? Representation? Specialities? Import and Export or—'

'I am, Mr. Carver, representing.'

'Who?'

He sipped again at the glass. 'Damn fine whisky. Would I imagine be a good proprietary brand?' He squinted at the bottle. 'Yes. Very good mark.'

'Who?' I repeated.

'Let us say friends of friends who have friends who have very delicate susceptibilities towards matters which affect their political, industrial, commercial and international reputations, etcetera and etcetera.' He smiled. 'You see I have need to be discreet. So, naturally—'

I lay back in my chair and shut my eyes. 'Wake me,' I said, 'when you come to the point.'

He laughed.

I opened my eyes.

He winked at me, and said, 'Five hundred pounds?'

I shut my eyes.

'Guineas, Mr. Carver. That would be—'

'Five hundred and twenty-five pounds.'

53

'Ah, then you agree? Good. Very sensible, Mr. Carver. And if you wish for some advice as to investing such a sum, I have a proposition which would double your money in six months. After that, another proposition that would double that amount in a similar time, and so on ad nauseum. In some years you are a millionaire, thanks to Jimbo Alakwe.'

'Esquire, or Mister?'

I opened my eyes.

He genuinely looked a little crestfallen but it didn't last long, the thick lips spread, the fine teeth shone, the pudgy nose wrinkled and the bright eyes spun in their sockets promisingly as though when they stopped the whole jackpot would come spouting out of his mouth. In a way, it did.

'One thousand. Not pounds, Mr. Carver. Guineas. Which is one thousand and fifty pounds.'

I stood up and said, 'The only word you've said so far which makes sense is the word "millionaire". I suggest you take it from there very quickly.' I moved to the door. 'Not that I want to be rude—especially to a man of your ebullience. But I want my supper. Okay?'

'Okay. Ebullience. Splendid word. Yes, that is me. Okay. These friends of friends, etcetera and etcetera, would like you to relinquish your commission with a certain gentleman. Then you get the money. Okay?'

He stood up, and I had no doubt that he thought that it was going to be as simple and painless as that. Only a fool would turn down one thousand guineas.

I held the door open. 'What was their top limit, Mr. Alakwe? Surely more than a thousand?'

He said, 'I think I am smelling a good aroma. Your supper, no doubt? The cheque will be sent.'

I shook my head.

'Don't bother. When I take a job I stay with it.'

He was genuinely concerned for me, surprised, no doubt, at my lack of common sense.

'Please, Mr. Carver, for your own sake. This is not a situation which calls for any high-mindedness or lofty idealism. Just

54

work and money, Mr. Carver. Perhaps one thousand five hundred pounds.'

'No. And don't make it guineas. Just tell them I'm not interested in their money.'

'Absolutely?'

'Absolutely.'

He came by me, as near stunned as he had ever been, I imagine. In the hall he stopped, eyed me, shook his head and said, brightening a little, 'Yes, now I understand. There can only be one explanation. You are eccentric. Very eccentric.'

'Something like that.'

'Well, Mr. Carver, all I can say is that it is your privilege to be that. But it is dangerous. These people—you understand, I only act for them—please be polite they say, this man is intelligent, good mannered and understanding. But these people may now take other action. D for drastic action, Mr. Carver.'

'And you would act for them?'

'Well, naturally, if they pay me. One thousand five hundred pounds or guineas—for the first time I meet a sensible chap who says no to it. You know—' hope sprang briefly to life—'it would be arranged, the payment I mean, so that you would not have to pay tax.'

'Goodnight, Mr. Alakwe.'

I opened the door for him and he went reluctantly past me and paused on the doormat, carefully scuffing his shoes on it.

'Tell me,' I said, 'in your dealings with these friends of friends, etcetera and etcetera, did you ever come across a countryman of yours called Joseph Bavana?'

'Bavana? Why of course. He is my husband-in-law.'

'Your what?'

'Well, if that is not right . . . I mean, he is married to my second wife. Who now, of course, is a widow. So now, of course, maybe, I shall take her back.'

'You know Bavana's dead? How he died?'

'Of course. I tell them not to use that way first of all. Joseph always was accident prone. This Mr. Carver, I tell them from

55

reading their first report, is not a man to deal with like that, but Joseph persuaded them.'

'And what are you going to advise them now?'

'I like you, Mr. Carver. You are polite and respectable with me. I shall tell them you ask for five thousand pounds. That gives you a few days to think about it. I know them. They will say, "God man, five thousand—for doing nothing? Offer two thousand five hundred, guineas if necessary." Then I come to you. You accept—' his face began to beam—'and we shall be happy. You should expect me tomorrow. Don't worry, Mr. Carver.' He thumped his chest with the handle of his umbrella. 'A willing heart is mine. For a friend I go all the way.' He tipped his bowler and turned away, borne on a euphoric cloud of human kindness.

I went back into the flat to be greeted by the smell of burning from the kitchen.

Mrs. Meld woke me with a thump on the door and a few exuberant lines of *Yellow Submarine*. I'd noticed recently that she'd slowly been bringing her repertoire up to date.

'Good morning, Mr. Carver. How was the pie?'

'Splendid,' I mumbled, rubbing my eyes.

'What you need,' she said, 'is a woman to look after you—not that you can't cook as well as any woman, but it's the cooking that does it. Time you've done it, as I tell Meld, it puts you right off. And then things like laundry, you never think about them. You going to stay a bachelor all your life?'

I said, 'Go away. I want two eggs, lightly fried, and some bacon, crisp.'

'Ten minutes, then. And I'll fix a nice steak and kidney for tonight.'

I got out of bed. 'Don't bother. Tonight I shall be in France, eating *omble chevalier*, straight from the lake. You know what *omble* is?'

'Well, if it ain't fish, I don't know what it would be doing in a lake. But anyway, that accounts for the spade across the road maybe. He was there when Meld went off at seven. France, is

56

it, and more of your larrikins? You have a nice life, Mr. Carver, but you need a good woman to share it with.'

I pulled on a dressing gown and went into the sitting room.

From the kitchen Mrs. Meld said, 'He's in the Mini, parked by the letter box.'

From the window I couldn't see much of him, just his bulk behind the wheel and a pair of brown hands spread over the wheel rim. The bulk of his body looked too big to be my friend Jimbo. But I had no doubt that they were connected. While Jimbo Alakwe tried to negotiate new terms for me, they were keeping an eye on me.

At half past nine I dropped my travelling case out of the bathroom window at the back of the flat. Mrs. Meld caught it for me from below in her garden, and then I followed, moving into her kitchen, pausing to admire the new washing-up machine that she'd finally persuaded Meld to buy for her, and then through the house and out of her side door which opened into the next street. It was a route that I'd used many times before, so many times in fact that I'd probably established a permanent right of way by now.

I took a taxi to Miggs's place and got him to send a boy up to the office to collect my air tickets and passport. If they were watching the flat they could well be watching the office. I phoned Wilkins and told her what was happening, and then asked her to have someone check at Somerset House and get all they could on Athena Holdings Ltd. Wilkins was in a better mood, and made me run over all I'd packed for my trip to make sure that I hadn't forgotten anything.

She finished, 'You're not taking a firearm?'

'No,' I said, 'I'm not taking a firearm.' Mrs. Meld would call a spade a spade, but not Wilkins. 'Why? Do you think I should have a gun?'

'No, I do not. You're much too bad a shot for it to be any use.'

Well, maybe she had something there. But, now and then, they were comforting things to have to hand.

I then phoned Guffy and told him about Mr. Jimbo Alakwe,

Esquire. At the moment I considered this a frank, open approach which might be useful.

'If there's anything about him or his employers which you know, which could be helpful to me, I would appreciate it. Let Wilkins know.'

He said he would consider it.

At two o'clock I was in Geneva, and there was a red Mercedes 250SL waiting for me. What it is to work for a millionaire and be able to use his name and credit rating.

I went south like a red streak on the wings of fantasy. I had fishing loughs, grouse moors, town and country houses and reserved hotel suites where I was not to be disturbed after eight. I had a yacht and a handful of cars of which this was my favourite. I daydreamed my way down to Annecy and Aix-les-Bains along a road I knew well. My hands had a millionaire's firm grip on the steering wheel with its large, padded safety boss, and—thanks to the single joint, low-pivot swing axle, the separation of wheel mounting and wheel suspension—the car held the road like a high-speed leech, gentling down the moment I put a foot on the two-circuit servo-assisted disc brakes. Oh, I knew all the jargon. I'd done a year as a car salesman before I had moved into business on my own, chasing other people's troubles and generally ending up with a bag full of them for myself.

Below Aix-les-Bains, at the end of the lake, I swung across country and then up to the west side of the lake. The Ombremont Hotel sat on the hillside above the lake, looking across to Aix. I had a large, bright, chintzy room overlooking the water and when I phoned down for whisky and Perrier water I got it within five minutes, which was something near a record. For records, it was going to be my lucky day. Within the next two hours I had found out something about Zelia which went a long way to convincing me that she had no more lost her memory than I had lost mine—not that there weren't a lot of things in my past that I would have liked to have forgotten. But there it is, things happen to you and things are done by you which are forever on the record.

Just before dinner I went down to the reception desk and cashed a traveller's cheque with the girl who was on duty. I didn't need the money because I had picked up cash at Geneva, but it was a way of opening a conversation and letting her get a few minutes of my warm, affable, engaging nature before I started on the small deceits and oblique questions which were part of my other, second, nature.

She was a girl of about twenty-plus with a little mole at the right corner of her mouth, a pair of dark, wise eyes that had an occasional flash of humour, and she had time on her hands, for all the evening transients had booked in. Her English was streets ahead of my French. I complimented her on it and asked where she had learnt it. It worked, of course. It always does. There's nothing people like more than to have it acknowledged how well they speak a foreign language. In no time we'd got to the point where she asked me whether I was in France on holiday or business. I said that I was on business, that I was the private secretary of one Mr. Cavan O'Dowda, and I didn't have to tell her who he was. She knew. If you're in the hotel business, you probably know all the millionaires and, anyway, the French have this natural reverence for money which makes the names of the world's millionaires as familiar to them as football players are to the differently oriented Anglo-Saxons.

Confidentially, shuffling my franc notes slowly into my wallet, I said that I was making some enquiries about his step-daughter Mademoiselle Zelia Yunge-Brown who was at this moment suffering from loss of memory which had come on at the moment she had left this hotel some weeks ago. For a moment her dark eyes were sad, at the thought of a million-aire's daughter being so afflicted—every memory must be golden, what unhappiness to lose even one.

I agreed and asked if I could see a copy of Zelia's hotel bill. I didn't think it would give me anything openly to prove a theory which I was nursing, knowing human nature, and that Zelia had been off the direct route down to Cannes. But there was no harm in checking. The girl produced a carbon copy from a file. It was for Room 15 and she had paid for the apartment and breakfast. No dinner charge. Well, she might have eaten out somewhere. I was about to hand it back when I noticed that there was no charge for an item which should have been there.

'While Mademoiselle Zelia was here she put in a call to her father in England, at about nine o'clock in the evening. There's no charge for it.'

The girl agreed that there wasn't a charge.

I said, 'Do you keep a record of phone calls?'

'From the rooms, when they are to be charged, yes.'

'Can you check the long-distance calls that evening? From all the rooms.'

'That would mean checking the copies of the accounts of all the guests who were here that night.' There was no sadness in her dark eyes now, just wisdom. A millionaire was fussing about his daughter and, while anyone in their right mind would be anxious to help, it would mean extra work.

I said, 'If it will take you a little time, then naturally Monsieur O'Dowda would wish me to acknowledge that.' I pulled out my wallet and handed her a hundred-franc note.

She took it with a quick, sensible nod of her head; no one in the French hotel business is anything but sensible about money. She said that if Monsieur would look back after dinner, no?

Monsieur went to dinner. There was no *omble*.

I made do with a *terrine de canard aux truffes*, and a *poulet aux morilles* with a bottle of Château-Rayas.

And, after dinner, the information was waiting for me. The only phone call to England made from the hotel that night—and it was just before nine—had come from Room 16 which had been occupied by a Monsieur Max Ansermoz who had booked in the same evening and left the following morning.

Not bothering with niceties, I asked, 'Is there a communicating door between Rooms 15 and 16?'

'Yes, monsieur. Normally it is locked but one would only have to ask the chambermaid.'

'What address did this Monsieur Ansermoz give?'

She had done her homework. It was a Geneva hotel, the Bernina, 22 Place Cornavin. Instinct told me that it wouldn't be any good making enquiries for Max Ansermoz there.

Quite genuinely, the girl said, 'I hope this information will not make trouble for Mademoiselle Zelia.'

'On the contrary. I think it will help her recovery. Her father will be most grateful to you.'

'It is a pleasure to help, monsieur. If you would wish it, some of the hotel servants might remember this gentleman. Maybe, by tomorrow morning, I could tell you what he looked like, no?'

I said I would be grateful for any scrap of information, no matter what the cost of the trouble, and then I went up to my room and sat on the little balcony, smoking, and looking across the lake to the lights of Aix-les-Bains.

So, Zelia had met Monsieur Max Ansermoz at the hotel. It had been careless of her to put a phone call through from his room, but then at that time she probably had not realized that there was any great need for care. Something had happened after leaving the hotel which had brought dull care on to the scene. After leaving the hotel, somewhere along the line, she had started losing things, her car, her luggage, her memory, and who knew what else . . . my guess was that Max Ansermoz knew. It would be interesting to know what Zelia's present feelings towards him were. It would be even more interesting —for this was my particular baby—to know what he had done with the red Mercedes.

I went back into the room, picked up the phone and booked a call to Paris 408.8230. It came through about twenty minutes later and I was put on to a duty officer, sitting bored miles away in 26 Rue Arnengaud, Saint Cloud, who was distinctly cagey about the call. I told him he could check my credentials with Commissaire Maziol or Detective Chief Superintendent Gerald Ulster Foley, but either way I would like any information Interpol was prepared to pass on about one Max Ansermoz, if he were on their files; either here if before nine in the morning or to my office in London if later. Reluctantly he said he would see what could be done and then rang off, no doubt to go back to reading his *Paris-Match*.

I didn't get my call before nine, but for twenty francs extra I had a description of Ansermoz. The hall porter remembered him well, a tall, dark gentleman between thirty and forty who had arrived with a young lady in a red Mercedes and had departed with her in the car the following morning—and he'd had with him a dog, a white poodle. He was a very nice, pleasant gentleman and was French, or at least he thought so, but, of course, he might well have been Swiss.

I tipped and thanked him, and then headed south down the Route Napoleon.

I reached Cannes late, largely because I had stopped for a very leisurely lunch and put a call in to Wilkins afterwards, which had taken over half an hour to come through.

She had had a message for me, through Guffy, from Interpol. There was no one of the name Max Ansermoz on their records, but he might easily be there under another name. Would I please supply a description if possible and any other details which might be helpful. I passed the description, the name of the Geneva hotel and the fact that he probably owned a small white poodle, for Wilkins to relay.

'And Miss Julia Yunge-Brown called on behalf of her father and wanted to know where you would be staying in Cannes. I'm to ring them as soon as I know.'

'Tell them the Majestic, if I can get a room there, which I ought to do because they've got three hundred. Have you looked into the Athena Holdings set-up yet?'

'I've got someone on it today.'

'Good. I'll phone you tomorrow about it.'

Between that moment and the time I arrived in Cannes somebody, I was to discover, had kept the wires busy. I got a room without trouble, ran the car around the corner from the Rue des Serbes and found a garage for it. I had two drinks, dinner, and then a short stroll down the street on to the Boulevard de la Croisette to get a whiff of the sea breeze and then back to bed. Somewhere in the port was O'Dowda's yacht, the *Ferox*—which was a name that had not surprised me, knowing his passion for fishing and knowing also something now of the nature of the man. . . . By any standards he was a cannibal trout preying on large and small fry.

In my room I dropped into a chair, lit a last cigarette before bed and began to think about Zelia and Max Ansermoz, and more particularly of the combinations of human experience and passion which, so soon after a no doubt romantic night at the Ombremont, could have made her decide to lose her memory of the events of the next two days and with it the red Mercedes. Somewhere along that line somebody had had a change of heart. I didn't get far with the obvious possibilities because the telephone rang.

There was, the desk informed me, a Mr. Alakwe to see me.

It was nearly eleven o'clock and my first instinct was to tell them to tell Mr. Alakwe to go to hell. Then curiosity as to how he could have traced me made me tell them to send him up.

He came in, dressed now for the Continent in a lightweight fawn linen suit, smiling all over his face, snub nose creased up like a wrinkled black plum. He carried a panama hat with an orange-and-silver ribbon round it. His tie was pale blue with a yellow horseshoe and hunting crop, rampant, over a bilious green shirt with a fine yellow stripe. He still wore his ginger suède shoes. He shook my hand and then presented me with his card.

I said, 'Don't let's go through that ritual again, Mr. Jimbo Alakwe, Esquire.'

He shook his head, his smile almost cutting his face in half, and said, 'Not Jimbo, Mr. Carver. Jimbo's my brother.'

I looked at the card. He was right. This was Mr. Najib Alakwe, Esquire—in the same line of business, but with an address in Cannes in the Rue de Mimont which, as far as I could remember, was somewhere behind the station. I turned the card over. The quotation on the back read: *Un bon ami vaut mieux que cent parents*. Well, I wasn't going to argue with that.

I handed the card back and said, 'Twins?'

'Yes, Mr. Carver.'

'How the hell am I going to tell you apart?'

'Very simple, I am always in France and Jimbo is always in England.'

I wanted to ask about the ginger shoes but decided not to because it would be some simple explanation I should have thought of for myself.

I said, 'How did you know where to find me?'

'Again very simple. Jimbo telephones me with the information.'

'And how did he get it?'

'This is not for me to know. We keep our departments very separate except in peripatetic cases like yours, Mr. Carver, where the subject is long-ranging. May I say already I have a great admiration for you. Man, you're a damned fast worker.'

I sat down, suddenly feeling very tired. Jimbo and Najib might look and act like a couple of clowns, but there had to be more to them than that. They had to be good for far more than a laugh. To prove it, Najib put his hand into his pocket and pulled out a gun.

I said, 'Is that really necessary?'

He said, 'Man, I hope not, because I am very bad at aiming.' He half-turned and called over his shoulder, 'Panda!'

From the little hallway outside the bedroom door, where she had been waiting, a young woman came into the room. Not that 'came' was the word. She breezed in like a whirlwind, smacked Najib on the back and waltzed up to me in a cloud of some very strong scent, ran her fingers through my hair, tugged the lobe of my right ear and said, 'Whoof! Whoof! Happy to know you, Rexy boy.'

Wearily, I said to Najib, 'She's not real, is she?'

Panda gave me a big grin. 'You betcha, daddy-ho. Every curve, every muscle, genuine human and jumping with life.'

She was over six feet tall, wearing a very short skirt and a gold lamé blouse. She was good-looking, with big, moist brown eyes and a laughing mouth full of the most splendid teeth I had ever seen, though I felt that there were too many of them. In fact there was too much of her altogether. Her legs were too long and her arms were too long, and as she pirouetted in front of me she gave off a hum as though she were driven by some high-powered dynamo. Her skin was a pleasant milky-coffee colour, and her hair was a mass of tight black curls. From her ears dangled gold ear-rings, each shaped to represent a man hanging from a gallows.

Najib said, 'My assistant, Miss Panda Bubakar. Pay no attention to her. Tonight she is full of beans.'

'Panda hungry. Panda want man,' said Panda.

'Panda search room,' said Najib, smacking her on the bottom. Standing, he could just reach it.

'Panda can search room,' I said, 'but what the hell is she looking for—apart from a man?'

'In England,' said Najib, holding the gun on me, 'you were given damned honourable offer of cash for non-co-operation with O'Dowda. Now, cash offer withdrawn. We just take the goods.'

From behind me, where Panda was turning over my bed, she said, 'Ra-ra! Ritzy pyjamas. Anytime you want those pressed, Rexy, just call for me.'

Something bit me gently on the back of the neck and I jumped.

'Leave Mr. Carver alone and get on with job,' said Najib.

I slewed round, rubbing my neck and watched her. Winking at me, she started to go through the room. She did it well—not as well as some people I'd seen, but good enough to prove she was no amateur.

Some of her remarks as she went through my case and the bathroom wouldn't have gone down well at a vicarage garden party, but there was no denying her high spirits and exuberant *bonhomie*. At a distance she was—once you got used to the length of her—quite good to look at, but I didn't trust the hungry man-glint in her eyes. After mating, she was the kind that topped it off by making a meal of her consort.

She came back from the bathroom and said, 'Nothing, Najib—except he wants a new toothbrush and he's almost out of sleeping pills. You sleep bad, honey?' She kicked out a long leg. 'Whoof! Whoof! Mamma has something for that, too.'

'Give me your number,' I said. 'The next time I have insomnia I'll ring. Now will the two of you get to hell out of here?'

'If it is not here, then it must be in the car still. The key, please?' Najib held out his hand.

Panda sat on the bed behind me and wrapped her arms around my neck. 'Give the man the key, honey.'

I said, half-choked, 'What's all this about a car?'

Najib said, 'The car you find. I wait here all this evening and see you arrive, but I am not quick enough to see which garage you took it to.'

One of Panda's hands had snaked down inside my jacket and now came out, holding my car key. She slid around me and handed it to Najib.

'Okay,' I said. 'It's in the Renault Garage just up the avenue and behind the Rue d'Antibes. Just leave the key with the hall porter when you've finished. I'm going to bed.'

It was a stupid thing to say.

Panda gave a couple of barks and high kicks and said, 'Mamma stay and tuck Rexy up.'

I said, 'Take this praying mantis with you, too.'

Najib looked at the key which lay like a fat tear-drop in the palm of his black hand, and then raised a pair of puzzled eyes to me.

I went on, 'It's not the car you want, but one I hired in Geneva to drive down here. Why didn't you check the registration number when I arrived?'

'Numbers can be changed, honey,' said Panda. 'You go check, Najib.'

'You both go,' I said. 'Check the car. There's one thing will tell you whether it's the right one. The secret compartment. You know where it is supposed to be?'

Najib grinned suddenly. 'I know where it is, Mr. Carver, sir. But I don't think you do. O'Dowda would never have told you. Damn right, yes?'

'Course he doesn't know,' said Panda. 'Mamma can tell from his eyes.' She made for the bathroom.

'That's not the way out,' I said.

'Man, I know that. I'm going to fix your bath and rub you down after.' She opened her mouth and snapped her fine teeth at me, her eyes rolling.

'You come with me, Panda,' said Najib. Then to me, he went on, 'I make the check and return the key. Sometime, also Mr. Carver, after you have seen Miss Zelia, we must have a man-to-man talk because it could be to your profit.' He got hold of Panda's arm and began to tug her towards the door.

'Mamma stay,' she cried.

'Mamma go,' I said. There was a moment's temptation, but I put it firmly aside. I just wasn't in her league.

From the door Najib said, 'While you are in this town, if there's anything you need, just let me know.'

'Double it for me,' said Panda.

'After all—' Najib ignored her—'we are in the same line of business, so no need not to be friends unless it becomes absolutely damned necessary otherwise.'

'Nicely put,' I said.

'Sleep well, Mr. Carver.'

'I don't like to think of you all lonely in this room, lover-boy,' said Panda.

'I'll survive.'

'Say, Rexy—' her eyes open wide with a thought—'you ain't discriminating about colour are you?'

I shook my head. 'I like your colour. But I need a lot of building up to deal with the size it comes in. Goodnight.'

They went. And I went to bed. Both of them were putting on a big fooling act. But neither of them were fools. And how the hell had they known that I was coming to the Majestic? Nobody had known until I told Wilkins, and she had phoned the O'Dowda place in Sussex. Within three or four hours of that time Najib had been on my trail. Somewhere in the O'Dowda *menage* there was somebody who was tipping off the other side. Somebody in the household didn't want O'Dowda to have his Mercedes back, and they weren't being very subtle about it. My guess was that it was Durnford. Working for O'Dowda, he could be expected to have a healthy dislike for him, but this went further, this was a horse called Revenge out of Dislike by Disloyalty. Good lines but obvious breeding. As far as O'Dowda was concerned something was really burning up Durnford, and quite clearly he wasn't overworried about what the man said, that you can hide the fire, but what do you do about the smoke? When O'Dowda saw that smoke Durnford was due for trouble.

CHAPTER FOUR

'Fate cropped him short—for be it understood
He would have lived much longer, if he could!'
WILLIAM BARNES RHODES

IT WAS A WARM, gentle, late September morning, full of soft
yellow light bouncing off the sea from a golden mesh of ripples.

The *Ferox* was anchored just outside the port, floating like a
fluffy white meringue, the final thread of confection piped out
to a narrow prow. For ten francs, a gross overcharge, a boy of
about fifteen rowed me out in a pram dinghy. He was bare to
the waist and the sight of his brown, muscular torso, not a spare
ounce of fat on it anywhere, made me consider the possibility
of starting my early morning exercises again.

I went up the gangway to the deck and blinked my eyes at
the white and gold paint, the polished brass and chromium,
did a quick sum in my head of what this outfit probably cost
O'Dowda a year, shuddered, and became aware of a woman
sitting in a deck-chair reading a copy of *Vogue*. She had silvery
hair, touched with a purple rinse, and was wearing red shorts
and a red blouse. She was somewhere around thirty, had a
baby face, a tiny pout to her full lips, and was smoking a long
thin cigar.

I said, 'I have a kind of appointment with Miss Zelia
Yunge-Brown. Carver is the name.'

She dropped the *Vogue* lazily on to the deck, studied me,
and in an American accent said, 'What kind of appointment?
Personal, medical, social or just hopeful?'

'Personal.'

'Well, that makes a change from head-shrinkers and social
boneheads.' She looked at a small gold watch on a slender
wrist and said, 'She'll be doing her jigsaw in the sun-lounge up
front.' She tipped her head forward. 'Don't knock. Go straight

69

in. If she's in a good mood maybe she'll let you stay. Before you go, come and have a drink with me. I might give you my autograph.'

'Is it worth anything?'

'Mercenary type, eh? On a cheque, value nil. On a photograph, value sentimental. But come and have a drink. You'll be helping my beat boredom campaign.'

She blew a cloud of smoke without removing the cigar, picked up the magazine, winked at me and began reading.

I went forward along the spotless deck, under the bridge-wing and had the run of windows of the sun-lounge on my right. They curved round in a wide semicircle above the forward deck. A seagull cut down through the warm air and screamed something at me in French. A man wearing a blue singlet leaned over the bridge-rail above me and nodded, and a Chris-Craft went by at speed, spewing a trail of wake like a plume of ostrich feathers.

I looked through the glass of the sun-lounge door and had my first glance of Zelia Yunge-Brown, the girl with the lost memory. She was sitting at a table, bending over a big tray on which part of a gigantic jigsaw was coming to life. At her right side the table was covered with a muddle of loose jigsaw pieces. All I could see at first was a sweep of long dark hair, the slope of a high, sun-tanned forehead, brown arms and hands and part of a simple blue-and-white-striped dress that looked like the stuff that butchers used to wear for aprons. I stared at her for a while, hoping she would become aware of me. The glass was proof against my magnetic personality, so I went in. She made a little clicking noise with her tongue, removed a piece from the tray and began searching in the loose pile alongside her, ignoring me completely either from rudeness or absorption in her work.

I walked across the lounge and sat on the arm of a blue-leather chair. There was a bar at the back of the lounge with a chromium grille pulled across it, through which I could see rows of glasses and coloured bottles. Either side of the bar were a couple of paintings of old-time tea-clippers, and above the bar in a glass case a stuffed swordfish with a stupid grin on its chops.

I said, 'What's it going to be when it's finished? The Houses of Parliament? George the Fifth's coronation? Or one of those old hunting scenes with chaps in red coats drinking port while the hunt servants pull off their boots and the inn servants are charging in with boars' heads and poached salmon three feet long. Those were the days. Everywhere by horse and coach. None of the roads stinked up with motor cars. By the way, talking of cars—my name is Carver and your father has hired me to find the red Mercedes which you carelessly mislaid.'

I said it all coolly, in my best unruffled manner, but, I hoped, getting a little hint of something not quite friendly in it to show that I wasn't in the mood for moods. Halfway through she raised her head, and that made it difficult for me to maintain my even manner because she was one of the most beautiful women I had ever seen. She had this wonderful black hair, pale blue eyes, and perfect classical features, and she was as cold as ice. An ice maiden from the frozen north. There was something of Julia in her looks, but only just enough to tell they were sisters. She settled back in her chair to get a good look at me, and I saw that she was a big girl, tall, statuesque and as strong as an ox. All she needed was a winged helmet, a shield and a long boat, and Eric the Red would have gone crazy over her. Personally, she made something quietly shrivel up inside me and die.

In a voice, steely and cold, straight from the refrigerator locked somewhere inside her, she said, 'I don't care particularly for your manner, Mr. Carver. And I have already given all the information I can about the car.'

I gave her a big smile, trying to get the atmosphere above zero, even feeling that maybe I had judged her a little hastily. After all she was beautiful enough to merit a second opinion. Could be I was wrong.

'So,' I said, 'you're sorry you can't help me?'

'I can't help you, Mr. Carver.'

She moved forward and studied the jigsaw.

71

I stood up, and the movement brought her head up a little.

She said, 'I'm sorry you've had a wasted journey—but I did tell my stepfather that it was unnecessary for you to come.'

I walked round her to the bar, gave a bottle of Hines a quick, frustrated glance through the grille, and said, 'I'd like to make one thing very clear.'

She had to turn a little to get me in focus and the movement showed off the splendid shoulders and torso to more than advantage.

'Yes.'

'I've been hired to do a job of work. I like to finish what I've started. It's a kind of thing with me. Stupid pride. Professional prejudice. Call it what you like. But I'd like you to know that I am only interested in the car. I want to get it back for your stepfather. But when I hand it over I don't have to give a blow-by-blow account of the recovery. Anything revealed to me in confidence by anyone along the line remains that way. You understand?'

'Perfectly. But I can't help you.'

She turned back and began to fiddle with the puzzle. I walked round the back of her and finished up full circle in the blue-leather chair. She glanced up briefly as I sat down.

'I would like you to go, Mr. Carver.'

'I will,' I said, 'when I've done what I'm being paid to do. For some reason your stepfather sets great store by this car. As his daughter——'

'Stepdaughter.' The word was snapped at me, like icicles breaking.

'—I should have thought you would have wanted to help him.'

She gave me a cold stare, and said, 'I have every reason in the world for not caring a damn about him.'

'You can't really mean that, otherwise you wouldn't be sitting here enjoying all the luxuries he provides. No girl with any spirit would. Now, come on, what happened to the car?'

I was pushing her, hoping to break her down a little; but it didn't work.

She got up from the table and began to move towards the bar. In the woodwork at the side was a bell-push. I was so absorbed in watching her walk, this frozen, beautiful Amazon, that I almost let her reach the bell-push.

'I wouldn't do that,' I said. 'Not if you want me to help you. It won't do you any harm to listen to me for a few moments. Then, if you want to, you can push the bell.'

She was silent for a moment or two, then she said, 'Go ahead.'

I stood up and lit a cigarette. Having her towering over me made me nervous.

'I'll be frank with you. You may or may not have lost your memory. Personally, I don't think you have. But if it suits you for good and private reasons to have people think that, then that's okay by me. But one thing is for certain—you haven't been truthful about your stay at the Ombremont Hotel. If you'd known what was going to happen after you'd left it, then, of course, you'd have naturally been more . . . well, discreet.'

'I don't know what you're——'

'You do. I'm talking about Room 16.'

'I was in Room 15.'

'But you telephoned Durnford in England from Room 16.'

'I certainly did not.' Big and frozen she might be, but I didn't have to have a trained eye and ear to know that she was holding something down inside, probably a desire to shout at me to clear out and go to hell. And it wasn't something that was pleasant for me to be aware of. Quite suddenly I had become sorry for her.

I shook my head. 'There was no telephone charge on your account. On the other hand there was on Room 16's account. And the person in that room—a man—paid for it without any fuss. So where do we go from there?'

She moved back towards the table until she was almost alongside me.

'We don't go anywhere, Mr. Carver. I know nothing about Room 16. If the hotel desk got their accounting mixed up and somebody paid for my telephone call because they were in too much of a hurry to check their account, I'm not interested. The only thing I'm interested in is that you get out of here and leave me alone. Go back to my stepfather and tell him to forget his car.' She paused and I could see the fine tremble all over her as she held on to her control, and I knew that she only needed a push from me—the mention of Ansermoz's name or a reference to a white poodle and her leaving in the morning, laughing and happy—to go right over the edge. With a lot of people I would have happily given the push. But I couldn't with her. Julia apart, there was some barrier in me that wouldn't let me do it. Whatever I wanted from her I would have to get some other way. This job made you think of and see people as jigsaw puzzles; you had to piece the parts together and not mind what sort of dirty or unholy picture came out. But I couldn't rush it with her. She was big and dark and as solid as an iceberg but she'd come too far south in the warm currents and was ready to topple. I didn't have to be the one to give her the final push. But now I was determined to find Ansermoz. Oh, yes, I wanted to meet him.

I moved to the door.

'All right. Just forget I ever came.' I gave her a brotherly grin. 'But if ever you want a shoulder to cry on, somebody to talk to—just get in touch.'

She dropped a hand and touched one of the loose pieces of the puzzle and, without looking at me, said, 'Thank you, Mr. Carver.'

Hand on the door, I said, 'Think nothing of it. But don't forget I've got a broad pair of shoulders.' So they were, almost as broad as hers. I went out, thinking of what Robert Burns had said about waiving the quantum of the sin, the hazard of concealing. If ever a woman had hardened all within and petrified the feeling, then Zelia had done it since leaving the Ombremont Hotel. And I meant to know why.

But first I had to get by the silver-haired, purple-rinse number in the red shorts. I didn't have a hope and in the end I was glad of it, because although I couldn't use Zelia the way I

74

ought to have done, it was easy with Mirabelle Heisenbacher, née Wright, stage-name Mirabelle Landers, age thirty-eight, friendly, bored, and all set to marry O'Dowda when she got her divorce from Mr. Heisenbacher, a rot-the-bald-headed-bastard-of-a-shoe-manufacturer (her words).

As I stood by the gang ladder wondering where my boy with the pram dinghy was, she came down the deck, changed into a green silk beach-suit, cigar in one hand and the other reaching for my arm as she said, 'Unless you have a drink first, you've got to swim back. Come on.'

She led me up to the stern where, under an awning, chairs, tables and drinks waited. She was as friendly as a puppy and just as restless.

She said, 'Did you get anything out of Zelia?'

'No—she's still in some kind of personal deep freeze.'

'I can't think why Cavan is riding the child about the damned car. He's so loaded, what does a car matter?'

'He was tough with her, was he?'

'Originally. I thought he was going to go into orbit. Gave me a few moments' doubt. Such a temper. After all, he's the guy I'm going to marry. Then I thought, what the hell? All men have something and, unlike most, he's got millions so I didn't see why love's blossom should be allowed to wither Why's he so stuck on getting the car back?'

'I wish I knew. You known him long?'

'Three, four years. Nice guy—except I don't like the side he's been showing since the car went. It's got to be more than the car. You know my theory?'

'Tell me.'

'Sometimes I think Zelia lost the car on purpose to annoy him. She must have guessed there was more to it than the car and she ditched it to get back at him. Some kind of emotional compensation for something or the other.'

'You've been talking to a psychoanalyst.'

'Not me. Any time I spend on couches is strictly for pleasure. Not that I'm like that now. I'm strictly a Cavan O'Dowda girl these days.'

'If he got that car back he'd be nicer than he is at the moment, wouldn't he?'

'Sure. And I wouldn't be stuck here, keeping an eye on Zelia. I hate boats. She wants to be out here. She hasn't been off this yacht for weeks. What are you driving at?'

'Was I?'

'Come off it, buster, I know the look in a man's eyes when he wants something and at the moment you've got that look —though it isn't asking for the usual thing which, in a way, is no damned compliment to me.'

'I just want to satisfy O'Dowda.'

'Snap. So?'

'Is there a shore-going telephone from the *Ferox*?'

'No.'

'What happens about the mail? When you write to O'Dowda, for instance?'

'Now we're getting down to business. Why not be direct? You think Zelia might want to write to someone now that you've seen her?'

I looked at her over a large gin-and-tonic she'd fixed for me. She was a woman who knew where she was going and how to handle herself. She was going to marry O'Dowda. What she didn't know about men would probably make only two dull lines of addenda to a large volume of personal reminiscences. She had to be like that because I hadn't said anything of note yet and already she was with me. I gave her a wink. She tossed the end of her cigar over the rail and winked back.

'Level,' she said, 'and Mirabelle might help—just so long as it all adds up to making O'Dowda sweet and getting Zelia out of the doldrums.'

'I've mentioned a little fact to Zelia which may make her want to write to someone. If I could have the names and addresses of all the people she writes to in the next twenty-four hours it could help a lot. Difficult?'

'No. All the ship's letters are put in the mail-box in the saloon and one of the stewards takes them ashore late afternoon. Any name and address in particular?'

'Not really.'

'Liar. Where are you staying?'

'The Majestic.'

'You like your kind of job?'

'I travel and meet people, and help some of them.'

'Then I wish to God you'd help Zelia to come out from under the glacier. I'm liable to be stuck here for weeks and that adds up to a lot of lost fun. It's a man, of course, isn't it, that she'll be writing to?'

'I wouldn't bet on it.'

'Why not, it's an even money chance? Anyway, it's got to be. Any girl ever needed a man, she does. My bet is she found one and he went bad on her. For the first time in her life she went into it starry-eyed and then—bam! the bastard ran true to form. They all do, even the nice ones, but she didn't have any experience to help her ride the punches. Correct?'

'You'll make a first-class stepmother.'

'Wife is all I'm interested in. I thought I had it made with Heisenbacher, but he developed nasty habits, and when I broke him of those he just withdrew and started collecting Japanese ivory carvings, netsukes, and all that stuff. I gave up. You like to stay for lunch?'

I said regretfully that I couldn't and it took me another half-hour to get away. I was run ashore in the yacht's launch and on the quayside waiting for me was Mr. Najib Alakwe, Esquire.

He fell into step alongside me, handed me the ignition key, and said, 'Okay, Mr. Carver, wrong car. You get anything from Miss Zelia?'

'No. But why should I keep you up to date on things?'

'Two thousand pounds, Mr. Carver. Damn generous offer. Cable from Jimbo this morning. Two thousand pounds you resign from Mr. O'Dowda's employment now, or three thousand you go on, find car, and hand same over to us intact.'

I shook my head.

His eyes spun in just the same way as his brother's had.

'This is a serious refusal, Mr. Carver?'

'Absolutely.'

He took a deep, sad breath and said, 'Then all I can indicate is that the consequences for you, Mr. Carver, may be——'

'D for drastic?'

'Absolutely.'

I had lunch at the hotel and then went up to my room and lay on the bed and stared at the ceiling. It was a boring kind of ceiling to stare at, not a crack or a stain on it, so I had to fall back on pure thought. What kind of people, I asked myself, would employ the Alakwe twins? The best answer I could come up with was probably people of their own race. O'Dowda, for instance, would never have employed them—except on an African assignment where they would not be conspicuous, though I had an idea they would still be just that even in an Accra bazaar. In Europe they stuck out like a couple of sore black thumbs. Probably their employer or employers didn't mind this. The Alakwes wanted whatever was hidden in the Mercedes, and they knew that O'Dowda knew they wanted it and—almost certainly—that O'Dowda knew who their employers were.

Then I had a think about Zelia. I was beginning to get some kind of picture of the nature of her amnesia. Max Ansermoz, I hoped, if I ever reached him, could fill in the blanks.

The phone went about four o'clock and it was Wilkins, with a list as long as my arm of companies and holding companies, subsidiaries, agencies and property investments which were all wrapped up in Athena Holdings Ltd. Most of the information I knew had never been got from Somerset House. It was the kind of stuff that came from a good city man working the pubs around Mincing Lane and Fleet Street. As I finished taking down the list, Wilkins said, 'Are you interested in any particular one?'

'Should I be?'

'In view of Joseph Bavana and a certain gentleman called Mr. Jimbo Alakwe who called round here for a general chat about you this morning, I should have thought that——'

'How did you get on with him?'

78

'He said he could get me an electric typewriter brand new at a discount of 50 per cent. Do you want me to get more details about United Africa Enterprises?'

I said I did. It was on the list she had just dictated to me.

Half an hour later I had Durnford on the line. Mr. O'Dowda, he said, wanted a progress report up to date, and with particular reference to my visit to Zelia. He assumed I had seen her.

'I've been with her, and I've got nothing from her.'

'Nothing?'

'Absolutely nothing. But I'm following a different lead which may help me.'

'Mr. O'Dowda would appreciate some indication of this new line. You realize that?'

'Sure. I'll give you details very soon.'

'So, in short, you've made no real progress at all?' I could imagine his cold agate eyes blinking.

'Yes, I'd say that was a fair summary. But don't worry. I'm not downhearted. A willing heart goes all the way, your sad tires in a mile-o.'

'I beg your pardon?'

'Never mind. But you can do something for me which might help. I'd like a complete list of guests, friends, or family who might have been staying at Mr. O'Dowda's Evian château for the two weeks before Zelia took off on her trip in the Mercedes. Can you let me have that?'

There was a little longer than natural silence at the other end, then he said, 'Yes, I suppose so.'

'Now?'

'No. I'd have to make enquiries.'

'Okay. I'll phone sometime tomorrow or the next day. Oh, there is one thing you can tell Mr. O'Dowda. I've been offered two thousand pounds by a certain Mr. Jimbo Alakwe—my secretary will give you his address—to drop this job. Interesting?'

'You refused, of course.'

'With a struggle—yes.'

Around six I was still on the bed, thinking of having a

79

shower before going down to the bar for a drink, when the phone went. The desk said that there was a Miss Yunge-Brown wanting to see me.

I was at the door waiting to greet her. She came in with a warm, flashing smile, a passing whiff of *Jolie Madame*, and a silver mink cape draped over one arm. After staring at a bedroom ceiling all the afternoon she gave my eyes trouble in focusing for a while. She dropped into the bedroom chair, crossed two beautiful long legs, fingered the fall of her black dress smooth, and said, 'I've never seen a man's eyes look so pouchy. Drinking at lunchtime?'

'They go like that when I sleep in the afternoons. A couple of whiskys and everything soon shakes back into place. Where shall we go for dinner?'

'We don't. Why don't you give up?'

'You've decided I'm not your type?'

'It's under review. What did you get out of Zelia?'

'Zelia,' I said, 'is a woman who needs understanding. I might make something of her if I could get her away from that jigsaw long enough.'

She gave me a cool, long look. There was in it even a hint of something a little warmer than a review-board stare. She topped the look with a little shake of her head so that one coral-pink tip of an ear showed against a raven wing of smooth, loose hair and then slid back shy as a sea anemone.

'Zelia,' she said, 'has spent most of this afternoon on her bed crying. That's something I've never known her do before. What the devil did you say to her?' The last sentence came curt and hard.

'When did you arrive?'

'Lunchtime. What have you done to Zelia?'

'Nice drive down in the Facel Vega?'

'Yes. And don't hedge. You bloody well leave Zelia alone if all you can do is to twist her up. Yes—' she eyed me with angry thoughtfulness—'maybe I am going to dislike you a lot.'

'Pity. I'd prefer it the other way. And don't get so het up about Zelia. Between ourselves she brings out the Sir Galahad in me and I'm looking forward to going into action. I like big, beautiful girls. But I don't like them frozen. They should be warm and full of bounce. So why don't you belt up and give me that envelope you're fiddling with?'

She looked down at her right hand and seemed surprised to find the envelope there which she had drawn from her handbag.

'I wish I didn't keep changing my mind about you,' she said.

'Give it time. The needle will settle down soon and show you the right course.'

She handed me the envelope.

'It's from Mirabelle. She asked me to deliver it.'

'Now there's a woman who's going full steam right ahead, armour-plated, reinforced bows and god help any pack ice that gets in the way.' I turned the envelope over. She'd made a reasonable job of it, but it was quite clear that it had been opened and then stuck down. I raised my eyebrows at her.

'I opened it,' she said. 'I couldn't imagine what Mirabelle could have to say to you.'

'You couldn't? Well, given a million pounds, I could have her lisping in my ear for the rest of my life and I wouldn't mind at all, except that she'd have to get rid of that purple hair-rinse.'

It was a half-sheet of plain notepaper and Mirabelle had written—

One letter an hour after you left.
Now she's taken to her bed. Letter went
ashore five o'clock with yacht's mail.
Max Ansermoz, Châlet Bayard, St. Bonnet,
Hautes Alpes. Don't you do a damned thing
to hurt the kid.

Mirabelle.

I put the letter in my pocket. Julia eyed me like a child watching a conjuror. I pulled out my cigarettes, lit one, and she watched the first curl of smoke fade away.

'Thanks for trusting me,' I said.

'What makes you think I do?'

'This.' I waved the letter. 'You'd have torn it up if you hadn't.'

'Well?'

'Well, what?' I said.

'Who is this Max Ansermoz—and what's he got to do with Zelia?'

'You've never heard the name before?'

'No.'

'Then forget it,' I said, hard. 'If you're fond of Zelia, really forget it. And when you get back to the *Ferox*, thank Mirabelle and tell her to do the same. Okay?'

'If you say so. Are you going to see him?'

'Yes.'

'When? Tomorrow?'

'Yes.'

'I'll drive you up.'

'I've got my own car and you'll stay here. I've just told you to forget Max Ansermoz.'

She stood up and came across to me, slipping the mink over her shoulders, the diamond setting of her watch pinpricks of brilliance with the movement. Mink and diamonds, Facel Vegas and yachts, Mercedes and châteaux in the Haute Savoie, *paté de foie gras*, caviare and pink champagne, dream stuff . . . but it didn't isolate her or Zelia or Mirabelle or any other woman from life . . . from the nasty little habits that some men are born with and others develop. Men were hunters and, no matter how much they kidded themselves otherwise, women were the prey. Just at that moment I didn't like the idea; wished I could be outside it, but knew I couldn't. The only consolation was that most men reluctantly observed the game laws and the close seasons. Some didn't. Max Ansermoz I was sure was one. So, I had an idea, was Cavan O'Dowda. Someday, somebody, I told myself, ought to shoot the pair, stuff and mount them, and hang them above a bar.

'What on earth's got into you?' she said. 'You suddenly look as though you wanted to hit somebody.'

'Don't let these puffy old eyes fool you.'

82

She came closer. 'They're not as puffy as I made out. And I'm really beginning to think that they don't fool me as much as you would like. Would you like me to break my dinner date?'

'Not on my account. I'm going early to bed. I've got a busy day tomorrow.'

She wasn't fooling me. I knew exactly what was in her mind, and had been ever since she had steamed open the letter on the yacht or wherever it was.

She was as anxious to see Max Ansermoz as I was. That didn't suit me. I wanted to see him first, and alone. In fact, I was already looking forward to it.

She said, 'I really want to come with you tomorrow.'

I said, 'I'm going alone. If you queer that I'll toss in this job—and then O'Dowda will get someone else, some fast slick operator who'll probably make a juicy story out of it afterwards for all the boys in the bar to laugh at. So keep away!'

Deep and warm inside me, heating up fast every moment, was a feeling that I didn't have very often, wouldn't wish for often, but which when it came just had to be obeyed. Somebody had to be hit. . . . Oh, yes, somebody had to be hit hard and the name was clicking through my brain like a ticker tape. She knew, too, what was there. Slowly she put out a hand and gently nipped the cloth of my sleeve between two fingers.

'All right,' she said. 'I won't interfere. . . . Poor Zelia.' She turned away to the door. Then, her fingers on the door handle, she turned and said, 'Do me a favour.'

'What?'

'Don't bother to be polite with him.'

She went. I gave her a few minutes, and then I called the desk. I wanted my bill made up. I was leaving right after dinner and would they send someone up to get my car key so that the Mercedes could be brought round for me. With any luck I might arrive at the Chalet Bayard just about the time Max Ansermoz got Zelia's letter. One thing that I knew for sure I wasn't going to find at the Chalet Bayard was a *chevalier sans peur et sans reproche*.

I left just after ten. There was a light drizzle falling and I could see no sign of Najib Alakwe being on the watch outside. If he had been I wasn't going to worry. In the Mercedes I was reasonably confident I could shake any tail.

St. Bonnet was about twenty- or thirty-odd kilometres north of Gap, and my route was back along the road by which I had come down from Grenoble. From the map I worked out that it gave me something over seven hundred and fifty kilometres of driving. I had time on my hands and took things slowly.

I gave myself an hour's sleep, somewhere well south of Gap, and then drove on to Gap for an early breakfast, coffee laced with cognac and a couple of crisp croissants spread with apricot conserve. Fortified, I left Gap and drove up and over the Col Bayard, thinking that if I had a troubled life, the *chevalier* had had the edge on me, every head of his family for two centuries having fallen in battle, and he himself likewise in the end—to an arquebus ball, whatever that was. From the top of the pass I rolled down into St Bonnet and got directions for the Châlet Bayard. It was a small, rough road, doubling back out of the village along the course of the river for a while and then climbing steeply through pine and oak woods by way of a series of *virages* that made me keep my eyes strictly on the road and ignore the views.

It was a wooden-built chalet, fairly new, with pink-and-green shutters, and the roof barge-boards decorated with pink-and-green stripes. It stood to one side of a steep green alp, on a plateau about the size of a couple of tennis courts. There was no garden, just trees and scrub running either side of the rough drive and then spreading back from the house itself. There was a garage beyond the open space in front of the house. The doors were shut.

I parked the car close under the verandah which ran along the front of the house, and went up the steps. There were petunias and geraniums in flower-boxes all along the front of the verandah and the front door was wide open to show me a small hall of narrow, polished pine boards, the odd rug and a grandfather clock with a loud tick, announcing that it was five minutes past nine.

There was an iron bell-pull at the side of the door. I gave it a couple of jerks and way back in the house a bell clanged, loud enough to wake the dead. But it didn't wake anyone in the house. I tolled again and still no one came to answer it.

I went in. There were two doors off the hall. I tried them both. The first led down a corridor to the kitchen quarters. It was a neat bright kitchen and there were the remains of a breakfast on the table, and a ginger cat curled in a wicker chair. The cat eyed me for a moment, stood up, stretched its legs stiffly and then collapsed on to the cushion, rolled itself into a turban and ignored me.

I went back and tried the other door. It led into a large lounge which ran the full length of the far side of the house with a view across part of the alp and away beyond to the valley peaks and crests, some of them already smudged with a patchwork of snow. It was a good, big comfortable room, polished pine boards, skin rugs over them, two big settees, four large armchairs, a wide, circular table adzed out of oak and ornamented with a bowl of multicoloured dahlias that would have had Jimbo in ecstasies. In one corner was a desk, and against the false wall that made part of a staircase that ran up to an open gallery with doors along it, was a bookcase and a long sideboard with drinks, cigarette box and a pile of old newspapers. I lit a cigarette and went upstairs. There were three bedrooms, all the beds neatly made, and a bathroom. The sponge on the side of the bath was damp, and so was one of the toothbrushes and the cake of soap. I went down to the lounge and started a more detailed inspection. The bookcase was interesting. One shelf had as big a collection of cookery books as I had ever seen in half a dozen languages. If Max were the cookery expert he had something for a guest of any nationality. There were three shelves full of thrillers, French, English, American and German. It was nice to know that Max was multilingual. We wouldn't have difficulty communicating.

The desk was neat and tidy, and contained very little. It

was clear that Max didn't care to leave any private papers lying around. There were some cancelled cheques, paid bills, most of them local, a list of shares and securities, some American, most French, which had been added to from time to time. He didn't seem to have sold any for there were no deletions. I didn't try to make out what they were worth. In one of the drawers was a pile of estate agents' leaflets and they were all concerned with restaurant and café properties as far apart as Paris and Marseilles. Another drawer held a 9 mm. Browning pistol, the magazine full, and alongside it a box of ammunition and a spare magazine. I pocketed the lot as a safety precaution.

I went across to the window, admired the view, and wondered how long Max would be. My guess was that he had gone off for his morning constitutional. He was a neat orderly type, bed made before he left the house, not a speck of dust anywhere, ashtrays emptied. Neat and—normally—regular in his habits, fond of the culinary arts to the point of already owning, or contemplating owning, a restaurant or a café, kind to animals—the cat seemed well content—and with a nice touch of expertise in flower decoration as the bowl of dahlias testified. Turning from the window and looking at the flowers, I noticed something I had not seen before. Lying on this side of the bowl was an envelope.

I picked it up. It had been slit open along the top and the letter tucked back inside. It was addressed to him and post-marked Cannes the previous day. I had to hand it to the *Postes et Télégraphe* boys. They had had five hours' start on me and beaten me to it.

I dropped into an armchair by the fireplace. It was so deep and wide I wondered for a moment if I was ever going to hit bottom. I did, bounced a bit, and then took the letter out of the envelope. It was to him from Zelia and read without benefit of any superscription, no glad 'Darling' or 'Dearest one'—

I had hoped that I would never have to communicate with you in any way. Circumstances now make it necessary.

86

For some reason my father is highly concerned about the loss of the car and has employed a certain Mr. Rex Carver of London to trace it. This man saw me today. Although he did not mention your name, he must know it, because he knows that you stayed in the next room to me at the Hotel and that I made my phone call to home from it. I denied everything. I shall continue to deny everything. I just want what happened to become a blank in my mind. If this man should trace you, you will do the same. You have never known me. You have betrayed me once. For this I do not hate you, or forgive you. I have simply made you nothing in my mind. Betray me to this man, or anyone else, and I swear that I will have you killed. You have destroyed something in me. Make this in any way public and I will destroy you.

Zelia.

I put the letter back in the envelope and slipped it into my pocket. Nothing she had said was news to me. She meant every word she said, and I was sorry for her. That was the hell of it. I was sorry for her, but I had a job to do. If I possibly could, I wanted to do it without hurting her more. She might want what had happened to be a blank in her mind, but I had to know what had happened. Once I knew, I could pass on to my real concern, the car, I would make it a blank in my mind. I sat there, wondering how Max Ansermoz had felt when he had read the letter. Not overmuch concerned, I imagined, or he would not just have chucked it across the table.

At this moment there was a yappy bark from the open door of the lounge behind me. Something white skittered around the side of the chair on the polished boards, leapt on to my knees and began to lick my face. It was a small white poodle. I'm not going to upset anyone by saying I'm no dog-lover, but I like my dogs big, discriminating, and with a certain secret contempt for mankind. I was just about to chuck this one into the empty fireplace as undersized when a breathless voice from the door called, 'Otto! Otto—*tu es fou venir ici avec cette sacrée auto? Tu voudrais que tout le monde——*'

He broke off as I stood up with the white poodle in my arms and he saw me for the first time

I said, 'You're rushing it, Max. That's not the car Otto went off with. Same colour, different number.'

I dropped the poodle to the ground and it began to walk around on its hind legs like some circus number.

'Cute,' I said. 'How is it as a gun-dog?'

He had a shotgun under one arm and a couple of pigeons hanging from his right hand.

'Who are you and what are you doing here?' He said it in English, not much accent, and his voice under control.

'Carver,' I said. 'Rex Carver of London. I think Miss Zelia Yunge-Brown mentioned me to you in a letter.'

I had to hand it to him. He didn't faint or have palpitations or collapse into a chair. He just stood there and for the fraction of a moment his eyes glanced at the big circular table. He was taller than me, slim, not an ounce of fat on him, and he had one of those dark, unhealthy-looking tans which come from chromosomes more than the sun. He wore a loose shooting jacket with a fur collar, a black peaked cap, and black breeches tucked into the top of gum-boots. He had an intelligent, good-looking face and sparkling teeth and eye-whites. I didn't like the look of him at all, but I could see how in a bad light, after a few glasses of champagne, some women might have called him a dreamboat. Not Zelia, I shouldn't have thought. But there you are—when a woman finally decides to drop the barriers you never know which way the water will flow.

Calmly, he said, 'I don't know what you're talking about. Kindly get out of my house.'

He dropped the brace of pigeons on to a chair and eased the gun into both of his hands, the muzzle low, pointing to the ground. He was over his surprise now, and had me sized up What could I do while he had a gun in his hands? I decided to see how far he would go.

I shrugged my shoulders, and said, 'You can take that

attitude if you like. But it won't get you far—and I'll be back.'

I moved up towards the door and he swung slightly round to keep my fully under observation. When I was abreast of him, he said, 'Before you go I'd like the letter which I left on the table.'

I stopped moving, eyed him as though I might be going to make an issue of it—which I certainly wasn't while he stood at the ready with a double-barrelled twelve bore—and then with another shrug I slipped my hand into my pocket for the letter and handed it out to him.

He smiled, just the faintest edge of white teeth showing, and shook his head.

'Put it on the chair there.'

I moved to the chair, put the letter on one of its arms and then gave the chair a hard push towards him across the slippery pine floor. The far arm caught him on the thigh, knocked him off balance and before he could gather himself together, I jumped him. Miggs, I'm sure, would have said I was slow, but I was fast enough for Max Ansermoz. I chopped down at one of his wrists, broke his hold on the gun, grabbed the barrel in my other hand and twisted the weapon free from him. I could have stopped there, I suppose, but a nice warm feeling flooded through me and I didn't see why I shouldn't take the opportunity to put him in a co-operative mood. I jabbed him hard in the stomach with the butt of the shotgun and, as his head came forward, I slapped him sidehand across the neck and he went down with a crash that had the fool poodle dancing and yipping with excitement.

He was game. He came up twice at me and I put him down each time, not bothering about the Queensberry rules, remembering Miggs saying, 'Don't be nice, be nasty, but leave 'em so they can talk.'

I let him crawl off his knees and into a chair. He flopped back, murdering me with his eyes, blood trickling from one corner of his mouth. I sat on the edge of the table and faced him.

I said, 'Before I begin the questions, let's get one thing clear. Everything you say to me about Miss Zelia will be in the strictest confidence. Think of me as a confessional. It comes to me—and goes no further. Okay.'

He spat something at me in a language I didn't know. To gentle him down I smacked the butt of the shotgun across the top of his kneecap, just not hard enough to break it. He gasped with pain, doubled forward and the poodle jumped up, trying to lick his face. He shoved it away roughly and dropped back into the chair.

'Bastard.'

'I don't expect you to like me. I'd take it as an insult if you did. Just answer me—or I'll break every bloody bone in your body. Ready?'

He said nothing and I took it for assent.

'Okay,' I said. 'Let's start at the end. Maybe that way we can skip some of the dirty middle. Who's Otto?'

He considered this, and he was considering more. I knew the look and that slow pulling-together movement of the body as they decide to go along with you, hoping that their co-operation will make you so pleased that you'll drop your guard for a moment.

'Otto Libsch, a friend of mine.'

'Age, nationality, description, residence and occupation.'

'Thirty-odd. Austrian. He's tall, biggish, fair hair, going slightly bald. Walks with a bit of a limp and has the lobe of his left ear missing.'

It was too glib, too fast, so I smacked him on the back of his right hand with the gun barrel. He shouted and swore with the pain.

'Try again,' I said. 'From the start.'

He sucked the blood off the back of his hand, and then, his eyes full of the comforting fantasies of what he would like to do to me, he said:

'Twenty-five. French. He's short, dark-haired, thin, weedy looking. God knows what he does, or where he lives. He just turns up.'

'Not quite good enough. If you wanted to get in touch with him what would you do?'

He balanced that one for a moment, eyed the gun, and decided to give good measure.

'I'd ring his girl friend, Mimi Probst. Turino 56.4578. That's 17 Via Calleta.'

Keeping my eyes on him, I backed to the sideboard and picked up the telephone and carried it to him, putting it on the ground where he could just reach it.

'Ring directory enquiries and ask for the telephone number of Probst, 17 Via Calleta, Turin. Then let me have it.'

He picked up the phone and dialled, saying to me, 'I'm telling you the truth.'

'The one thing I always check is the truth.'

I waited while he put the call in. It took a little time and I lit a cigarette one-handed, keeping the other on the gun.

After a time he spoke, asking for the information, then he nodded to me and put the phone with the loose receiver on the floor. I retrieved it, eyes on him all the time. After a few moments the girl at the other end came on and my French was more than good enough to follow her. He'd given me the right number.

I shoved the telephone on to the table and said, 'Otto was here when you were here with Miss Zelia, yes?'

'Yes.'

'He stole the car?'

'Yes.'

'And her luggage and any loose stuff she had lying around, watch, jewellery and so on?'

'Yes.'

'Nice man. Weren't you worried?'

'No.' There was the faintest shadow of a smile about his lips, and I was tempted to smash if off his face.

'Was he interested in this car particularly, or was it just a car like any other, fair game if he could see a way of driving off in it?'

'Otto would steal anything. He's my friend. He's amusing —but he is a born thief.'

He was coming back fast, I could sense it.

'How long had you known Zelia before you came here with her?'

'Quite a while—on and off.'

'Where?'

'Geneva. Whenever she was staying at her father's château.'

'You read her letter carefully?' I nodded to where the letter lay on the floor by the chair.

'Yes.'

'Then take my advice. She wants the time she spent here to become a blank. That's how it's going to be. You step out of line over that and I'll do the job of wiping you out for her free. Understood?'

'Don't you want to know what happened here?'

'No, I bloody well don't. I'm only interested in the car.'

He grinned and I began to see red.

'You don't want to know what she's like, this beautiful iceberg when for the first time a man gets his hands on her and warms her up? When for the first time—'

I should have sat tight and blasted his head off from a safe distance. I should have known that he was deliberately provoking me, hoping for some advantage from it. Christ, I should have known, but I didn't care. I just went for him, to stop the dirty words in his throat, and he played my own trick on me, suddenly swivelling the chair round on the polished floor so that the arm crashed into my hip as he leaped from the chair and kicked my legs from under me.

I went sliding across the floor and almost before I had finished moving, he was standing over me with the gun pointing at me.

'Just stay there,' he said. 'You move and I'll blow your head off a little quicker than I intend.'

I lay where I was, and said nothing. It was one of those times for inaction and silence. He had a finger crooked round the lead trigger and I saw his thumb slide the catch off *safety*.

'And I do intend to,' he said quietly. 'You've annoyed me, assaulted me and entered my house unbidden. I shall say that I came back, found you robbing the place, that you attacked me, and the gun went off accidentally. The police won't make any trouble about that.'

'Other people might.' I felt that I ought to make some case for myself.

'No. Not Miss Zelia, as you so nicely call her. Or her father —because she will never say a word about me.' He gave me a warm, evil grin. 'She wants to forget she ever knew me—or Otto. You know she knew Otto as well, of course? No? Well, I want you to know it. I want you to know everything before I shoot you. When I met her in Geneva she was ripe, you know. Ripe to explode—and she did, like a wild thing after a few drinks here, in this room. We all finished up together, upstairs in the one big bed: Otto, dear Zelia, and me—'

'Shut your dirty mouth!'

'Move—and I'll shoot you. It doesn't matter to me now when I do it. Yes, she was wild. She suddenly woke up and began to live and she tried to put all she'd missed in the last ten years into two days.' His eyes sparkled as he spoke. He was thoroughly enjoying himself. 'There were times when even Otto and I found it hard to handle her. But if she went up like a rocket—are you enjoying this?—the charred stick came back to earth eventually. But before it did Otto moved out with everything she had—the car, her luggage, everything. He didn't tell me he was going to do it. At six o'clock on her last morning he was gone from the communal bed. . . . No, no, hear it all. It amuses me to see you hating me and every word I say. He went and she came back to earth, back to what she'd been before I met her. And she walked out too. Just walked. I didn't mind. Except when she was wild, she was rather boring.'

I said, 'It would be a pleasure to kill you.'

'Happily you're not going to have that pleasure. Mind you, I don't want you to get the wrong idea of Zelia's character. Everything was perfectly correct, all those times in Geneva.

They were just warming-up exercises. And here . . . well, just drink wouldn't have released her to such wild heights of inhibition. Oh, no—Otto and I doctored her drink. In a way, you could say it was an act of mercy, a form of therapy which she needed. You know, ever since she left I've been wondering whether to be content, altruistically, with having helped her to discover herself, or whether I shouldn't make a charge. Blackmail, I suppose you would call it. What do you think?'

I wasn't thinking. I was just aware of the twin muzzles of the gun a few feet from my face, and of a maddening pressure of rage inside me, mounting to a point which in a few moments would take me off the ground and at him regardless of what happened to me.

He said, 'I asked you what you think? I did it with other women before, of course—until I had enough to set myself up in business. After that I promised myself I would help the cold, frustrated ones like Zelia just for the pleasure of it. But with a millionaire's daughter, perhaps it would be silly not to make a charge——'

At this point I jerked the poodle at him. It had come dancing up on its toes to me as he talked, licked one of my ears and then had begun to worry playfully at my left hand. I grabbed it by its skinny loins and threw it, rolling sideways and jumping to my feet as he staggered back a few yards and fetched up against the table. But I wasn't quick enough to get at him. The gun barrel was out, levelled towards my face.

'Good monsieur,' he said. 'Now I kill you. But first I tell you I have made my decision. I shall blackmail Miss Zelia. Yes, I shall make her pay, and each time she does it will be necessary for her to bring the money here in person. You understand? Part payment in money and part in——'

I began to move for him. There was no time to get at his gun in my pocket, no time or thought for anything except blind action. But as I felt my muscles contract, the hollow of my guts squeeze tight with the moment of taking off to get at him, there was a *zip* past my shoulder like the clumsy whirr

94

of a June bug. Max's head jerked as though he had been struck violently under the chin and upwards. He stared at me stupidly, his mouth rolled open and then he fell backwards to the ground with a neat little hole drilled an inch above his nose, dead centre between his dark eyebrows.

A voice I knew said from behind me, 'Damn necessary, and no great regrets. In fact, Mr. Carver, sir, no regrets at all.'

I dropped back into an armchair, shaking all over like a man with Parkinson's disease. After a moment or two a glass was put into my right hand.

'Here, lover-boy, down this and get the roses back in your cheeks.'

Panda's long fingers patted my shoulder. The glass was full to the brim.

I had to steady my wrist with my left hand to get the glass to my mouth. It was cognac and went down like lava and the shaking in my body stopped.

Mr. Najib Alakwe, Esquire, stepped back from me and said, 'It is a nice little dog, but I think not right for it to lick dead master's face.'

Panda picked up the poodle and moved out of the room with it. She was wearing sky-blue ski-trousers and a short red acket and her legs seemed to have grown in length since I had last seen them.

Najib sat on the edge of the table, one leg swinging and showing a flash of purple sock above his ginger-suède shoe.

I put the glass down, almost empty, and said, 'Thank you very much, Najib.' If any man deserved to be promoted into the first-name category he did.

He beamed at me. 'Yes. I saved your life. It is a good feeling for me since I do not often do good deeds. But also I am sad.' He looked down at Max. 'What good is damned dead body? You get much information from him?'

I said, 'How did you know about him?'

Panda, coming back into the room, said, 'That is my department, lover-boy. There is a steward on the *Ferox* who

95

likes Mamma. I say to like Mamma and have Mamma like him then Mamma likes names and addresses of all people Miss Zelia sends letters to. So everything ends up very likeable. One day soon I'll show you.' She sat on the arm of my chair and twined a long arm around my neck.

Najib said, 'But there never are any letters until you visit Miss Zelia. Then there is the letter to this gentleman and you are gone from your hotel, so we come up here. We have damned fine car, American Thunderbird, hired, you understand, because I cannot personally afford to own such a luxury. You wish more cognac?'

'No thanks.'

Panda patted my cheek. 'Good. Complete recovery.' She looked at Najib. 'I shall take him up to the bedroom for some liking and then he will tell me all Mr. Max tells him?'

I said, 'It's not such a complete recovery as that.'

'Nevertheless,' said Najib, 'in return for life-saving you will tell what he said about the red Mercedes. Personal details of Miss Zelia, of which I hear a little before I shoot, do not interest my good self. I read between the lines why she said nothing about whereabouts of car. But it is damned reasonable now to tell me what you know. Yes, sir?'

He was dead right, of course. It would have been only damned reasonable to repay him with the information he wanted. I wanted to do it. But, like most people who have been hauled out of trouble, once the shock of crisis has passed, I knew that life had to go on in its same old sordid, double-crossing way. Gratitude must never get in the way of bringing home the bacon. The best place for sentiment was on Christmas, birthday and get-well cards, Najib was on the other side. I wanted to help him. But I had a job to do, fees and a bonus to collect, so there was never a moment's doubt in my mind.

I said, 'I didn't get much out of him—and I don't know that what I did was the truth. I think I'd have needed a few hours to work him up into a state of frankness. You know how it is.'

Panda stood up, stepped over Max, and helped herself to a cigarette from the box on the sideboard. She turned and winked at me. 'Try, honey, try hard to remember all the lies he gave you. We'll sort 'em out. You want that Mamma takes you up to the bedroom and works you up to a state of frankness. Whoof! Whoof!' She did a couple of high kicks.

I said, 'The car was stolen from here by a friend of his called Otto Libsch. He's a pretty undesirable character, I gathered. If you have a way into police records, you'll probably find him there. Because of what happened here with Miss Zelia, he was pretty safe in taking the car. But he didn't have any dea—nor did Max here, I imagine—that there was anything special about the car.'

'This man, Otto—you have an address for him?' asked Najib, and I noticed that when he was getting down to facts his pidgin English slipped.

'No.' I decided to play hard to get, because if he had to drag it from me he wouldn't suspect, perhaps, that it was a false address.

Najib fingered his tie, took off his panama and laid it on the table by the bowl of flowers.

'Splendid dahlias,' he said. 'I am very fond of flowers.'

'Runs in the family.'

'Maybe,' said Panda, 'I should break the bowl over his head? Eh, honey?' She came back and sat on the arm of my chair.

Najib shook his head and smiled at me, his dark eyes full of understanding. 'You are, of course, Mr. Carver, stuck on the horns of a dilemma, no? In thanks for your delivery, your heart wants to be generous. But your brain is a professional man's brain. Tell nothing, it says.'

'In my place, what would you do?'

'The same.'

'Stalemate, then.'

'But you have an address for Otto Libsch?'

'Well . . . I've an address but I wouldn't know whether Max had just made it up.'

'That we can check. The address, please, Mr. Carver.'

He produced his gun from his pocket and nodded at Panda. She slipped a long arm round me and took Max's Browning out of my pocket, kissing my left ear as she did it.

'Damned big bulge these make,' she said. 'You should have used it on the late gentleman.'

'I didn't get a chance.'

Najib said, 'You get no chances now. Personal feelings are disqualified. I want the address.'

'And if I won't give it?'

I just caught the flicker of his eye towards Panda and then it happened. She grabbed me by the wrist, hauled me up, dropping her shoulders as she did, and I went cartwheeling over her and hit the floor on my face. Her weight dropped on my back and a pair of long legs took a scissors grip round my neck, almost choking me.

'For proper likings, honey,' she said, 'we begin with gentle love play.' She twisted my right arm hard and I shouted.

'Let him up,' said Najib. There was nothing phoney about him now. He was crisp, cold and determined and there wasn't a thing wrong with his Queen's English.

Panda let me get up. Najib faced me, pulling at his pudgy nose. Panda straightened my tie for me.

'You ought to meet a friend of mine called Miggs,' I said. 'You've got a lot in common.' Then, out of sheer pique, I kicked her feet from under her and she sat on the floor with a bang. For a moment she stared, disbelieving, at me, and then she began to laugh. 'Oh, Rexy-boy,' she chuckled, 'I got you wrong. You got promise.'

Najib made an impatient movement of his gun-hand.

'Give me the address. If not I shall shoot you so that you cannot take advantage of it. The situation will then be that I still do not know the address, but you will be dead, and I shall be able to find it some other way without trouble from you.'

'That'll leave two bodies here. Could be embarrassing.'

'If you have a coloured skin like mine, Mr. Carver, and live

in a white man's world, then you know all about embarrass-
ments, most of them more damned awkward than a couple
of cadavers. Give me the address or it is D for drastic.'

He waggled the gun. Panda got up off the floor.

'Be reasonable, lover-boy,' she said. 'You gonna miss all
them lovely things otherwise. That extra drink you shouldn't
take. Lovin' arms around you in the night and the first
cigarette with your hangover in the morning. Why, I just
couldn't bear to see so much good manpower go down the
drain.'

She was right of course. And anyway, I felt I had stalled
long enough. I flapped my hands and let my shoulders
collapse.

'Okay. I'd hate to arrive at the pearly gates next in the
queue to Max Ansermoz.'

'Splendid.' Najib beamed. We were all friends again.

'Otto Libsch,' I said. 'The Bernina Hotel, Geneva. That's
in the Place Cornavin.'

Najib beamed. 'Thank you, Mr. Carver. This Max may
have lied, of course. That I accept. But if I find that you have
lied then you go right down the drain. Now, please, turn
round.'

'Why?'

'Do like Najib says,' said Panda.

I turned.

Najib hit me on the back of the head with his gun and I
went down and out.

When I came to, I was lying on the floor with my head on
a cushion. My face was wet and my shirt-front was soaked
with water. Sitting on a chair close to me was Julia Yunge-
Brown, holding a glass jug of water in her hand. She flicked
half of it into my face as my eyes blinked at the light.

I said, 'If you really want to help you might find something
stronger than water.' This was my morning for girls and
cognac. As she moved away I sat up and looked around.

'Where's the body?' I said.

Over her shoulder, she said, 'What body?'

I didn't answer. What a nice chap Najib was. He had carted off the body to save me embarrassment. I really felt bad about lying to him. But I knew that the next time we met he was going to be anything but nice, and would want to take all the lovely things away from me.

CHAPTER FIVE

'We ride, and I see her bosom heave.'
ROBERT BROWNING

IT WAS A PLEASANT enough family scene. Ten o'clock on a
Sunday morning, the sound of church bells coming through
the open kitchen window, the smell of coffee from the per-
colator on a small electric ring, and over everything the warm,
steamy smell of baby clothes half dry, strung out on a line
across the top part of the window.

The man was lounging in a broken-down cane chair,
nursing the baby in his arms. I couldn't tell its sex and never
asked, but it had a red face, screwed up like a toothless old
man's, and a fluff of soft black hair on its head that looked
like the combings from a dog's coat. It was sucking away at
the business end of an old fashioned feeding bottle, slipping its
mouth sideways from the teat now and then to give a milky
belch.

The man manoeuvred a cigarette one-handed from his shirt
pocket, struck a match, one-handed, on the sole of his sandal
and said, 'After the business with Otto, Mimi lost her milk.
Big shock—but she's over it now. In good hands.'

Mimi Probst—I was sure about her because she had
answered the door and identified herself—was ironing on the
kitchen table. She wore a loose apron affair and had bare legs
and bare feet. Her red hair was untidy, and her blue eyes
were quiet and mild. She had a thinnish face with high cheek-
bones and a narrow chin. She looked about eighteen but was
probably more. She gave the man an adoring look when he
said 'in good hands', smiled and made a silent kissing movement with her mouth. Happy, contented couple, baby giving
no trouble for once, all Sunday, the day of rest, before them,

and on her wrist she was wearing a small diamond-set watch that was right out of her class and an identical number to the one which Julia wore. When I got back to Julia I wasn't even going to ask if Zelia had a watch like hers. Cavan O'Dowda had probably unloaded a couple on the girls at some time to mark some coup he'd pulled off.

I said, 'You know who I am. And I know who Mimi is— but who are you? Otto is the man I want, and you know why.'

My card was lying on the edge of the chair he sat in. I'd just said that I was looking for Otto to try and recover a Mercedes that belonged to a client of mine. No more, no less, not even how I had come to trace Otto. Right from the start I'd been troubled by their manner. There hadn't been the slightest edge of resentment at an intrusion on their Sunday morning. Every time I'd mentioned Otto so far, they had looked at one another and giggled.

Mimi tested the flat of the iron by spitting on it, was dissatisfied with the heat and dumped it on another ring alongside the coffee. She turned back, put her hands on her hips and looked at me. Dolled up, she would never have passed unnoticed in a crowd.

She winked at the man. 'What do you think?'

His English accent would have passed, but hers was surprisingly thick. She could have had a mouth full of sticky toffee.

The man nodded, and eyed me affably as he slipped the teat from the baby's mouth, hunked the infant gently over one shoulder and began massaging its back through the shawl to ease up wind.

'He's doing a job,' he said to no one in particular. 'Been frank. Right to the point. Broad-minded, too, I should say. Would have to be in his job.' Then to me particularly he went on, 'I'm Tony Collard. You're wrong about Mimi. It ain't Probst. We were married last week. I can see you're wondering about my English. No need. My father was a Canadian, volunteered at the beginning of the war into the British Royal Artillery, came over here, changed his mind about war, deserted, settled down, married and eventually had me. He died two years back. I run the garage and repair shop that never made him a fortune.'

I said, 'You jump about a lot. And you're giving me a lot of information that I don't want. Otto is my bird. Where's he roosting now?'

At that they both gave out high squeaks of laughter. When the paroxysm was over Tony said, 'Like some coffee?'

'No thanks.'

He massaged a final burp from the baby and then stuck it back on the bottle. He had nice, easy, comfortable hands, gentle, but I had a feeling that there was far more to him than a smiling frankness of manner and an occasional mad laugh. He was about twenty, plump and big built, and with a face like a young Pickwick, made more so by the steel-rimmed glasses he wore. He had thin, blond-white hair, and would be bald before he was thirty.

'What's the score on the car?' he asked.

'My client wants it back. He's a millionaire. They get touchy about property. You and I worry over the pence. His kind worry all the way up through the cash register. That's why they're millionaires. I understood, from a gent I met recently, that Otto regarded Mimi as his girl.'

Going back to the pile of baby-clothes and diapers, iron in hand, Mimi said, 'I was. That's his baby. I had a bad time with it.'

'Caesarian,' said Tony, proudly almost, and I thought at any moment he would ask her to show me the scar. He gave her a loving look and she angled it back with that silent kissing motion of the lips. I began to feel out of place in so much domestic bliss.

'Being Otto's makes no difference to Tony,' said Mimi.

'Not a scrap,' said Tony. 'I loved Mimi long before Otto came along. Old faithful.' He chuckled. 'But then every girl's due for one stupid infatuation. Come to that, so's a man. More than one, perhaps. Eh?' He winked at Mimi and she brandished the iron, mock angry at him. I began to get the idea that they were either playing with me, or just glad to have a diversion on a warm, happy Sunday morning before they put the kid in its bassinet and wandered down the road to some *trattoria* for lunchtime *spaghetti Milanese* and a couple of glasses of Chianti.

I put some lira notes on top of the refrigerator and said, 'Don't be offended. Good information—particularly about bad characters—is worth paying for. And it isn't my money, anyway. Just tell me about Otto. Description, habits, and, maybe, present whereabouts.'

They both went into their side-splitting-giggle act, and then recovered themselves and looked a bit self-conscious.

'We don't need the money,' said Tony, 'but we'll take it on principle. Money is always something you take even if you don't need it. Money, as my old man used to say, is like music. No matter where or in what form it comes we should be glad of it. It cuts across international and cultural barriers and it is a sad person who gets no joy out of it. The other thing he used——'

'Don't start about your father,' said Mimi, shaking her head at him, smiling indulgently, and finishing again with that silent kiss.

He said something to her in rapid Italian beyond me. She blushed in a swift curtain fall from the roots of her red hair down to the point of her pert chin and said something back in Italian, and Tony squirmed in the chair and rolled his eyes behind the spectacles. It was a horrible sight. The baby burped slipped the teat and was sick all down the front of its shawl. Tony took out his handkerchief and mopped up the mess with the loving unconcern of a devoted stepfather. In my book, there was something wrong about Tony and Mimi. I had the feeling that not only outwardly, but quietly, inwardly and even sadistically, they were laughing their heads off about me. There was, I felt, some monstrous, side-splitting joke going on so that when I left they would collapse on to the floor, rolling over and over as the pent-up mirth oozed out of them.

Tony got up and took the baby to a wicker cradle that

stood on a side table. He began to tuck it away, making father noises. Without turning, he said, 'What kind of car did you say?'

'I told you. A red Mercedes 250SL. Number 828 Z–9626. 1966 model.'

He turned, smiled at me and nodded.

'That's the one. Otto brought it to me almost a month ago. I did it over for him. Only an outside job, no fiddling about changing engine numbers and so on. Just a respray and new number plates. Let me see.' He screwed up his eyes in thought, staring at the ceiling. He was a big man, bigger than he'd looked in the chair. 'Yes.' He came back to earth, having remembered, walked to his chair, patted Mimi on the bottom as he passed, and collapsed into the cane chair so that it creaked like a building about to come down in a high wind. 'Yes. I did it up cream, and the new number was something like 3243 P 38. Or it may have been 3423. But it was certainly P and 38. The last two numbers, you know, show what department a car is registered with and he particularly wanted it to be Isère—that's up around Grenoble.'

I said, 'You don't mind sitting there and telling me you did this?'

'Why should I? But you try to put it on the record—which I don't think you will—then I'd deny it. I run an almost honest business. That's as much as any garage can say.' He chuckled, and winked at Mimi. Thank God, she spared him the silent kiss on that one.

'What would he do—resell it?'

'With Otto, he could do anything. Enter it for Le Mans perhaps. Give it to his old mother for a present—if he ever knew who was his mother.'

'What does Otto look like?'

He didn't answer at once. He glanced at Mimi and I could sense the joke bubbling silently between them like a dark underground stream while their eyes lightened with merriment.

'He's four foot nothing and built like an ape. Very strong.

Brown hair, long, always tossing it out of his eyes. Smart dresser. About thirty-five. Good dancer. Women fall for him, God knows why, but it never lasts because he's so selfish and unreliable with money. Still owes me for the repaint job.'

'That's all?'

'What more do you want?'

'He's got two heads,' said Mimi.

I sighed as they went into a convulsion of laughter. In fact, I was a bit annoyed. If there's a good joke going I like to be in on it.

I said, 'Anything else you've overlooked? Hare lip, forked tail, or a club foot?'

Mimi said solemnly, 'On the inside of his left thigh he's got a birthmark shaped like the cross of Lorraine.'

They both laughed again and when Tony had squeezed the last tears of delight from his eyes, he said, 'Pay no attention. Just Mimi's jokes. She's a good one for a giggle.'

I said, 'How come Otto let you walk in and take over Mimi?'

'Because he knew I was going to do it anyway, and break him in half if he made trouble. Oh, he knew it. But trust Otto to get out without trouble. A week after he took the car off he phoned, long distance somewhere, saying he was through with Mimi. Right, *cara mia*?'

'Just like that.' Mimi began to put away the ironed clothes. 'Just phoned. Everything was over. It was not unexpected. The baby was a mistake. He never loved it. Never wanted it— but I am naturally shocked until Tony comes and says marry me. Tony is a good man.'

'The best,' said Tony. 'True love triumphs. You know what we're going to do—when the baby's a little older? Sell the garage and go to Australia. No more garage. I'm going to farm. With animals, I am good. Like with children, like with women.' He reached out as Mimi passed and held her by the left knee under the apron and they both made silent kissing motions at one another as though I were not there. He let her go and she moved over to the baby.

I said, 'Any idea where Otto might be now?'

106

Tony choked on his mirth, pursed his lips, gave it thought, and then said, 'Sitting comfortably somewhere without a care in the world.'

I wasn't meant to see it, but there was a mirror on the wall over Tony's chair. In it I could see Mimi's back as she bent over the cradle. From the movement of her shoulders and head, I thought she was about to have a convulsion. She just stood there, holding down a great, pulsing pressure of laughter.

I was glad to get out of the place, to get away from the homely shrine they'd built to their true love. Going down the street, heading for the nearest bottle of beer, I knew that up in the flat they were letting the laughter flow like red-hot lava. I didn't believe a word they'd said about Otto. But what they hadn't said didn't make me feel sorry for him wherever he was sitting—comfortably and without a care in the world—because always at the back of my mind was the thought of Zelia with him and Max at the Chalet Bayard.

After the beer I took a taxi to the Via Sacchi and the Palace Hotel. Lying on my bed, I put in a call to Paris and got the duty man at Interpol. I had a brief up and down with him, establishing my credentials after he'd told me that Commissaire Maziol wasn't available. I threw Guffy's name at him—told him that my *bona fides* had already been checked through him once, and what was the matter, weren't they interested in suppressing crime and bringing the riff-raff of Europe to book? He said it was a beautiful day in Paris, and would I make it as brief as possible. So I said in *précis: Otto Libsch. Could be Otto Probst. Possible descriptions. Four feet high, strong as an ape, brown, floppy hair. Or, maybe, six feet high, round happy face, steel-rimmed spectacles, fair hair, going bald. Associate Max Ansermoz—enquiry already made viz same. Otto floating around possibly in cream-coloured Mercedes 250SL. Index number—3243, 3234, or 3423 P 38 according to latest inaccurate information, probably different number altogether, possibly car not cream, but green, blue, black or maroon. But certainly Mercedes.* For a moment or two I debated dropping in the names of Mimi Probst and Tony Collard and then decided against it. They were a couple I'd like to have up my sleeve just in case anything definite came up about Otto.

Just as I was finishing, Julia came in without knocking and sat at the end of the bed. She wore a cream-coloured silk dress with a little snatch of red scarf at the throat, and I could see by the set of her mouth that she was determined to have things out with me. I looked at her watch and checked it against Mimi's—they were both the same. Otto, before taking off, or Tony, before settling in, had made it a love gift.

I put the phone down and Julia said, 'I've driven you all the way down here. When do I get let into your confidence?'

I should say that Najib had taken my car. He'd left a note on Max's round table saying that Panda was driving it off, and he gave the name of a garage from which I could collect it in Geneva. That was merely to get a head start on me in the chase after Otto. At this moment he was probably a damned angry man without any doubt that I was anything but a *bon ami* of his.

So Julia had been press-ganged into driving me to Turin and no explanations. She'd been content to wait for the right moment which, as she swung her legs up on to the bed, I saw she had decided was now.

I said, 'There isn't any need for you to know anything. You want to protect Zelia. So do I. Let's leave it like that.'

'I want to know about this Max Ansermoz.'

'He's dead—and I'm heartily glad. A sort of friend of mine shot him just before he could shoot me, and then this friend conveniently carted the body off—and my car. All I need say to you is that Zelia spent a couple of nights at the chalet. Okay?'

She looked at me, head lowered a little, and then slowly nodded.

'Okay. But why are you here?'

'I've got a job to do. Remember? I have to find your father's car.'

'Can't I help you with that?'

'You have, by driving me here. But that's as far as it goes.

Look, your concern was Zelia. You've got my word about that. O'Dowda's not going to know anything. But there's still the car, and that's my job. It isn't a game. I'm paid to take bumps on the head and stupid risks. I've a defect of character which forces me to accept it as a way of life. I'm a hard case, hooked. I can't afford to have you along all the time. Somebody might flatten you—and then what chance would I have of a bonus from step-daddy? Business to me is money, and I don't want you involved just for the kicks. Let me finish this job and then, if you like my company, I'll give you two weeks you'll never forget.'

'God, you're impossible.'

Her bosom heaved. It was something I had never seen happen before. She almost burst.

'I dislike you,' she said, 'more than I can say.'

I said, 'The top button of your dress has popped.' It had, too.

She swung off the bed and made for the door, her hands up, buttoning her dress. Halfway there, she turned towards me.

'By the way, while you were out I phoned my father. He wants to see you at once. That's an order.'

'Where is he?'

'Evian—at the château.'

I gave her a big smile.

'You wouldn't care to drive me back as far as Geneva?'

'Not bloody likely. Remember, you don't want any help from me.'

'Okay.'

She went to the door, and then paused before opening it.

She said, 'Tell me one thing—and I'm not asking out of idle curiosity. When you talked with this Max, did he tell you how he came to know Zelia?'

'No. He just said he met her in Geneva and Evian.'

'Secretly?'

'I imagine so.'

'Poor Zelia.'

'Well, she doesn't have to worry about Max any more. And

when I get hold of the other bastard I'll do something about him.

'The other?'

'Yes—it can't hurt you to know. There was another man at the chalet. He's the one who ran off with the car. I thought I might find him here, but I was unlucky.'

'What was his name?'

'Otto Libsch.'

There was a long pause, and then she went.

I didn't care for the pause. There was something unnatural about it. I had the impression that for a few seconds she was fighting within herself to decide whether she should move out at the end of the pause or say something.

Somehow I wasn't surprised when, ten minutes later, she phoned through and said that she had changed her mind and would be willing to drive me to Geneva. And that change of heart I was convinced had something to do with the name Otto Libsch.

A few minutes later my phone went again. It was a Paris call. The duty officer out at Saint Cloud was brisker this time, alive, alert, almost commanding. Somebody had not only confirmed my rating with him, but somebody clearly wanted something from me. Where, he asked, could I be found in the next twenty-four hours? I said that I was going to be driving through the night to Geneva, where I should be picking my car up at the Autohall Servette in the Rue Liotard, and then going on to Cavan O'Dowda's château above Evian, and what was the sudden urgency about? He said it was still a splendid day in Paris and wished me *bon voyage*.

At nine the next morning Julia dropped me in the Rue Liotard. The night drive had been quite an experience, like being crated up in the hold of a jet cargo plane. I croaked appropriate thanks and crabbed my way down the street on bent legs, my eyes gritty for sleep and my mouth dry with smoking too many cigarettes. She swept by me with a wave, smiling and as fresh as a dew-spangled rose.

At the entrance to the Autohall I was met by an old friend, looking, as usual, as droopy and sun-dazzled as a day-trapped owl. He was leaning against the wall, Gauloise dangling from the corner of his mouth, wearing a shabby brown suit, brown shirt without tie, and big brown shoes that turned up at the toes. Over his rusty brown moustache he blinked upwards at me in welcome. Upwards, because Aristide Marchissy la Dole was only just over four feet in height. He looked at his watch and said, 'Good timing. I heard it was a Facel Vega. I had you bracketed to the half-hour.'

I said, 'What the hell are you doing in Switzerland?'

The last time I'd met him he had been with the *Sûrete Nationale—Office Central des Stupéfiants.* Before that with *Renseignements Généraux.*

He said, 'I've moved on to higher and no better things. Let's have breakfast.'

He took me around the corner to a *pâtisserie* where he loaded his plate with a large slice of *gâteau Galicien,* oozing with apricot jam and stuck all over with pistachio nuts, ordered a large cup of hot chocolate into which he poured cognac from his own flask and then, butter cream fringing his moustache, asked, 'You are well?'

I was feeling sick, but said, 'Yes. And you?'

'I am in good health and appetite, despite a lack of sleep. But sleep is for weaklings. Tell me, are we going to have the usual trouble with you over this?'

'Probably.'

'You know what I mean by this?'

'No.'

He stoked up with more cake and through it said, 'I am very fond of *Galicien.* It was first made in Paris at the Pâtisserie Frascati, alas no more. It stood on the corner of the Boulevard Richelieu, on the site of what was at one time one of the most famous gaming houses in the city.' He sighed, blinked, and went on, 'I wish I were back in Paris at the Sûreté. I do not like International things nor anything that begins with Inter. Despite De Gaulle I am not even in favour of the Common

Market. I am parochial. And much as I like you, I am sorry even to meet you briefly on business because I know you will only give me trouble as before.'

He held a brief silence in memory of the troubled past. I lit a cigarette and, reaching for his flask, put the rest of his cognac in my coffee.

He said, 'Let us now play the frankness game. I will be frank with you.'

'And I will be frank with you.'

'Up to a point.'

'Up to a point where individual ethics, self-interest, etcetera, etcetera, demand otherwise. So?'

'We have no information on one Max Ansermoz.'

I said expansively, 'Forget him. *Requiescat in pace*.'

He gave me a look and said, 'We will not pursue it unless it mes up. Without a *corpus* there is no *corpus delicti*. Something like that, no?'

'Something,' I said.

'Tell me,' he said, 'before we get down to the real business. Have you engaged yourself—on the side—in another commission which concerns O'Dowda?'

'Like what?'

'Possibly from some member of his family?'

'I've enough on my hands with his Mercedes job. I just stick to one thing at a time—and often that's too much for me.'

He nodded approvingly, and I said, 'Tell me about Otto Libsch?'

'Willingly. He is about thirty-five years old, born in Linz, Austria, of course. Passes as a Frenchman. Five foot ten, dark-haired, good physique, various prison sentences, various names, same crimes—armed robbery. From a description given, and the method used, he is now wanted for a payroll robbery which he carried out with a companion two weeks ago. It was in France and they got away with the equivalent in English money of . . .' he thought, licking the fringe of his moustache with his tongue—'say ten thousand pounds.'

'Where did this happen exactly, and how?'

'At the moment my frankness doesn't reach that far.'

'How far does it reach?'

'Let us see. Ah, yes. A car was used in the robbery. It was a black Mercedes 250SL. Index number—different from any that you named.'

'I'm not surprised. Has the car been traced?'

'No. Nor Otto.'

'Or his companion?'

'No. He was tall, six feet, big build, round, plump face, steel-rimmed spectacles and he had fair hair. He doesn't fit anyone in our records. Naturally we are interested in anything you might have to say about any person of your acquaintance who fits this description.'

I was silent, trying to figure the best way out because I didn't want to declare as good an ace as Tony Collard yet. He got up and went over to the counter and came back with a concoction that made me feel I would never want to eat again.

Seeing my look, he said brightly, 'It is a *Saint-Honoré*. He was, you know, once Bishop of Amiens and is the patron saint of pastry-cooks for no good reason that anyone has ever been able to discover. So, a big man with big face and cheap glasses —you met someone like that in Turin?'

'No. I got Otto from Max Ansermoz. He also gave me an address for Otto in Turin—but it was a phoney. Nobody knew of Otto.'

Aristide chuckled.

'You want the car,' he said. 'And we want Otto, plus friend. Please try to find a way around this which will trouble no one's ethics.'

'I'll do my best.'

He nodded. 'Of that I am sure. The trouble is that you produce such a poor best at times. Now me, for example, for a friend I always try to give of my best. Take your car in the garage around the corner. The same kind of car that your employer is so mysteriously worried about. You should not drive it away without having a good look under the bonnet. While waiting for you I took the trouble to inspect it only because I am interested in engines . . . purely that. How large events sometimes hang on the smallest of human curiosities.'

I stood up. 'I'm sure,' I said, 'you'd like to be left alone in peace with your *Saint-Honoré*. But thank you for everything.'

'Nothing at all. I have left my card in your car. When you are ready—just give me a call.' He raised a large round of sugar-iced *choux* to his mouth and crunched on it hungrily. Then, mouth full, he added, 'By the way, there is one other small point.'

'Nice of you to save it for last. That means it's the real point.'

'Possibly. When you locate this car—you will notify me at once, and say nothing to your employer until I give you permission.'

'And if I don't?'

He gave me a beaming smile, his mouth flecked with crumbs.

'If you don't—then many people more important than me will be angry. Very angry. Influential, official people, who could make life hard for you.'

'When has it been any other?'

He took another bite at his *Saint-Honoré* and winked, his mouth too full for words.

I went and collected my car, but before driving it away I inspected the engine as he had suggested. In the long run, professional ethics are one thing. But if there is going to be a long run there's nothing like friendship.

The Château de la Forclaz was about ten miles due south of Evian, out along the road to a place called Abondance. It had a mile of road frontage, a high wire fence studded with the usual notices, *Chasse Interdit*, *Défense d'Entrer*, *Propriéte Privée*, and so on. There was a lodge, a lodge gate with a wide cattle-grid across the road, and then half a mile of private drive up through pine woods, curving and banking, and with more notices telling one to take it easy on the curves and not exceed thirty kilometres an hour. The rich are great ones for notices telling you what not to do, which is odd, really, when you consider that they take no account of warning notices themselves.

The château, with a façade almost as long as that of Buckingham Palace, was big enough to give a millionaire a feeling of not being too cramped. From the corners and roof spaces of the building—which was built of a pleasant grey-yellow stone —a series of round towers with blue slate roofs fingered their way skywards. There was a terrace along the front with wide steps leading up from either end. In the centre of the terrace a bronze fountain spouted water twenty feet high over a centrepiece of mixed-up mermen, mermaids and dolphins engaged in some nautical frolic that in real life would certainly have led to trouble. Naturally, being O'Dowda's place, there were no goldfish in the fast swirling waters of the fountain's bowl. Just brown trout.

I had a room in one of the towers with a view reaching way back to Lac Léman. I took lunch in a small, sub-guest dining room with Durnford, who was still twitching his eyes and was not particularly friendly towards me. He told me that O'Dowda was in residence and would send for me after lunch.

I said, 'Did you get that list of people in residence here at the time Miss Zelia left?'

'I am working on it.'

It occurred to me that it wasn't something that required all that much work, but I made no comment because I could see that he was in no mood for comments.

I lingered over my coffee much too long for him, so he got up and excused himself, making for the door. But from the door he did a Wilkins on me, turning and saying, 'I think I should warn you that Mr. O'Dowda is in a particular mood today.'

I looked at him enquiringly.

'You care to enlarge on that?'

'No.' He opened the door. 'But I thought it only fair to warn you. His staff are used to him but it sometimes disconcerts strangers.' He went.

I sat there and, for a few moments, it occurred to me that perhaps he wasn't as unfriendly as he always appeared and sounded. If he disliked me he would have been happy for me to meet any awkward mood of O'Dowda's head on.

Half an hour later a footman in green livery, silver buttons, and with the face of a professional mourner, came to conduct me to O'Dowda. We went through and up what seemed a quarter of a mile of corridors, picture galleries and stairs and finally landed up in front of a tall pair of doors covered in red leather and ornamented with copper studs.

From a niche in the wall alongside the door he pulled out a hand microphone and announced, 'Mr. Carver is here, sir.'

Almost immediately, the double-doors slid back, and the footman nodded to me to enter, looking as though he were muttering a requiem for me under his breath.

I went through the door, heard it whisper to a close behind me, and faced a long room full of people, not one of whom took the slightest notice of me.

It was an enormous room, originally intended for stately balls, masques, routs, assemblages, minor coronations or, maybe, indoor joustings. Tall mullioned windows ran along one wall, draped with heavy red velvet curtains. From the barrel-vaulted ceiling hung three Venetian glass chandeliers. The floor under my feet was polished Carrera marble, and on the wall opposite the window hung four Velasquez portraits.

Although the place was full of people there wasn't a sound to be heard. There were about fifty of them—men and women, more men than women, some black, most white and a few yellow. Their dress was everything from evening gown and tiaras, court dress, rough old working suits, shirt sleeves and denims, military uniforms to national costumes. Some of them were sitting, some standing, and one couple were down on one knee in the act of obeisance, and they were all looking towards the far end of the room. Not a muscle among them moved because they were all made of wax. Nearest to me was a woman in a low-cut evening gown whose shoulders wanted dusting.

At the far end of the room was a raised platform, half-crescented at each side with a pierced marble balustrade. Three low steps ran upwards to a final dais on which was an enormous throne-chair in gold stucco with a back that ran up into a kind of baldachin affair overhead from which fell silver-

and-gold curtains. On either side of the throne-chair stood a pair of seven-branched candelabra, all the candles lit. In the chair sat a wax figure, double life-size, of O'Dowda. The big head was decked out with a chaplet of laurel leaves, a purple toga swathed the huge body, and there were gold sandals on the big feet. One fat hand held a silver drinking goblet and the other a long roll of parchment. Take the parchment away and stick a lyre in it and you could ring the changes: Caesar or Nero, according to mood.

Just at that moment, having got over the shock of the Madame Tussaud collection in the room, I was wondering what was the particular mood of the man who sat on the edge of the platform below the effigy. Normally it might have been difficult to guess. It could have been his day to be Caesar, Nero, Hitler, Napoleon, Karl Marx, Sam Goldwyn or Kruschev. But it wasn't. He was all togged up from ankle to neck in one of those blue siren suits Winston Churchill used to wear, and there was a fat cigar stuck in his mouth and a fat scowl overhanging his eyes. In his right hand he held a whippy little cane with which he was gently smacking his right leg.

He just stared at me across a hundred yards of marble floor, waiting for me to speak, I imagined. But I knew my place. You do not speak to royalty until they speak to you first. I knew something else, too. Despite this show, he wasn't mad. He wasn't even eccentric. Everything he did, he did from reason; cold, hard, cash-registering reason. Only the failures in life go mad. It's their way of opting out of the rat-race.

He got up and slowly made his way down the room. He stopped once alongside the figure of a London policeman and gave the blue serge of the man's seat a whippy slash with the cane.

Then, coming up to me, he said, careful all the time to keep the scowl on his face, 'Know why I did that, Carver?'

I said, 'I should think because years ago he was the one who around midnight nobbled you as you came out of the neighbourhood grocer's with the contents of the till in your pocket.'

O'Dowda grinned, but he still managed somehow to keep the scowl going.

'Bad guess. Sure, before I had real hairs on my chest I knocked off a till or two. How the hell do you get capital to start otherwise? No—he nobbled me for drunken driving when I was twenty-two. Licence taken away for six months, meant I couldn't drive the van. Business kaput. They're all like that.' He waved the cane around the crowd.

'You brought me all the way up here to tell me about the people who've crossed you in your life?'

'You'll learn why I brought you up here soon enough. Sure, yes, they are all people who crossed or tried to cross me. I like to come in here sometimes and talk to them, let 'em see where I am now. You know how much one of these figures costs?'

'No.'

'Kermode does them. Clever sod, is Kermode. Used to work for Tussaud's once. Two hundred quid, he charges me.'

'You could save money by having them done in miniature. Keep 'em all in a glass case. That way the dust wouldn't settle on them.' I ran my finger down the V-back of the tiara number and showed the tip to him. 'Now stop trying to impress me.'

'You're fired, boyo.'

'Splendid.'

'You were going to cross me up.'

'You should have let me do it—then you could have stuck me in here. I'd have sent you one of my old suits to make it authentic.'

'Watch your tongue when you speak to me. You're just the hired man.'

'You fired me a moment ago. Remember? Anyway, hired or fired I speak as I find. Stop playing games, O'Dowda.'

For a moment I thought he was going to hit me with the cane. He stood there and bulged his big face at me, little blue eyes boring at me, the afternoon sun sparkling on the short copper scruff of his hair, the end of his cigar glowing like a Stop light. Then he wheeled away and went up to the figure of a coloured gent wearing a tarboosh and ten yards of white

Manchester cotton robe and swiped the tarboosh off with his cane.

'What did he do?' I asked. 'Sell you a dud lot of dirty photos?'

'As a matter of fact it was a dud lot of industrial diamonds during the war. He lived to regret it. And don't think I'm trying to impress you. For me this is therapy. Every so often I like to review 'em, talk to 'em. Afterwards I feel as clean and pink inside as a baby. And when I'm not here they still have to face me.' He nodded towards the outsize Caesar figure.

I said, 'You should open it to the public. Cover your costs in a couple of years. Kermode could sell hot-dogs and ice-cream on the terrace.'

He scowled at me.

'You're fired,' he said.

I turned and made for the door. He let me reach it, and then said, 'Don't you want to know why?'

I looked at him over my shoulder. 'If you feel you've got to tell me—okay. But in that case let's do it over a drink and a smoke.' I fished out my cigarette case. 'The drink,' I said, 'is up to you.'

He gave me a grin then.

'You're a lippy bastard. But it's a change. You're still fired, though.'

He went back to the other end of the room, smacking the odd rump and shoulder here and there and stopped in front of what was probably a Louis-the-something console and produced brandy and glasses. Again, he gave himself the bigger helping. I went up and sat in an armchair with an elderly, diplomatic type in court dress resting one elbow nonchalantly on the back. (He'd probably blocked O'Dowda's bid for a knighthood.)

I breathed the brandy aroma, sipped, let the liquid roll around my mouth like a mixture of ginger and fire, swallowed it, and felt it like the beginning of a young volcano in my stomach.

I said, 'This is bloody awful stuff.'

O'Dowda said, 'You think I'd waste my best brandy on a man I've just fired?'

I said, 'Why am I fired?'

'Because, Carver, when I employ someone I demand complete loyalty for my money. Nobody has to love me for it. But they have to earn it.'

'So far as I know I haven't even got round to cheating you on a hotel bill yet. But I'll make a note to do so when you reinstate me.'

He whipped the cane through the air in front of him angrily and said, 'Bejasus, you try me hard.'

I said, 'You're the first Irishman outside of a music-hall I ever heard say Bejasus. Just let me have a few facts about my disloyalty.'

'Two days ago I had a visit from a black number called Alakwe——'

'Was this in England or over here?'

'Why?'

'Because then I'll know whether it was Jimbo Alakwe or Najib.'

'In London.'

'Good old Jimbo, still trying hard. Don't tell me—I can guess the kind of line he would take. I've taken a bribe of, say, two thousand guineas, not pounds, to double-cross you by letting him know before you where the Mercedes is when I find it? Something like that?'

'More or less. You're damned frank about it, aren't you?'

'I'll be even franker. Jimbo's the simpler of the two brothers —twins actually. God knows what the people he works for make of him. He should have known that my price for a double-cross like that would be in the region of ten thousand. I'm happy in my work with you. It gives me a change of scene, luxury living, new faces—some of 'em pretty and feminine— and a life expectancy that would have me booted out of any insurance office. Take a look at this.'

I reached into my pocket and tossed it across to him. It was the size and shape of a half grapefruit, but a good deal heavier. He held it in one gorilla paw and said, 'What's this?'

I said, 'It's a magnetic limpet bomb, thermo-activated. There's a little sliding pointer on the side which you can set against the scale to any temperature. The temperature readings are calibrated in Fahrenheit. Centigrade and Reamur. No detail overlooked. At the moment it's set to "safe". It was stuck on the side of my car engine in Geneva, set to a reading that would have blown me sky-high after a couple of kilometres.'

'Boyo, what a damned useful gadget.'

'You can keep it. But if I'd taken cash to double-cross you, why would they want to knock me off? Waste of money. They were annoyed because I wouldn't double-cross you. I suppose you've now paid Jimbo good money to double-cross them, whoever they are?'

'Yes, I have.'

I shook my head. 'You'll have him all mixed up. He isn't the kind to carry a double disloyalty in his mind without getting the wires crossed. All right, am I back at work?'

He reached round and put the bomb on the console affair behind him. Then he slewed his big head back at me, lowering it like a bull sighting on the middle point of a matador's cummerbund, and heaved a great sniff of air out of his nostrils.

'What the hell goes on?' he said. 'I just want that car back.'

I said, 'You're going to get it. It was pinched by a crook called Otto Libsch.' I paused, watching him closely as I mentioned the name. It had, I was sure, meant something to Julia. It could mean something to him. If it did he didn't show it. I went on, 'He had a respray job done on it and some weeks after used it to carry out a payroll hold-up somewhere in France. Since then, neither he nor the car has been seen. But I'll lay you ten to one in hundreds—pounds not francs—that I find that car in the next few days. On?'

'No.'

'It's nice you have such confidence in me. Am I reinstated?'

'Temporarily, yes. But by God—you put one foot wrong and——'

'You're jumping the gun,' I said. 'If you want me back, there's a condition on this side. No, two conditions.'

'Nobody makes conditions with me.' He said it with a rumble like a runaway steamroller. As I knew better than to argue with a steamroller I began to get up to leave.

He waved me down. 'Let's hear them.'

I sat back. 'First, I don't want to be badgered with questions about how I traced Otto and the car. And I don't want your stepdaughter Zelia badgered. Like she says, she knows nothing. Secondly, I want to know what's in the secret compartment of that car and who the people are who are employing Najib and Jimbo Alakwe. This I have to know for my own protection. What do you say?'

He stood up slowly and gave me a warm smile. You wouldn't believe it possible, but suddenly that big brute of a face was transformed. He was a solid, bearlike, father-figure reaching out his arms with a benign smile, ready to take and comfort the world's weary and sick at heart, the oppressed, the poor and the homeless. It didn't impress me at all, because I knew that he would take them all and make a profit out of it somehow.

'What I say, Carver, is that I've obviously been mistaken in you. Just get on with the job. I've complete trust in you, boyo. And as far as Zelia's concerned, I'll never mention the car to her again.'

'Good.'

He shook his head. 'I'll never understand why you haven't made a million for yourself already. You've got all the gall in the world.'

'What I haven't got is an answer to the second condition. What's in the car and who wants it?'

'Ah, yes, that. Well, that's a little more difficult. Delicate, in fact.'

'Try.'

He chewed the end of his cigar for a while, working up in his mind the lie he was going to tell me. After the write-up he'd just given me he knew it would have to be good. He wasn't long about it.

'In the car,' he said, 'is a very considerable parcel of bonds. Gold bonds. To be exact they're Imperial Japanese Government external loan bonds of 1930, sinking fund 5½%, which are due for final redemption in May 1975, but these bonds are ones that have been drawn for redemption in January of next year. Naturally no further interest accrues to them after that date, but their redemption value is around twenty thousand pounds. Originally they belonged to me. But I was passing them over to a friend in return for services rendered. You with this, so far?'

'Yes. But I shall check that there are such bonds, naturally.'

'Do that, you careful bastard.' He grinned.

'And the friend?'

'He is an important figure in the opposition party of one of the new African states. At the material time this opposition party was the ruling party. Times change. The present ruling party considers that the bonds belong to them since, they argue, the favour done for me by my friend when he was in power was done in his official, not private, capacity.'

'What do you think of that argument?'

'I don't care a damn. I promised him the bonds, and he gets them. And that's all the damned details you're going to get about it.'

I said, 'Where do these bonds have to be delivered for redemption?' It was a quick one but he was up to it, the answer rolling out smoothly.

'The Bank of Tokyo Trust Company, 100 Broadway, New York, N.Y. 10005. Naturally you'll check that, too. But do it on your own time, not mine. Now get the hell out of here and find me that Mercedes.'

I stood up. 'And where is the secret compartment in the car?'

He puffed his cheeks out like a grotesque cherub, exploded air gently, and said, 'That's no affair of yours. You're all right in my book so far, but not so far that I would trust you with twenty thousand pounds' worth of bonds. '

I looked sad, but only for the record, and I went towards the door, past the bobby who had flagged him down for drunken driving, past the Syrian diamond merchant who had switched stones on him, past a slick looking South American type who'd probably sold him a salted gold mine, past men and women who once, for a brief while, had got in his way, shaken him down, held him up, and had eventually lived or died to regret it. And not for one moment did I believe a word about the bonds . . . that is, that that was what was in the car. Imperial Japanese Bonds existed all right. He'd just used the fact to get rid of me. And I'd accepted it. Why not? A job is a job, and this one paid well, and when I got the car somebody—I wasn't sure who yet—was going to pay well for whatever was in the secret compartment.

I went back to my room, panting up the spiral stairway to my turret, anxious to pack and be away. Waiting for me was Miss Zelia Yunge-Brown.

She was sitting in a chair by the window, in a blue anorak and a blue skirt and wearing heavy walking shoes, looking as though she'd just come back from a long tramp through the pine woods.

I said, 'So you finally decided to come ashore?'

'Yes.' She put up a hand and ran it through one side of her dark hair and did a little brow-knitting act; no smile on her face, but not, I thought, as cold and glacial as she had been at our last meeting.

She stood up as I dumped my case on the bed and began to pack my pyjamas which some flunkey had already laid out.

'I was stupid about the Max Ansermoz letter. I should have guessed that was what you wanted me to do. You must have enjoyed yourself.'

I said, 'Between ourselves, Max is dead.'

'Dead?'

'Yes. You want me to look unhappy about it?'

'But you——'

'No, I didn't do it. But Max is dead and I'm dry-eyed about the whole thing. I'm only interested in a motor car. So's your father.'

'Stepfather.'

'Well, yes, if you're sticking to niceties. He knows nothing. Nobody knows anything, except me—and for some things I have no memory at all. Now stop doing an ice-maiden act on me. Write it off to experience and get into gear again.'

'You have said nothing to anyone?'

'That's right.'

She was a big girl, and she was embarrassed suddenly, and she wasn't very good at carrying it off. For a moment I was afraid that she would come across and embrace me, crushing me in those lovely long strong arms. However, she got it under control and slowly held out a hand to me.

'I am very grateful to you.'

She had my hand in hers and now I was embarrassed.

'Just forget it.'

I got my hand away. She clumped to the door in her heavy shoes and paused before going out.

'I wish there was something I could do to show you how grateful I am.'

I said, 'You could try smiling again. It's a knack that comes back easily.'

'It's not easy to smile in this house. It has too many memories for me . . . of my mother. I have decided to go away and get a job.'

'I'm all for the job. You'll land one easier though with a smile on your face. Try it.'

It came back easily. She gave it to me, a slow warm smile that was followed by a little shake of her head and then a laugh. Then she went.

I snapped the lid of my case down, glad that Max was dead.

In the hallway, down a long perspective of green and white marble slabs Durnford was waiting for me. He came up to me with the practised glide of one used to walking in marble halls, and said, 'You're going?'

'Be glad,' I said. 'Besides, I don't like staying in a wax-works. I presume you've heard from the boss that I'm reinstated?'

'Yes.'

'In that case, could I have the list of people who were staying here before Miss Zelia took off with the Mercedes.'

He handed me a sheet of paper and said, 'I think you should know that I had been given strict instructions from Mr. O'Dowda that I was never to make that guest-list available to anyone.'

'Then why me?'

'That's not a question I'm prepared to answer.'

I slipped the paper into my pocket and gave him a cocked-eyebrow look.

'You don't like him, do you?'

'He is my employer.'

'You'd like to see him come a cropper, a real trip-up, flat on his face?'

He gave me a thin smile then, and said, 'I'm hoping for more than that. And I've been waiting a long time. Contrary to what you imagine, I have no animosity towards you. I think you may turn out to be the *deus ex machina*.'

'What you mean is that if I find the car, you hope that I will walk off with whatever is in it. Or hand it over to some-one else?'

'Possibly.'

'You really hate his guts, don't you? Tell me, have you ever written any anonymous letters about him to Interpol or Scotland Yard?'

'Why should I?' He was well in control.

'It's just a thought I had. Anyway, whatever game you are playing I think it's a dangerous one. You watch it, unless you want to end up in the waxworks with all the others.'

I picked up my case and went outside to my car. Standing alongside it was Julia.

She said, 'Was everything all right?'

'Fine. Your father almost trusts me, Zelia's grateful, and Durnford is full of hints. What are you registering?'

She said, 'Why is it that you can't talk to me without being cross or vulgar?'

'It's something you do to me. There's nothing I'd like better than a beautiful relationship but I always seem to knock on the wrong door.'

She lit a cigarette as I put my case in the car.

I paused at the door before getting in and said, 'Don't do anything stupid like trying to follow me.'

'It wasn't in my mind. Where are you going, anyway?'

'To find Otto Libsch. Any messages?'

She gave me a quick, almost apprehensive look. 'Why should there be?'

'I had the impression that you knew him, or something about him.'

'I don't know why you should think that.'

'No? I'll tell you. When you came to my room that first night, there was more on your mind than just protecting Zelia. When I mentioned his name in Turin, it was no surprise to you, and right now you haven't said you don't know him. Don't worry, I'm not going to force anything from you. I just want to find a car. That's my brief.'

'Did you mention him to Zelia?'

'No. The less said to her about either of them the better. But I mentioned him to your father, naturally, and his big happy face remained quite unchanged. Now, do you want to talk about Otto, or do I get moving?'

She blinked at me a little and bit her lip. Then she shook her head, and said, 'There's no point. Absolutely no point whatsoever . . . it couldn't change things from being what they are.'

Then, her manner hardening, she went on, 'You go. Go and find your car. That is important. That's money, that's business. Things that really count in this life.'

She turned abruptly away from me and made for the house.

I drove off, not pleased with myself, knowing that she needed help, and knowing too that it was no moment for me to get involved in anything else. This car business was all my hands could hold at the moment—particularly with Interpol sticking their noses in.

CHAPTER SIX

'And Laughter holding both his sides.'
MILTON

I DROVE WITHOUT HURRY south from Evian. In Grenoble I went into the Post Office and found the Botin for the Gap-St Bonnet district and turned up Max Ansermoz's number at the Châlet Bayard. I rang through—it was now about seven o'clock—and the phone rang for ten minutes without being answered. That was good enough for me. With any luck the only living thing in the house was the white poodle and by now it must be damned hungry.

I had a quick meal in Grenoble, and then went south down the N 85 towards St Bonnet and Gap. I didn't try to push it. This was my second night on the road and my eyelids had begun to feel like heavy shutters that every bump in the road brought down. I pulled up for a couple of hours' sleep somewhere around a place called Corps, and then drove on to the Châlet Bayard. I came to it at dawn with little wisps of mist lying between the trees and the air full of bird-song, which shows how isolated the place was because normally if a bird gives out with an aria anywhere in France some *chasseur* promptly blows its head off.

The front door was still open and I walked straight in and was greeted by the poodle lying curled in an armchair. A few days without food had taught it manners and it came to me, trembling and with all the bounce gone from it. I gave it some water in the kitchen—the cat had disappeared, which didn't surprise me, cats can knock spots off any dog in the independence and survival stakes—and then fed it a bowl of scraps which I had scrounged in the restaurant where I had fed. In half an hour I knew it would be its same old jaunty, face-licking self. While it was tucking in I went upstairs and had a bath and shave, and then came down and carted Max's typewriter and some of his stationery to the round table, and wrote a letter to Otto. I had to write it in English because my French would never have been good enough to fool anyone that it had come from Max. And the fact that it was in English wouldn't matter to the people who opened it because I guessed they wouldn't know much about the way Max usually wrote to Otto.

The letter read:

My dear Otto,

Going off like that with the Mercedes almost landed me in a great deal of trouble, and I have been very angry.

I decided to have nothing more to do with you, until yesterday it came to my attention—through Aristide, you will remember him, always two ears to the ground—

(That was safe enough for Mimi and Tony when they read it because they would assume Aristide was some genuine nark known to both Otto and Max.)

—that you in fact used the car to pull off a neat little job in your usual line with a companion who—from Aristide's description, and you know how reliable he is in the matter of police dossiers—sounds just like the Turin type, Tony Collard, you were telling me about. I presume he did the respray.

Well, dear Otto, my friend, since I virtually provided the car and as times are never as good as they should be, I've decided that I should have my cut. And no argument.

I shall be here for the next two days, and shall expect you. If you don't turn up I shall let Aristide—to whom I owe a favour—have a few details of you and this Tony Collard, and where to find you. (My love to the delightful Mimi, by the way, though how you stick that baby I can't think. Not your style.) I am sure Aristide will promptly find a market for such information with the police. So don't let me down, dear friend. I promise to be reasonable about my share—but don't think I don't know how much you two got away with.

Salutations,

I found a wad of cancelled cheques in the bureau and without much care forged the signature 'Max' to the letter. I addressed it to Otto Libsch at Mimi's flat and then drove into Gap and sent it express. When I got back I was greeted by the poodle, all its elastic reset, gave it a stroll through the pines and then shut it up in the kitchen.

Back in the main lounge I settled down with a large glass of Max's brandy and pulled out Durnford's sheet of paper, which I had already glanced at, knowing that it demanded a lot of thought. Before I could start on it, the ginger cat walked in from nowhere and came and sat in the empty fireplace and stared at me, accepting a new owner without comment.

The list of guests was in Durnford's handwriting. The château had been given over to them completely for five days. Durnford commented (the list was full of little comments, as though he were aching to say more, willing to wound but afraid to strike) that O'Dowda often let business associates and friends have the use of the château. Not all the guests had stayed for the full five days. The principal guest was a General Seyfu Gonwalla. Durnford commented that he did not have to tell me who he was. He did not. The General had stayed there in strict incognito—none of the servants had known who he was. (For my money, it was probable that he had made the trip to Europe in strict incognito, too.) He had stayed four out of the five days, missing the first, when there had only been one guest, the General's aide-de-camp, who had preceded him to see that all the appropriate arrangements had been made. And, surprise, surprise, the aide-de-camp was named as Captain Najib Alakwe. (I'd chewed that one over for a long time during the night drive, and for my money again, Najib had to be a Jekyll-and-Hyde character, though at the moment I didn't know which of the two I had had dealings with.) Najib had stayed the full five days. The next guest, and she had stayed for the middle three days, was a Mrs. Falia Makse (strict incognito). She was, Durnford noted, the wife of the Minister of Agriculture in General Seyfu Gonwalla's government. Also for the middle three days there had been present a Miss Panda Bubakar. There was no comment against her name —though I could have made one. For the last two days only— and no comment also—there had been present a Mr. Alexi Kukarin. And that was the lot.

At the bottom of the sheet, Durnford had added a note:

You realize that in giving you this information I am very much putting myself in your hands. I do so because I flatter myself that I am a good judge of character. The secret apartment in the Mercedes is behind the large air-intake opening on the right-hand side of the facia board. You just unscrew the circular vent with an anti-clockwise movement. You will, of course, destroy this communication. So far as the Press etc. are concerned, no one knew of the presence of the above guests at the château.

I destroyed it then and there, burning it in the fireplace while the cat watched without much interest. That I did destroy it didn't necessarily mean that Durnford was a good judge of character. It simply struck me as a sensible thing to do with people like the Alakwe brothers, Aristide, Tony Collard and so on around.

I sat back and gave some of my attention to the rest of the brandy. The other part I gave to O'Dowda and General Seyfu Gonwalla. If I were right, Gonwalla, as Head of State, was the guy who now thought he should have the twenty thousand pounds' worth of bonds. Odd that O'Dowda thought not, yet gladly lent him the château for a five-day conference, if that were the word for it.

I reached back and picked up the phone and booked a call to Wilkins in London. It came through much later.

Wilkins said, 'Where are you?'

'France.'

'I know that, but where?' She sounded cross and clucking like a disturbed mother hen.

'A chalet in the Haute Savoie, very comfortable, with a white poodle and a marmalade cat, well, ginger, to keep me company. No women—glad?'

She said, 'I thought you must be dead.'

'Why?'

'Because that Mr. Jimbo Alakwe was here this morning offering to buy out your share in this firm.' She paused, enjoying the moment to come. 'He said that with imaginative and efficient running he could make a real success of it.'

'He's a comic—but not as much as he would like people to think. Anyway, I'm alive and kicking, and I want a *précis* of all the press comments you can get on General Seyfu Gonwalla, Mrs. Falia Makse, and possibly though I doubt it, a Miss Panda Bubakar. And I particularly mean the outer-edge comments that run near libel. You know the kind of stuff, "great and good friend of". Also—I hope you're getting all this down?'

'The tape is on, naturally.'

'Also any record you can find of dealings, difficulties or troubles that any of O'Dowda's companies, especially that United Africa job, may have had, or are having, with Gonwalla's regime. Also, ring Guffy, or invite him out for a coffee and Danish cakes, and see if he'll admit that at some time or the other, meaning fairly recently, he's had some more anonymous letters suggesting that O'Dowda is worth investigating from a personal point of view, that is to say——'

'You needn't elaborate. But I doubt if Superintendent Foley would tell me anything like that.'

'You try. He goes for blue-eyed redheads. Or offer to darn his socks, the heels are always gone.'

'Is that all?' The old tartness was back.

'No.' I gave her the telephone number of the chalet, so that she could ring back, and went on, 'And don't fuss. I'm well and happy and not lonely. In fact I've an interesting guest arriving soon who will be able to tell me, possibly under duress, where the Mercedes is located. Isn't that good?'

'You sound,' she said, 'too pleased with yourself. That means you're probably up to your neck in trouble.'

'Well, so what? That's life. Didn't the O.T. expert on it say that Man is of few days, and full of trouble?'

'Or else you've been drinking. Goodbye.'

She was right, of course. It's funny how you can sit in a chair occupied with your thoughts and the brandies go down unnoticed.

I had a great night, ten hours of dreamless sleep with the poodle at the foot of the bed and the cat on the spare pillow. The cat woke me by kneading determinedly on my chest, and when I blinked at it said it was time to let him out to forage for his breakfast which I could hear singing in the nearby scrub. The poodle slept on, knowing there was no point in moving until I was down slaving away in the kitchen at his and my breakfast.

After that it was a matter of waiting and taking what precautions I could. The moment my letter arrived in Turin I was sure that Mimi and Tony would open it. Tony would come, as fast as he could, to make sure that Max never got anywhere near grassing on him to any Aristide. If the letter arrived by first post, it meant Tony would be at the chalet by the evening. If by the afternoon post, then he could make it by midnight or early morning. Whenever he came I just couldn't afford to be sleeping and not give him a welcome.

I spent the morning making a reconnaissance of the surroundings of the chalet. At the back, which I had not noticed on my first visit, well up in the pines, was a wooden shack which held a small Volkswagen saloon, Max's. I ran it down to the front of the chalet and put my Mercedes in its place. I didn't want Tony arriving and being confused by the sight of the Mercedes. Then I went down to St Bonnet and bought some supplies, but I had to cuff the poodle out of the car—my car—because someone in the place might recognize it.

When I got back the telephone was ringing. But instead of Wilkins it was some French woman asking for Max. It took me a little while to put over to her that Max was away in Cannes on a property deal and had lent me the chalet for a few days.

We all three had lunch together, sharing everything except a bottle of Clos-du-Lyon *vin rosé*. After that we took a long siesta, very long, until it was gin-and-Campari time, strictly one, because there was soon to be business ahead. Then I shut the animals in the kitchen, found a warm hunting coat of Max's, borrowed his twelve-bore and a handful of shells, and went and sat in the Mercedes where I could catch the lights of any car coming up the road to the chalet. I didn't want to be inside when Tony arrived. It wasn't going to give me any points as a host, but I felt that for this visit protocol could be dropped.

By midnight nothing had happened, except that I was colder than I thought I would be and wished I'd brought some brandy out. I sat there, thinking about a quick nip and how it was only a few yards away. The more I thought the colder I became—the chalet was up around the twelve hundred metre mark where the nights are chill at the end of September—and I was tempted to go and serve myself. It was only fifty yards to the chalet. I'm glad I didn't because Tony would have walked in on me as I had my hand on the bottle.

I had to give him full marks for his approach. Either he'd been to the chalet before or Mimi had briefed him. He must have parked his car well down the road and approached on foot. The first sign he gave me was a quick flicker of a torch away in the pines, a hundred yards to my right. I got it out of the corner of my eye, which, in my job, is what corners of eyes are for. Then there was just the darkness, the odd hoot of an owl and the noise of a plane droning overhead. The next flicker was when he hit the drive; brief, but enough to give him his surroundings.

I slipped out of the Mercedes and went cautiously down through the pines on my right. Ahead of me somewhere he had to be crossing left-handed to the chalet, even if he were going to avoid the front in favour of a side or back entrance.

Actually, he opted for the front entrance. When I was down level with the parked Volkswagen, I saw the torchlight come on and stay steady as he cowled it with one hand and examined the door. I'd locked the door and the key was in my pocket. That wasn't giving him any trouble. The torchlight went off and I could make out his bulk against the night sky as he worked on the door. He jemmied it, and well. There was just one quick scrunch of wood and steel going and then silence, and Tony standing there, waiting and listening. Nobody could tell me that this number was an amateur. I kept my fingers crossed and hoped the poodle wouldn't set up a racket inside and scare him off. The poodle was silent, stuffed with food still, and sleeping secure on that phoney reputation which dogs have conned mankind with since the first cave. Ask any T.B.N. man.

Happy in his work, Tony pushed the door open and went in. I gave him a few moments and then I went after him. I slipped through the front door and at once saw his torch doing a low sweep round in the main room, the door of which was wide open.

I went gently to the door, flicked on the lights and raised the twelve-bore, holding the sights on his head as he turned quickly.

'Just keep your hands where they are. It's not my house and I don't mind blood on the carpets.'

He blinked at me through his steel-rimmed glasses and then gave me that babyish grin of his and a fat chuckle. It didn't fool me. He had only one way of expressing any emotion.

I went up and around him carefully. He was wearing rubber-soled canvas shoes, black trousers, a thick black sweater and, for relief, a pair of white cotton gloves. From the corner of his left-hand pocket the handle of the jemmy stuck out. From behind him I reached out and retrieved it, slipping it into my coat pocket. Standing back I tapped his trouser pockets with my left hand, holding the gun in the right, barrel end pressed hard against his back. There was nothing bigger than

136

a packet of cigarettes and a lighter in his pockets by the feel of it.

He said, 'I've got nothing but the jemmy, but I can see you're the thorough type, like my old man. Nothing on chance.'

I said, 'You can tell me about your father some other time. Turn around.'

He turned, beaming a Pickwick smile at me.

'Pull your sweater right up, but keep your hands in sight.'

He pulled his sweater up. He wore a singlet underneath and a leather belt round his trousers.

'Anyway, I've got nothing against you.'

I nodded to him to drop the sweater and said, 'Now, sit on the floor, keep your legs crossed and your hands at the back of your head. It's a tiring position but if you talk fast you won't have to hold it long.' I had memories of this room with its polished floor and sliding chairs.

He sat on the floor and I went three yards away from him and sat on the edge of the table, the shotgun cradled in my lap, covering him. Just then the poodle began to bark its head off. They time it well—the moment real trouble is over.

Tony, hands behind his head, said, 'That's a dog.'

'Don't be fooled. It's only the impression it likes to create. Now, give me the story from the moment you held up that payroll and then went away like bats out of hell in the Mercedes. I don't want any colourful matter about your emotions of the moment or unnecessary details. Just a plain unvarnished tale. I want to know what happened to the car, and what happened to Otto. Not that I care about him—the car's my concern. But it would be nice to hear that he's dead. And don't worry about my saying anything to the police. I'm in private business and I just want that car.'

'Wow! You had me fooled. That letter from Max, so-say.' He rolled his eyes in his horrible laughing manner. 'Yes, you're a number.' His face went serious. 'But you know, you got Mimi really upset with that letter. I had a terrible time with her, 'cos I didn't really want to do it. But she says if it's true bliss and a bright future we want, which it is, then there's nothing but come here and knock this Max off. I had to give in.'

I said, 'Why be squeamish about Max? You'd already got your hand in with Otto. Come on, now. Start talking.'

'But I didn't do anything to Otto. He did it to himself.' He started to chuckle. 'Yes, he did it to himself. I never laughed so much in all my life. It was real funny. Mind you, it was convenient, too. I mean, seeing that Mimi and me had decided anyway to give Otto his cards—on account of we loved one another. He was wanting out anyway, chiefly because of the baby. Even so, he'd have made trouble. But we were prepared to face that. Course of true love. Two hearts beating as one. My old man was pretty cynical about all that, of course. You'd think I'd be, too, wouldn't you? You know, just four legs in a bed, any bed, any four so long as two of 'em are yours and the others are a nice shape. But in our family sons must go by opposites. I'm a faithful man, you know. One woman's all I want.'

'Congratulations. Now get on with the bloody story.'

'Of course, of course.' He started to laugh, tears squeezing out of his eyes, and there was no doubt that it was genuine. I couldn't wait to be let in on the joke. There's nothing more annoying than people laughing and you right out in the cold as to why. He looked up at me, hands behind his neck, sitting there like a Buddha, and he wobbled his big head with joy. 'He was drunk, you know. Not stoned. But . . . well, well away. That's why it happened. Mind you, he was always like that after a job, excited, wings on him. You know, feet right off the ground. It takes you all ways after a job. Me, well, I don't alter much—except I get bad heartburn. Never anything more.'

I said firmly, 'If you don't come to the point I'll——'

'All right. All right now. Just wanted you to know how it was. Yes, Otto was well away. That's why I never liked him driving, but he always would. Anyway, we took off in the car. We were only going to use it for about ten kilometres. Not safe otherwise. We had another waiting for us up in the mountains,

ready for the switch and the ditch. The switch and the ditch!'
He started to chuckle again and it rumbled around inside his
throat like a caged bear trying to get out. I sat there and
ordered myself to be patient. He had only one way of telling a
story and there was nothing I could do about it. If it had been
his gallows-side confession he would have laughed through it
in his own good time until any priest would have wanted to
crack him one and skip the final absolution.

He looked up at me, tears in his eyes, and said, 'It was the
funniest thing you've ever seen.'

'It wasn't—because I didn't see it. But come on, tell me,
and make me laugh.'

'Well . . . there was this place up in the mountains. Up a
dirt road through woods to a lake. We'd left the other car
there. Otto sang like a bird all the way there. Man, he was
wild. You know, I think when he did a job there was something sexual about it for him. I was talking to Mimi about
it——'

'Come to the point.'

For a moment he looked piqued, really hurt, like a fat, jolly
boy who'd been reprimanded unjustly.

'Well . . . the other car was there, so we off-loaded the stuff
into it, and then Otto ran the Mercedes close to the edge of
the lake. It was an open slope, about ten yards of it, down to
the lake edge and over a ten foot drop into deep water. Nobody
goes up there much. Just a few fishermen. It's a beautiful spot.
A good place to spend a day . . .' He rocked with a sudden
outburst of fresh giggles. 'A great place to spend the rest of
your days.'

In a minute he was going to tell me what size the trout
ran to and I was going to clout him over the head with the
shotgun.

He saw the look in my eyes and sobered up a little.

'Well, all you had to do was let off the hand brake and start
her rolling. And that's all Otto did. He opened the door,
reached in and let off the brake—and the Merc started rolling.
Lord, I never saw anything so funny. The car went off before

he was ready for it . . . really it did. Rolled away and the door swings back a little against him and somehow his jacket or something got caught up inside so that he was dragged with it, half in half out. You've got to believe me when I say I tried to get to him. It was instinctive. You see a man in trouble and you go to help—but it was too late. The tipsy bastard lost his head and he yells and pulls his feet up, half in and half out. I think he was trying to get at the brake again to hold the Merc. Before I could do a thing, he was over the side in a damn great splash.' He looked up at me, shaking his head at the comic wonder of it all, his plump face beaming, the little eyes shining with happy tears behind his glasses.

'And what did you do?' I got to my feet. 'Just stand there and read the service for those lost at sea?'

'I couldn't do a thing. I can't swim. And the lake, right off the edge there, is about twenty feet deep. Anyway, I knew Otto could swim, so I just waited for him to come up. But he didn't. I gave him fifteen minutes, but no sign of him . . . so what would you have done? What would any man have done in the circumstances? He was out of my hair, no trouble to Mimi anymore—he really didn't like that baby, you know—and I got the full share of the payroll we'd taken. I just got into the other car and drove back to Mimi.'

'Laughing all the way.'

He grinned. 'Well, I had to chuckle now and then. Don't tell me you're upset about this? You said you hoped he was dead.'

'Frankly, I'm delighted. It's just that I'm old-fashioned enough not to show it by a good belly-laugh.'

Keeping him in sight, I went to the desk and got a pencil and a sheet of paper.

Tony was a bright boy.

'You want me to draw a map?'

I dropped the paper and pencil at his feet.

'Do that. And make it accurate. If you shove me off with any phoney details, I'll laugh my way to the nearest phone and ring a friend of mine at Interpol. Play ball—and you can shove off from here and I'll forget that I ever met you. You'd be surprised how easy that will be.'

'You can rely on me. Besides, I got Mimi and the baby to think about now.'

He sat on the floor and began to sketch out the details of the road and the track up to the lake, giving me a running commentary as I stood behind him.

Once, he looked up and said, 'What's all the fuss about this car anyway?'

'My client wants it back.'

He shrugged. 'Why—O'Dowda could make a better deal with the insurance company.'

I went poker-faced.

'How did you know my client was called O'Dowda?'

'From Otto, of course, and the car. All the registration papers were in it when I did the respray.'

'Did Otto know O'Dowda?'

Tony shook his head at me sadly.

'You haven't done your homework. Up to about two years ago Otto was second-chauffeur at O'Dowda's place near Evian. Used to drive the wife about. News to you?'

It was news to me—and news that suddenly made sense of a lot of things that had quietly puzzled me.

I said, 'Give me the map.'

He handed it over his shoulder and I stood back from him.

'What now?' he said.

'You blow,' I said. 'I'm not having the spare bed mucked up and I'm not making breakfast for two. On your feet.'

I escorted him to the front door and covered him as he went down the steps. At the bottom he turned and beamed up at me.

'Done you a good turn, haven't I? And all for free. No charge. Just goodness of heart. Know what, too? I've complete confidence in you. About that Interpol thing, I mean. Keeping your mouth shut and so on. I'm a good judge of character. I said to Mimi after you left, "Now, there's a *buono ragazzo* who——" '

'Skip it. I've got all the character references I need.'

'Okay. And when you finally lift that car out, just say hello to Otto for me.'

He went and I could hear his rich laughter burbling all the way down the drive. Life should have more characters like him, simple, uncomplicated, always ready to look on the bright side of things, and good with children, too.

I went back in and packed up my stuff and made myself a cup of coffee against the journey ahead. I should have skipped the coffee because then I would have missed Aristide.

As I picked up my suitcase in the main room and made for the hall door, I saw the headlights of a car wheel across the window. Not knowing who it was, but having various possibilities in mind, I had only one thought. Almost any visitor at four o'clock in the morning might be interested in the location of the Mercedes. I whipped out the plan which Tony had drawn and shoved it under one of the chair cushions. Then I picked up the shotgun from the table. It was a good gun, a well-used Cogswell and Harrison hammerless ejector with nicely engraved strengthening plates on the walnut stock.

I opened the door to the hall, prepared to welcome guests.

The main house door swung back and Aristide came through. He took off a beret and gave me a half wave with it, and then stood there, shaking his head either in sadness at the sight of me or to get the sleep out of his eyes. Behind him was his driver, a big fellow in a tight blue suit and a peaked chauffeur's cap.

'The shotgun, my friend,' said Aristide, 'will not be necessary. You were just leaving?' He nodded at the suitcase inside the room door. Then he sniffed the air and said, 'Coffee?'

'In the kitchen. Help yourself.'

'You must share it with me.'

He came down the hall, took the shotgun from me and handed it to his driver.

'Have a good look round, Albert. Miss nothing.'

He took me by the arm, steered me into the main room, glanced round, nodded approvingly, and said, 'Always it has been a dream with me to have such a place. Secluded, the mountains, peace, and the air so clean you can wear a white shirt for a week without dirtying it.'

Albert clumped by us, and I led the way into the kitchen. The poodle greeted me as though I had been away for a month. The cat opened one eye, and then closed it, dismissing the interruption to its sleep.

Aristide said, 'Excuse me,' and began to make fresh coffee. I found a tin of chocolate biscuits and put them beside him. Not to get into his good books but because I knew he would have found them for himself anyway.

I said, 'How did you know I was here?'

He said, 'I didn't, but I am glad you are. I was merely informed that this was the address for Max Ansermoz and that the place might be of immediate interest. Personally, I am sure that behind it all was a desire to embarrass you. You are embarrassed?'

'No more than usual. Who informed you?'

'It was a woman—on the telephone—and she gave her name as Miss Panda Bubakar. A fictitious name, of course. It is always that, or they remain anonymous.' He gave me a warm smile, and went on, 'There is cream somewhere?'

I found him some cream.

'Did you know,' he said, 'that coffee, which is held in such high esteem in the Middle East, used once to be taken during prayers in the mosques and even before the tomb of the Prophet at Mecca? And at one time the Turks, on marrying, used to promise the woman that in addition to love, honour and a daily bastinado or whatever, she should never go short of coffee, and that we owe that filthy instant stuff to a country-man of yours called Washington who, while living in Guate-mala—yes, Albert?'

Albert had appeared in the doorway.

'It is there, *monsieur*.'

'Good. Go back and stay with it. We will be with you in a little while.'

'What is where?' I asked as Albert disappeared.

Aristide stuffed a chocolate biscuit into his mouth, generously tossed one to the poodle who was walking around on its hind legs, and then said, 'You have had a visitor tonight?'

'No.'

'Then it was you who jemmied the front door? The jemmy is on the table out there.'

I said, 'Do me a favour, Aristide—don't save the main point till last. I've got a long drive ahead of me and want to get off.'

'You have found where the Mercedes is?'

'No.'

'A pity.'

'Why?'

'If you had, I might have stretched a point. The main point you were talking about. This is good coffee. Martinique. It was a great countryman of mine, one Desclieux, who under severe hardship brought the first coffee seedling to Martinique. You can always tell Martinique coffee, big grains, rounded at both ends and it is greenish in colour. Did you see Max Ansermoz at all on this visit?'

'No.'

'You are becoming monosyllabic.'

'What do you expect at this hour of the morning?'

'That you would be in bed, sleeping the sleep of the just. However, it is convenient that you are already dressed. Are you sure that you do not know where the car is?'

'Frankly, no.'

'Splendid. If you tell me where it is, you can go, and I shall ignore all that this Miss Panda has said, ignore even the evidence of Albert's and my eyes, and even the fact—which I have no doubt the laboratory experts will establish—of your fingerprints.'

I said, 'I'd better have some coffee to clear my head.'

Graciously, he poured me a cup and another one for himself. Then he gave me one of his warm, owlish smiles, and said, 'Just tell me where the car is and I will smooth away all difficulties for you. I have the power—and after all I have, too, a certain affection for you. You have had a visitor tonight

—otherwise you would not be leaving at this hour. The car, *mon ami*, where is it?'

I lit a cigarette and shook my head.

'You insist?'

'I insist,' I said. 'And what is more I insist on my rights. Unless you are going to make some charge against me, I wish to leave. Okay?'

I turned to go.

Aristide said, 'I think we had better join Albert first. He is a good man, Albert. Solid, a little slow-thinking, but a first-class driver. He comes from Brittany where they make a coffee substitute out of chickpea and lupin seeds. This way.'

He held out a hand with a gun in it and pointed towards the door on the far side of the kitchen through which Albert had gone.

I went through the door and he followed me. At the end of the corridor I could see Albert waiting. I'd been down here before when I had first reached the house. There were a couple of store-rooms and a cellar. Albert was standing outside the cellar door.

As we approached he turned the key in the lock and opened the door for us. They stood aside and motioned me in first, Aristide switching the light on behind me.

One wall held racks of wine bottles. There was no window and there were empty crates and cartons stacked against another wall. Along the wall that faced the door was a big deep-freeze unit. The lid was pushed back, resting against the wall, and an internal light was burning in it, throwing a soft glow up to the ceiling.

One of them prodded me gently up to the deep-freeze. Lying inside, knees bent up, head sunk between his shoulders, was Max Ansermoz. On a pile of frozen spinach cartons rested the gun with which Najib had killed him, and I didn't have to be told, because I already had been, that my finger-prints would be on it, placed there by Najib while I lay knocked out in the main room. Najib wasn't the kind of man to throw anything away that one day might come in handy.

'Well?' said Aristide at my side.

I stepped back. 'You'd better get the lid down,' I said, 'or the rest of the stuff will spoil.'

'You killed him,' said Aristide.

'I didn't—and you know it.'

'I only know it if you know where the car is. Otherwise we go to an examining magistrate. Your prints will be on the gun.'

'That won't surprise me.'

'If you know where the car is it will save endless complications . . . the slow progression of the law to establish innocence . . . the *procès-verbal*. Have you any idea how long it all takes?'

'How,' I asked, 'can I tell you where the car is if I don't know?'

Aristide studied me, shook his head and said, 'If only one could tell whether a person is telling the truth or not.'

'It would make police work simple, and cause a lot of confusion in domestic life.'

Aristide nodded and then said, 'Search him, Albert.'

Albert came over, turned me round, perhaps out of respect for the dead, to face the door, and then went through my clothes. He did it very thoroughly and handed his find to Aristide. Aristide shuffled through the stuff, passport, credit cards, wallet and so on, and then handed the lot back to me.

I said, 'Look, Aristide, you know I didn't kill Max. That doesn't mean to say I'm not glad he's dead—but I didn't do it. What you are doing is just falling for a gag—from another interested party—to keep me from finding that car.'

'It could be true, *mon ami*, but it is equally true that I don't want *you* to find that car, so . . . it is very convenient to have something to keep you busy elsewhere for a time.'

At this moment there was a bark outside the door and the poodle came bounding in. It ran a circle round the three of us and then got up on its hind legs and danced, begging, in front of Aristide.

He beamed.

'*Mignon, non?*' His calloused, police heart was touched.

'Don't fool yourself, Aristide. He just sees you as one big

chocolate biscuit.' But as I spoke I was glad of the diversion. Both the men were watching the exhibition from the fool dog with happy grins on their faces. I stepped back to give the poodle more room for its act and, putting my hand behind me, got hold of the neck of the nearest bottle in the wine-rack. I jerked it out and slung it at the naked electric light-bulb. There was a crash and the light went out, followed by another, louder crash and a roar from Albert, but by this time I was at the door and out, slamming it shut and turning the key in the lock.

I sprinted for the kitchen and was beaten by the poodle. Trust a dog to get the hell out of danger before anyone else.

I dashed through into the main room, picked up the shotgun, the map from under the cushion, and my suitcase and headed for the door, the poodle following. The cellar door was stout but I couldn't give it more than five minutes of pounding from Albert's big shoulders.

Outside I pumped both barrels of the shotgun into one of the rear tyres of Aristide's car. The noise sent the poodle, yelping hysterically, streaking for the woods, and then I ran for the Mercedes, wondering whether it was burgundy or claret which I had slung at the light. Either way Aristide was going to be angry. Wine, I was sure, was something which he always treated with respect.

The place where Otto and Tony had carried out the payroll robbery was St Jean-de-Maurienne, a small town of about seven thousand inhabitants on the N6, which is the road that runs eastwards from Chambéry across Savoie to the Italian border at the Col du Mont Cenis and then on to Turin. It had been well chosen because it left them only about seventy-odd kilometres to reach the border. Fourteen kilometres east of St Jean there was a town called St Michel and some way out from this on the road to the border they had turned left-handed up into the mountains to their lake. From St Bonnet it was quite a drive, and no direct route to it. I reckoned I would make the lake sometime in the early afternoon. The payroll robbery, I learned later, had been from a small light engineering firm which had set up business on the eastern outskirts of St Jean-de-Maurienne. And later still, I learned that Otto had had this fixed pattern of hold-ups—knocking off a payroll in eastern France and then making quickly for the Italian border.

Dawn came up with a slight drizzle as I left St Bonnet and headed north. The rain slicked the road and cut down my speed. I stopped for coffee around nine o'clock in a small town and also bought myself a face-mask and snorkel, swimming trunks and a rubber-jacketed hand torch. For all I knew the lake water might be as clear as gin, but I wanted to be prepared. One thing I knew was that it would be as cold as hell.

I reached the lake soon after midday. It was two miles up a side track that climbed all the way through pine woods. It was still drizzling and, as I got higher, wisps of cloud began to sweep through the trees. The track ended, clear of trees, on a wide grassy plateau that overlooked a lake almost as big as the one O'Dowda had back in Sussex. On this side the ground was fairly level, broken with large grey boulders pushing through the bracken and scrub. On the other side—visible now and then through the mist—the ground rose steeply to a small crest. The surface of the lake was still, and the colour of gun metal.

I got out and walked to the edge of the plateau. Faintly in the thin grass I could make out the marks of Otto's car, and at the edge a big piece of ground had been broken fairly recently. There was a sheer drop of about fifteen feet into deep water. Looking down into it I could see nothing. It looked cold and uninviting and I felt a thin rise of goose pimples move across my shoulders and arms. I went back to the car, turned it round, and then stripped and put on the bathing trunks and the mask and went back to the bank. The cloud mist was thickening fast.

Somewhere down there was the car and Otto. I could rely on that because I knew Tony would never risk a lie with me. I didn't have to dive down and say 'hello' to Otto. I didn't have to grope about and recover what rested behind the air-intake grille. I could just go to the nearest phone and give O'Dowda the location and then send in my bill. All I'd been hired to do was to find the car. Whatever was hidden in it was no business of mine. O'Dowda and Aristide wanted it, and Najib wanted it for his employers. They could get on with it. It was no day for swimming and diving. All I had to do was to mind my own business. Simple. Except that few of us can resist minding other people's business—because just now and again it gives the chance of taking a commission on it. If Wilkins had been there she would have put her foot down firmly on ethical grounds and ordered me back to the car before I caught double pneumonia.

I scrambled down the bank until I was two feet above the water and then I jumped in feet first. I went in and nearly didn't come up. The cold hit me like a great hand squeezing the life from me. I surfaced, gasping for breath, blowing and swearing and in no mood to waste time. I didn't want my fingers to drop off before I could get down to that car.

I swam out a few yards, adjusted the mask and snorkel, took a deep breath, and went down, rubber torch in hand.

Underwater it wasn't as dark as I had imagined it might be, and I saw the car almost immediately. It was about ten feet away from me on the angle of my dive. It was lying tipped over to one side on the slope of the lake-bed. The driving-wheel side was the farthest away from me. I made it to the right-hand door, grabbed it to anchor myself and flicked on the torch. The window of the door was wound down. I beamed the torch around the inside and saw Otto at once. He wasn't a nice sight. He was wedged up like a grotesque carnival balloon against the roof of the car, his arms and legs dangling, marionette fashion, from the movement of my grasping the door. I took the torch off him quickly, swung it to the air intake to locate its position and then I let go and surfaced.

I trod water for a moment or two, wondering whether I was going to be sick, then took a deep breath and went down again. This time I worked without the torch, not wanting to see

Otto buoyed up against the roof. I held the door with my right hand, shoved the torch into my trunks and reached in with my left hand. I got hold of the circular grille face and turned it. For a moment or two it wouldn't budge, then as the last of my breath was going, I gave it a jerk and felt it move.

I went up for a fresh supply of air and hung on the surface for a while like a played-out fish. The clouds had come lower and there was a dense, moving succession of mist wraiths wafting across the water. Somewhere up the slopes on the far side of the lake I thought I heard the soft tinkle of a cow-bell.

I went down again, and this time the grille turned easily and came away in my hand. I dropped it and reached into the aperture. I felt something flat and thick and pulled it out. It was about the size of a good fat book. I groped around to make sure there was nothing else in the compartment and then went up quickly without taking time for a goodbye to Otto.

I surfaced, pushed the mask back, sucked in great gulps of cold, misty air and looked at the object in my right hand. It was wrapped in thick brown oiled paper and banded all over with scotch tape. Shivering, hardly able to feel my hands or feet, I turned to make for the bank.

It was then that I saw—standing up above me on the plateau edge, a little fogged with the mist patches that swept by them—Miss Panda Bubakar, and Najib Alakwe. They stood there and watched me as I stopped swimming and trod water.

Panda had a short leather coat flung open, her hands on the hips of a green mini-dress, her long, tight-encased legs seeming longer from the angle at which I viewed them. She was so tall that at times her head was lost in the moving patches of mist. But when her dusky face was clear I could see that she was giving me a cheerful, predatory smile and a chance to admire the sparkle of her white teeth. Najib, though I had little time to be surprised about it, was wearing a neat, sober grey suit and a dark tie on a white shirt. He stood back a little so I couldn't check whether he still had his ginger shoes. But I could see clearly that he was holding a gun in his right hand.

'Hello, hello, Rexy-dexy boy,' called Panda. 'Just keep swimming. You're on the right track. Big welcome awaits.'

'And be careful not to drop the parcel,' said Najib. Just to emphasize the need for care, he fired a shot into the water two feet from me which made me leap like a running salmon, and he called, 'No need for any alarm over personal safety. Just hand over the parcel and all is forgiven.'

'And Mamma will come up with a big brandy and nice rub down with rough towel. Whoof-whoof!' She gave that big, dark brown laughing bark of hers and did a couple of high kicks that would have left a Bluebell girl grounded.

I shook my head. 'Sorry,' I said, 'but I promised myself I would do a couple of lengths before I came out.'

'You come on straight out, lover-boy,' said Panda, 'otherwise you gonna freeze and lose all your accessories. Come on, come to Mamma. Mamma soon make baby warm.'

'Come on in,' I said. 'It's lovely. Don't know what you're missing.'

I turned, stuck the parcel between my teeth and flattened out into the nearest thing to a fast crawl that I could manage, heading away into the mist. I knew that Najib wouldn't fire at me. He didn't want me to drop the precious parcel. On the other hand that wasn't much consolation. I might make the other bank before they got round to it but I didn't fancy being stuck up in the mountains wearing only a pair of trunks. Even if I made a road I was going to have trouble thumbing a lift. The French aren't all that broad-minded.

After about twenty yards or so, I stopped, took the parcel out of my mouth and got some air. The mist hid the grass plateau now. That was good. But it also hid everything else. I hadn't the faintest idea which way to go. You can blindfold some people, dump them down in the dark and they can always tell where north is. Well, I could have been a homing pigeon but it still wouldn't have helped because I didn't have any home. Then I heard Panda's delighted bark-laugh come through the mist and there was the crisp sound of a body diving into the water. That scared me. She was after me, over six brown feet of human torpedo, impervious to cold water, and with a built-in radar device that could pick up a man and home on him from any distance. Once she got her long arms and lovely legs around me in the water I would have less chance than a minnow with a pike.

Parcel in my mouth, I went full ahead for a hundred yards, hoping to hit the bank. But I couldn't find any bank. I stopped, panting, no sensation in my body at all, and wondered how long it would be before Otto had company. From behind and to my right, some way away, I heard the water threshing as Panda screwed herself along. Then the sound stopped. All sound stopped. There was just the mist and the cold ripple of water around me. Then there was a sound. Up ahead of me I caught the brief tingle of a cow-bell. I got moving. I swam thirty yards and then stopped. Somewhere behind me I heard Panda swimming. She didn't sound as though she were going fast; just heading steadily in my direction, keeping the blip on her screen dead centre. Over the noise of her swimming I heard the cow-bell tinkle again, but this time it was away at an angle to my right and the unpleasant thought occurred to me that there could be more than one cow browsing along the far shore. I did the only thing. I took a mean between the two bells and swam down it. Very sensible. In the circumstances. But not good navigation. A mean course can land you in trouble. That's the catch with averages, they always give you a cock-eyed answer like the average English family has one and a half cars. I ran straight into Panda, simply because I hadn't allowed for the acoustic factor that sounds in a mist don't come from where they seem to come.

She came out of the mist four feet ahead of me, went astern to brake her way and gave me a big white tooth-flashing smile. Held in her teeth was a nasty-looking knife. She took the knife out of her mouth and said, 'Hiyah, honey. Come here often?'

I took the parcel out of my mouth, and through chattering teeth, said, 'You come a foot nearer and I chuck this overboard.' I held up the parcel.

She said, 'How we going to get warm if we don't get close?'

I said, 'Just switch your radar on the nearest cow-bell and lead the way.'

She shook her head and said, 'We do it side by side, lover-boy. And don't play no tricks on a poor girl what's achin' for love. You drop that parcel and I'm gonna slit you from gizzard to crutch and to hell with the waste of a good man.' She winked at me, and added, 'Anyone ever tell you you got nice shoulders? Kinda square and sexy—and I like 'em that blue colour. Goes well with the red face. Start tracking.'

We swam, four feet apart, and Panda just leading the way. I wasn't concerned with what was going to happen. I just wanted to get out of the freezing lake. My body was frozen, my mind was in need of de-icing, and my arms and legs moved as though I were swimming through mud. Only my eyes worked normally to help me keep station alongside Panda.

She grinned at me and said, 'Kinda nice, havin' the whole place to ourselves. Awful crowded in summer they say.'

I didn't answer. I had a mouth full of parcel. But I kept my eyes on her as we swam on.

She was stripped to her bra and long tights, pink, with a little balloon of trapped air swelling up over her backside, and every now and then she twisted her head to give me a beaming smile, which had a lot of mixed emotions bubbling in it. The least I could expect when we got to the bank was to be raped, then knifed. I thought of praying but decided against it. It never did a male mantis any good in the same circumstances.

Panda's radar worked. We hit the bank dead on the cow. It was a big brown-and-white beast, standing between two pines, blowing great gusts of vapour through its nostrils and it watched us with large, liquid, uncurious eyes.

Panda slid out of the water, and said, 'Hi, cow! Nice lake you've got here.' And then, water rolling over her brown arms and shoulders and rippling down her tights, she held the knife at me as I stood in six inches of water and mud at the verge. 'Just come out nice and easy, man, and then toss the parcel to Mamma. Business before pleasure, uh?' She threw her head back and bellowed, 'Najib! Najib!'

153

From somewhere through the mist distantly came an answering call.

Panda stood waiting for me. She was no fool. I might not know what was in her mind, but she knew what still dimly survived in the icy depths of mine. I didn't want to give her the parcel.

'No tricks, honey. I like you a lot and anytime you say the word we'll shack up some place with a big bed and make the springs work double time. But first Najib must have his parcel. Okay?'

'Okay.'

I moved out of the water, but she stopped me after the first two feet.

'No more. Just toss it over.'

Somewhere up to our left Najib shouted. Panda shouted back. I looked down at the parcel in my hand, and remembered a lot of routines I'd been through in Miggs's gymnasium. Somewhere or other I guessed that Panda had been through even more routines, and she could give me inches in height, seconds in speed, and probably just as much in muscle, and she had a knife.

'Come on, honey. Flip it over. After that it's no hard feelings and loving kindness all round. Najib likes you and, what's more important, I like you and that spells a rosy future somewhere.'

Giving myself time to think, I said, 'Great help you've been —keeping Max on ice for me.'

'That? Honey, that was just for laughs. Come on, goose-pimples—give!'

I gave. I tossed the parcel to her and I deliberately threw it a little wide and a little short. It landed on the ground a foot in front of her and to her left. She flexed her gorgeous legs and bent, reaching for it with her free hand, her ample breasts sagging against the wet stuff of her white bra, and her eyes never left me except for the split second when eyes and hand had to co-ordinate to locate and pick up the parcel. It was the moment I wanted. I already had my hand on my trunks covering the bulge of the rubber torch inside. I had it out and jumped for her as her eyes came back to me. She made a good try. In fact she gave me a three-inch slash on my left arm but it was too hurried to be serious, just messy. I hit her as hard as I could just at the side of the right temple, really hard, and to hell with chivalry, and she went over on her back and stayed there.

I grabbed the parcel and ran, away round the lake in the opposite direction from which Najib's calling voice was coming. I didn't run for long, not in bare feet. But I kept going, hobbling fast, and luck was with me. I struck a small path, coated with dry pine needles and finally came back round to the grassy plateau.

Najib's Thunderbird was parked alongside my Mercedes. He'd left the ignition keys in so I took them and chucked them into the water. Then, without waiting to get dressed, I drove away, turning the heater up full blast. I couldn't wait to get to the nearest hot coffee and lace it with cognac.

As I drove down the track in the woods, and when I was almost in sight of the main road, a beaten-up yellow Citroen pulled suddenly out of the trees on to the track ahead of me and stopped. I braked to a halt about ten yards from it. Through the back window of the Citroen I could see a woman at the wheel. I waited for her to move on and while I did so, reached back for my shirt and trousers. I had them in my hand when the beaming, bespectacled face of Tony Collard appeared in the window across from me. He opened the door and got in, and, with a smoothness that astonished me, picked up the parcel from the seat and stuffed it inside his Windbreaker, reached back and got the shotgun, broke it and checked that there were no shells in it, and then, drawing a gun from his belt, said amiably, 'Just follow Mimi.'

He reached over and pressed the horn. The car ahead started to move. He prodded me in the ribs with the gun and I followed.

I said, 'If we've got far to go I'm not dressed for it.'

'We'll keep the heater going.' He looked admiringly at me

and said, 'I had a bet with Mimi you'd make it. Five hundred francs. Great little gambler that girl. This is the thing there's all the fuss about?'

He held up the parcel.

I nodded.

'That's what your boss really wanted—not the car?'

'I wouldn't lie to you.'

'Course not, you're a *buono raggazzo*. But don't worry, Tony will take care of you and everything. You're my friend, in a sense.'

'What sense?'

'That I got respect for you. My old man always said if you want to succeed with people you got to work with their natures, not against them. How was Otto?'

'No complaints.'

'Good. Mind you, Otto had his points. The master mind—that's what he used to think he was, and he was to some extent. Do a job in France and scoot back to Italy. Do a job in Italy and scoot back to France. That's where we're going. A little hiding place we had this side of the border. Old mill, not working now, of course. Orchard with medlars and pears . . . lovely place for a kid to play. And a stream. Course, now Otto's gone that makes me the master mind. I can tell you, I had trouble with Mimi about it at first, but she's come round to my way. Did you have to rub out either of those two up there?'

We were out on the main road now and heading east.

'I was a bit rough with the girl.'

'Fix their car?'

'Yes.'

'Good. Then we can all relax.' He leaned back and lit a cigarette and began to hum to himself. After a while, he said, 'I don't mind being pushed around strictly in the way of business. Got to expect it now and then. Don't mind if anyone pushes Mimi around a bit, come to that. But—' he gave me a big smile and chuckled to himself—'I'm dead against any bastards that could push a little baby around. That long-legged, dark number just chucked the feed bottle out of the

156

window. It takes a woman, you know, to be really cruel to a little baby. You can see that's why I had to talk.'

'Absolutely.'

I knew it was no good trying to hurry him or force him to put events in order, and anyway, I was dog-tired and longing for something hot and fiery to be burning my gullet. I knew that I was going to have to deal with him but it wasn't the moment and I wasn't in the mood. His master brain had dreamed up some scheme but until I was dressed and in my right mind it would have to wait.

'My old man used to say,' he said, 'that a black child develops mentally faster than a white up to the age of twelve, and then it stops. They can't get beyond twelve. Something in it, I think, or that dark number must have thought I was an idiot. If he'd come down the road first I was going to take him. But I'm genuinely glad it was you.' He began to laugh. 'God, I'd like to see their faces now.'

Ahead of me, Mimi turned off the main road on to a B number.

Tony said, 'Make a lot of money in your job?'

'Enough.'

'Somebody asks you to do something, like, and you do it—no questions asked?'

'Sort of.'

'Must be interesting.'

'There's always something happening. Like now.'

That tickled him but he overlaughed it as usual.

Recovered, he said, 'I'd have liked working with someone like you instead of Otto. He was a randy, rotten runt. If you don't have nothing else in this life, my old man used to say, you've got to have respect for women. That's what he used to say, but he never acted like it. Some ways he was worse than Otto. Mimi's going to turn left up ahead. You'll have to get into low gear. Like the side of a house.'

I followed Mimi for a couple of miles up a steep, winding hill, and then we came out on to a wide plateau, fringed on three sides by woods. As Tony had said, there was an orchard, full of moss-covered fruit trees, a small paddock and a tall mill-house standing at the side of a stream. Attached to the mill-house was a low cottage with a paved yard in front of it.

I drew the Mercedes up behind Mimi's car in the yard. Ahead of us she got out, reached into the car and brought out a carry-cot, and then went into the house.

Tony said, 'If you don't try any tricks we'll get on well. Nothing's going to happen to you and your boss won't be able to blame you.' He grinned, winked at me, and added, 'Let's face it, we've all got to have our failures.'

He got out and, gun in hand, marshalled me into the cottage. The main room was large, stone-flagged, and with a kitchen range against one wall. Mimi sat on a chair, gave me a nod, and then opened her blouse and started to feed the baby.

'There's not much here, Tony,' she said. 'With all the upset. Get the fire going and warm some up. But you'll have to do something with him first. The baby-food's in the case in the car.'

Tony went over to her, kissed the top of her head and kept his eyes on me all the time. Then he went to a door at the far side of the room, drew back bolts and opened it, motioning me to him.

'I think they wintered the goat or cows in here once. Kind of central heating for the house.' He chuckled.

He waved me in.

The room was stone built with one window about six inches square high up at one end. There was a broken-down wheelbarrow in it, a pile of old straw in a corner, an iron bed without a mattress against the wall, and a row of cobweb-draped rabbit hutches along the other wall. He shut me in, but was back again after a few minutes carrying my clothes and a bottle. Behind him Mimi came to the door, baby crooked in her arm, its wet mouth searching for her nipple, Tony's gun in her hand to cover me.

Tony said, 'Make yourself comfortable. Ring if you want anything.' He laughed, dropped my clothes on the floor and put the bottle in the wheelbarrow.

I said, 'Is it a boy or a girl?'

'Boy,' said Tony proudly. 'Two months. Fair-sized little pecker on him already. Gabriel we're calling him. Like it?'

'Heavenly,' I said and reached with one hand for my trousers and with the other for the bottle.

They left me alone and I dressed and drank. Then I pulled some of the straw out of the corner and spread it across the wire-spring frame of the bed and flopped down on it. A cloud of dust, smelling of cowdung, rose around me, but I didn't care much.

I just lay there, bottle handy at the side of the bed and stared at the ceiling. I've stared at a great many ceilings in my time, and mostly in the same kind of mood, feeling debilitated and incapable of sustained thought. I knew enough about the mood to realize that there was nothing to be done but to wait for it to pass.

From the other room I heard the sounds of Mimi and Tony and the baby . . . the clanking of pans, the wail of the child, and Tony's big laugh and Mimi's occasional chuckle. After a time the baby stopped crying, and there was only the low murmur of their voices and then, suddenly, I heard Mimi give a loud exclamation and Tony began to roar with laughter.

I took another drink and went to sleep, but just before I went off I thought I heard the sound of a car starting up.

I woke late in the afternoon to find Tony in the room and with him a good smell of coffee and fried bacon. He'd put a plank across the wheelbarrow and there was a tray on it. He kicked an old box towards the barrow for me to sit on and then went and stood by the door, one hand inside his Windbreaker. I didn't have to be told what he was holding. He was friendly, but he wasn't going to take any chances with me.

He said, 'Keep your voice down. Don't want to wake the baby.'

I said, 'I'm not doing any speaking. That's up to you.'

I began to attack the coffee and fried bacon.

159

He gave it to me then, in his own laughter-punctuated, highly involuted way.

When he had come to visit me at the chalet, he had brought Mimi and the baby with him, leaving them parked in his car well down the road. He had brought Mimi, he explained, largely because they were inseparable and also because if there had been trouble it was easier to pass the frontier with a woman and a child in the car. Anyway, Panda and Najib had jumped him as he came back to the car. Najib had got into Tony's car, and Tony had to drive off with Panda bringing Mimi and the baby along in their car. Somewhere the other side of St Bonnet they had pulled up and the conference had begun. Najib had wanted to know what he had been doing at the chalet and who had been there.

'Honest, I tried to stall. Like I said, I got respect for you. He wanted to know everything—and he seemed already to know a lot—and then there was the baby. Mimi nearly went out of her head. Fact, I'm surprised she's got any milk left at all. That black tart was the worst, telling us what would happen. You can see, I didn't have any choice, and then on top of that he said he'd make it worth my while. Not that that by itself——'

'So in the end you told them about the Mercedes being in the lake?'

'Had to—and we had to take them there. Me with him, and Mimi coming behind with her. But I was thinking of you all the time. I wanted to give you a chance like, give you time to get there ahead. So I led him a dance, took the wrong roads and the long way round. You know once,' he chuckled, 'I took him round in a big circle and he never noticed it. You can see I tried to protect you, can't you?'

'I'm touched, Tony.'

'Well, I like you. You got a nice way. Still, I couldn't stall for ever, 'cause I knew Mimi would be fussing about the kid's feed, so I finally took him to the bottom of the lake road, and then he pays me off and tells me to get the hell out of it.' He chuckled. 'Which I pretended to do of course, but I didn't, and let me tell you if I could have got my hands on the gun Mimi had in the kid's carry-cot I would have blown their black heads off. Coloureds I always thought were crazy about kids. Anyway, I'd been doing a lot of thinking. Mimi and me wanted all the money we could for emigrating. Nice touch we had from that bank, and a bit more from the sale of the garage, but why not more? So I thought, what's in that car they're all crazy about? Not just the car—so I decided to hang around. First lot down the road will have it, whatever it is, and whatever it is it's worth money and I'm going to have it. So there it is. It was you—and I was real happy it was you. With them I'd have had to be real rough in order to please Mimi.'

I finished the coffee and said, 'Don't go on, you're breaking my heart. Just tell me what cock-eyed plan you've got now.'

'Nothing that will hurt you. Your boss will see that you tried and you failed—on his behalf. He can't grumble.' He pulled the gun from his Windbreaker. 'After all, what could you do? I'll explain it to him when he comes.'

'When he comes?'

'To collect the parcel. Mimi's gone off for him now. Be back tomorrow. Why you looking surprised?'

'Wouldn't you—if you saw a man jump into a bear-pit for a friendly game of tag? My boss will tear you apart. Tony, my friend, he's not the kind of man you can shake down. As your dear old father would have said, you're good but you're not in his class.'

Tony grinned, 'You're trying to frighten me. I can handle him. He's got to come alone. Mimi knows the terms.'

'Listen,' I said. 'He's eight feet tall, four feet wide, and he's got a fat touch of the Irish. He'll eat you.'

'Will he? Then he'll have to polish this off as a starter first.' He joggled the gun. Then he gave me a kindly shake of his head. 'Don't you worry. You did your best. More can't be asked of any man. You'll get your pay from him. You could sue him if not. And Mimi and I will get our price for the parcel. You know what's in it?'

'No.'

'And a good thing for you, too.' He started to laugh. 'You ain't old enough yet. You should have seen Mimi's face. She's a first-class mother and wife, but that's not to say she hasn't been around—but she was shocked. She didn't even want to take the little bit of film I clipped off to show him, but I said she must. He's got to know we're genuine sellers. Anyway, it's all wrapped up again out there, just as it was, and you don't have to bother your head about it. And he's getting it cheap, five thousand dollars, used notes, and no fear of the police about it or he wouldn't have hired you.'

I gave him a look and went back to the bed. I picked up the bottle and took a deep pull, swallowed, breathed hard, and said, 'Wake me when he comes. I wouldn't miss the show for anything.'

'I will. You'll be right out there so he can see it weren't any of your fault. As my old man used to say, you take advantage of someone, particularly someone you like, then the least you can do is make sure they don't get more than their proper share of the blame. You just got outsmarted. I want him to know that. Then he can't hold anything against you.'

I didn't tell him that I was deeply moved—not for me, but for him. He and Mimi were a couple of Babes in the Wood, and O'Dowda would enjoy every minute he spent in this house.

I said, 'Did Otto ever tell you why he quit working for O'Dowda?'

'Sure. He'd accumulated some capital and wanted to get back to his own line of business.'

'How did he get the capital?'

Tony laughed and winked. 'Never asked him. Like my father used to say—never ask questions you know won't be answered.'

He went out, chuckling to himself.

I lay on the bed, later, and stared at the little patch of window. Through it a few stars were showing and now and again a brown owl screamed in the orchard just to keep the voles on their toes. It wasn't all that way from here to Evian.

Mimi should be back sometime in the morning, and with her would be O'Dowda, alone. Mimi would insist on that, and O'Dowda would play ball. He would bluster and bully to begin with, threaten her with the police and so on, but in the end he would come, alone, and with the money because he wanted the parcel and he wanted it without any police interference.

He probably knew already that the police, or Interpol, wanted to get their hands on it. Najib wanted it, Interpol wanted it, and O'Dowda wanted it. What did I want? Well, I had to be frank. I wanted it, too. But, in the first place, out of sheer curiosity to see what was in it. After I knew that, I could decide what to do with it. Ethically, of course, I should —if I ever got it—hand it to O'Dowda. He was my employer. But he'd only employed me to find the car, not to recover a parcel. And ethically, before allowing me to take his commission, there was a lot he should have put me wise to for the sake of my own personal safety, and personal safety was something by which I set a very high store. For the moment, ethics apart, I was prepared to be taken along by circumstances —in fact I had no choice—until I got a chance to dictate the running again.

I went to sleep, deep, complete, dreamless sleep, and woke to daylight and the fact that Tony was sitting hard and square on my shoulders, had my hands drawn back behind me, and was cording up my wrists. If I had been one of those people who come fast out of sleep, brain clear, ready for action, I might have been able to take advantage of him. The truth was he had me trussed almost before I was awake. He got off me, rolled me over, and I yawned in his face. Outside the birds were singing and a shaft of sunlight came through the window.

Tony, beaming, said, 'It's a great morning. Come on out and I'll feed you some coffee.'

He did, too, while I sat in a kitchen chair, and he did it expertly holding the cup to my lips. He should have been a male nurse.

'Thought you'd like to be present when your boss arrives. Tied like that he can see there was nothing you could do.'

I said, 'You're happy about meeting him?'

'Why not? He's coming alone, and I've got what he wants.' He tapped the parcel on the table with his gun. 'What's five thousand dollars to him?'

'You'd be surprised. He's got a gallery of people like you. Some there for less than five thousand, I imagine.'

'A gallery?'

'Never mind. He just doesn't like handing over money under duress.'

'Who does? But it happens. Just you sit there and don't move. I got things to do.'

He had. He warmed up some baby food, fed Gabriel, and then changed its nappy. I said, 'You've skipped its bath.'

'Mimi said not to on account of its rash. All over its little arse. Powder's the job. Like I did before I put the fresh nappy on.'

He settled Gabriel down in the carry-cot and I watched him with interest. Seeing me following his movements, he said, 'Haven't got Mimi's touch. He goes down right away with her, but with me he always yells for five minutes before going off. Don't let it worry you.'

I didn't. Gabriel yelled and I sat on my chair and stared at the parcel I had fished out of the Mercedes. So far I'd done all the hard work and it didn't look as though I was going to get much out of it. I should have skipped this job and taken a holiday. I'd have missed Julia, true. But at this moment that didn't seem much to lose. I yawned. What I needed was a tonic, something to pep me up and set me going again so that there was a bounce in my stride and a bright cash glint in my eyes.

O'Dowda arrived three hours later. First there was the sound of Mimi's car. Tony went to the door and opened it. From where I sat I could see the yard. Mimi drew up alongside my car and came across to us, her red hair glinting in the morning sun, a spring in her step, and clearly everything all right with the world. As she reached the door where Tony stood, gun in hand to welcome her, O'Dowda's Rolls drew into the yard driven by him.

'He's alone?' asked Tony.

'Yes. I checked everything like you said.'

'Good girl.' He ran a hand down her back and pinched her bottom.

She came in, gave me a friendly nod, and went to the carry-cot and began to fuss over the baby.

I said, 'What was he like?'

'Very polite and gentlemanly. No trouble.'

In my book that meant that he was saving the trouble for later.

O'Dowda came to the doorway, carrying a small case in one hand. He had a little billycock hat perched on top of his big head and was wearing a thick tweed suit which made him look even bigger. He gave Tony a fat smile and then seeing me inside, said, 'So you made a mess of it, boyo? Seems I read somewhere in your prospectus that nobody could outsmart you. Well, you're costing me five thousand dollars. You think I should deduct that from his fees?'

This was to Tony.

Tony, in a business mood, said, 'That's between you and him—but he did his best. Just turn round, Mr. O'Dowda, and lift your hands.'

O'Dowda did as he was told and Tony ran a hand over him from behind. Then, satisfied, he backed into the room and O'Dowda came after him.

O'Dowda looked around and said, 'Nice little property this. Could pick it up cheap and do something with it.'

Tony moved around the table, picked up the parcel and handed it to Mimi, his eyes never leaving O'Dowda. Well, at least, that was something but he would need more than that to deal with O'Dowda. Nothing could convince me that O'Dowda was going to hand over five thousand dollars willingly and with that happy smile on his face.

Tony said, 'Your man did his best, Mr. O'Dowda. Remember that.'

'Good of you to stress it. I'm sure he did. But it was a damned poor best—going to cost me five thousand dollars.'

He put the case on the table and then waved a fat hand at it. 'Just count it,' he said, 'and then your wife can hand over the parcel, and I'll be going.'

Tony said, 'No. You open it up. I don't want that lid snapping up and something going pop in my face.' He chuckled. 'My old man was an expert on booby traps, Mr. O'Dowda.'

'You're right to be cautious, boyo. Let's be frank—if I could do you I would. But I know when to resign myself. I want that parcel too much to quibble over a few thousand dollars.'

He was too reasonable. I could sense that he wasn't worried, that underneath the mildness there was the real tough, don't-try-to-shake-me-down O'Dowda.

He opened the case, letting the cover flap back so that Tony could see the bundles of notes. I had a bet with myself that he would have a gun hidden under the notes. I was wrong. He picked up the case and turned it upside down, spilling the packets of notes on the table. From the far side Tony reached out a hand and picked up one of the piles. He handed it backwards to Mimi. She put the parcel in the carry-cot and began to count the notes. Then she came up to the table, and from a safe distance, counted through the piles.

'It's all there, Tony.'

'Give him the parcel. Don't go near him. Pass it to him.'

I had to hand it to Tony. He was taking no chances. He might not be a master mind, but he was doing his best. But there was one thing about O'Dowda he could never know, never believe, although I had in a way tried to tell him, and that was the man's courage. To be a millionaire you have to have it, you have to know that nothing can beat you, that anything you want is always in reach even if it means a moment or two of danger . . . for against danger there is always luck and, let's face it, luck is a snob and doesn't waste time on the poor and meek.

Mimi got the parcel and slid it across the table to O'Dowda. He picked it up and stuffed it into one of his big side pockets —and from that moment he didn't waste a second. The moment of pocketing the parcel was his deadline. As his right hand came out of the pocket he swept it forward, took the edge of the table and tipped it back at Tony, shoving it at him with all his strength.

As the table hit him Tony fired, but O'Dowda had already moved, and like a lot of big men, he moved fast. The bullet went high over him and hit the ceiling, showering plaster down. O'Dowda was round the table and, as Tony, on the floor, rolled over to shoot again, had one big arm around Mimi pulling her in front of him as a shield. Tony held his fire.

Panting a little, O'Dowda said, 'Now you bastard, push that gun over here or I'll break your wife's neck.' He raised his free hand and grabbed the nape of Mimi's neck, screwing it round so that she gave a cry of pain.

Tony, lying on the floor, was lost. The game had gone against him, and he had no idea of his next play.

'Tell him, Carver, that I'll do it,' said O'Dowda.

I said, 'He'll do it, Tony—and make it legal afterwards. Just kiss your five thousand goodbye. Do it, and don't be a fool.'

Tony looked from me to Mimi. Gabriel began to yell in the carry-cot. Tony slid the gun along the ground to O'Dowda. O'Dowda tipped Mimi over like a truss of hay and recovered the gun with his free hand. Straightening up, he gave a big smile.

'Well, now we can really do business.' He forced Mimi across the room to the open door of the cattle lodge. He shoved her in and then closed the door and shot the bolt across. Tony made a move to rise but O'Dowda waved him down with the gun and came back slowly to him.

He said, 'I'm a bit stiff from that drive, but I'm beginning to loosen up. All right, after business, pleasure; that's the order. Up you get.'

He put the gun in his pocket and stood back from Tony. Tony must have thought he was mad to give him the chance. I could have told him better. He came up fast at O'Dowda but before he was off his knees O'Dowda drove his foot into his chest and sent him sprawling and the shock whipped Tony's glasses from his face. O'Dowda followed him up, grabbed him by the shirt front as he rose, jerked him to his feet and smashed a fat fist into his face, slamming him back against the wall.

It wasn't pretty to watch. Without glasses Tony was half blind anyway. O'Dowda just used him as a punch bag. He held him in the corner of the room and beat him until he couldn't stand on his legs, and then he held him up and beat him some more, and all the time Mimi was screaming like a banshee from the other room, the baby was crying as though he had a fit, and I felt a murderous rage running through me. Tony was not only getting what he had asked for, he was getting far more.

I shouted, 'Lay off, O'Dowda. You'll kill him.'

O'Dowda, holding Tony, turned and looked at me.

'Not me, Mr. Bloody Carver. I know the exact limit.'

He turned and slammed another blow at Tony and then let him drop to the ground. Tony lay there, groaning faintly.

O'Dowda brushed off his hands, examined his knuckles and then, the baby still crying, he went to the carry-cot and gently patted its cheeks. 'Hush now, my darlin', your daddy will be with you soon, though I doubt you'll recognize him.'

He came over to me and pulled a penknife from his trouser pockets.

'Stand up and turn round.'

I sat where I was. Just at that moment I was enjoying myself. I wanted him. I wanted to take him more than anything else in the world, and the thought was doing things to my glands. Everything had gone into full production again inside me. The bastard had come in here, barehanded, and with just his mother-wit and the knowledge that he could get away with anything, and it had worked for him, as it had worked before. I just wanted to prove to him that or once it wouldn't always work.

'Stubborn, eh?' He smacked me across the face and the chair almost went over. 'And you think I believe his story about outsmarting you? It would take a better man than him to do that. No, it was a bright idea, boyo, right out of the old joke book. You two got together. He shakes me down—then you split, and you're still a hard-working but unsuccessful agent of mine entitled to full fees. You think I fall for that? Stand up, or I'll knock your bloody head off.'

He hit me again and I stood up because I still needed my head. I needed it badly. I knew what he was going to do. He was going to free me and then he was going to play the same game with me that he had played with Tony. And I had an idea that, while it might take him a little longer, he could do it. He was all warmed up and ready to go, looking forward to the fun.

I said, 'You've had enough exercise for one morning, O'Dowda.'

'Don't believe it. All he brought out in me was a light sweat. You got to do better. Think you can?'

'You want to bet?'

'Why not?'

'Five thousand—dollars?'

He laughed. 'You're on, you cocky bastard. Now turn round.'

Slowly I turned round so that he could get at my wrists, and I knew that from the moment he cut the cords I would have about four seconds in which to save myself. Four seconds. It doesn't sound much. In fact it's quite a long time, particularly against a man so full of self-confidence as O'Dowda was at that moment. In four seconds I had to finish him or he would finish me. I might be endangering my pay from him, plus five thousand dollars, but I was prepared to worry about that later.

He stood up against me at my back and sawed impatiently away at the cords and I kept the strain on them so that I would know the moment I was free. He was eager and impatient to be at me. I liked that. He was looking forward sadistically to his fun and an easy five-thousand purse, his mind full of it. That meant it didn't have room for too much caution. My only hope was to surprise and finish him in four seconds.

The cords went and I brought my arms round fast in front of me and, before he knew what I was doing, I had the back of the chair in front of me in my hands. I swung around, slamming the chair at him hard as I went. I got him full on the side of the head. He went over sideways and crashed against the floor. For once lady luck wasn't with him. Having seen him well and happily on his way, maybe she'd gone out for a drink. His head hit the stone-flagged floor with a crash and he just lay there, knocked out. I threw the broken chair from me and bent down by him. He was breathing. I took the parcel and the gun from him, and I didn't waste any time. He had a head like an ivory ball and he wouldn't be out long.

I let Mimi out, and said, 'Get out of here quickly, before he comes round. Come on.'

She didn't need urging. I helped her haul Tony to the car. Then I went back and collected the baby and my dollars. I put twenty per cent of the purse in the carry-cot with the baby, and dumped it in the car. Mimi drove off fast, sobbing to herself. I took O'Dowda's ignition key and then turned my car and sat, window down, watching the door of the house. A few minutes later he came staggering out, holding his head.

I called to him, 'Great fight. I've taken my winnings. When your head's better maybe we'll have a chat about things.'

I drove off and dropped his keys overboard a mile down the road.

I went north as fast as I could and by five o'clock I was at Talloires, which is a small place on the east side of Lake Annecy. I got a room at the Abbaye which overlooks the lake, and where I had stayed before. I put a call through to Wilkins and caught her just before she left the office. It was a long-winded conversation. She was fussing like an old hen because she hadn't been able to get me at Ansermoz's number. She had no information, other than was public knowledge, about General Seyfu Gonwalla or Mrs. Falia Makse; that is that he was head of his government and she was the wife of the Minister for Agriculture. She could find no information at all about any Miss Panda Bubakar. But our city contact had come across with the fact that O'Dowda's United Africa company set-up had been on the verge of obtaining monopolistic mineral rights and mining concessions from the previous government to Gonwalla's. However, a military *coup d'état* had brought Gonwalla in and negotiations for the concession had been broken off. I could see how annoying that must have been for a man like O'Dowda. That he would take such a set-back lying down didn't strike me as likely. I had an idea that the oiled-paper parcel on my dressing table would prove it.

She had seen Guffy, but had not been able to get anything more out of him about anonymous letters concerning O'Dowda. He had said, however, that he wanted to get in touch with me and would she pass him any location or telephone number she had. I considered this, decided there could be no harm in it, and gave the Abbaye's number, Talloires 88.02. I then told her I had found the Mercedes and would be back very soon to face the bills which had no doubt accumulated.

She said, 'Are you all right, personally?'

'Intact,' I said, 'except for a three-inch scratch on my left arm which I've bandaged with a very dirty handkerchief. I was chased by Miss Panda Bubakar. She was wearing just a brassière and pink tights. She's coloured, by the way.'

At the other end Wilkins cleared her throat but said nothing.

I said, 'Anything else to report?'

She said, 'A Miss Julia Yunge-Brown has telephoned three or four times wanting to know where you were. I decided it wouldn't be wise to say. Oh, yes, there is one other thing. There was an announcement in *The Times* yesterday of the forthcoming marriage of Cavan O'Dowda to a Mrs. Mirabelle Heisenbacher.'

I said, 'Remind me to send flowers,' and then rang off.

After that I rang Durnford at the Château de la Forclaz. I gave him the location of the car to pass to O'Dowda when he got back. My job was now finished. I would be forwarding my bill in a few days.

He said, 'Did you go down to the car?'

I said, 'You any idea how cold those lake waters are, even in September?'

He said, 'If you did recover the package I'd like to talk to you about it, privately, and soon. After all, I did tell you where it was. And it could be, would be, to your advantage.'

I said, 'I'll think about it.'

He said, 'Where are you?'

I said, 'I'll tell you if you promise not to hand it on to O'Dowda.' I knew I was dead safe on that one.

'I promise.'

I gave him the hotel address.

After that I had the hotel send up a bottle of whisky and a couple of bottles of Perrier water. I took the first drink into the bath with me and soaked for half an hour. Dressed, I fixed a second and undid the oiled-paper parcel. There was an inner wrapper of thick plastic sheeting, and inside this were two rolls of 16 mm. film and a tape recorder spool.

I took one of the films to the window and stripped off a couple of feet, holding the negatives up to the light. I wasn't really surprised. In this business you get to have a sixth sense, an instinct for anticipation that can sometimes take a great deal of pleasure out of life. The short strip of film I held up featured Panda Bubakar prominently, grinning all over her fun-loving face and stripped for action. The man in the background, a coloured gentleman, looked broadshouldered enough to take the brunt of anything but, even so, there seemed to be a slight nervousness about his attitude which I could well understand. I didn't unroll any more film. Personally I've found that if you must have pornography—and a little occasionally never did any harm except to make life a shade greyer than it need be—then it was better after dinner with a couple of brandies. I had promised myself that I would eat at the Auberge du Père Bise along the quay and I didn't want to spoil my *gratin de queues d'écrevisses*.

I wrapped the whole lot up, and wondered what I would do about security arrangements. The next day I meant to hire a projector and run the film and also a tape recorder to play off the tape. But that was the next day. It would come all right. But I didn't want it to come without my being able to take a dispassionate eye-view of Panda and her friends and also to hear the tape which, I had a feeling, would be more interesting because it would leave a great deal more to the imagination than the film would. So I took the whole lot, including my dollars in a separate packet, to the Auberge du Père Bise with me and asked if they would keep them in their safe for me overnight, which they said they would, without any demur, which is always the sign of a first-class, well-run establishment. My hotel would have done the same but I knew that that was one of the obvious first checks that any official busybody would make since I was staying there. The *écrevisses* were delicious. So was the *omble chevalier poché beurre blanc* which followed them—and although *ombles* are part of the great *Salmonidae* family, I didn't think of O'Dowda once.

The next morning I was glad that I had taken my simple security precautions. Around eight o'clock there was a knock on the door and the chambermaid came in with my breakfast coffee, hot rolls and croissants and two of those small pots of conserve, one apricot, the other raspberry, and a big dish of butter curls. Behind her came Aristide Marchissy la Dole. He looked as though he had gone without sleep for a week and hadn't had his brown suit pressed for a month. He had a little blue cornflower in his buttonhole and a shaving nick on his chin with a little fuzz of cotton wool stuck to it like penicillin mould.

He gave me a slow, dubious smile and lit a cigarette while he waited for the maid to go out.

I sat up in bed and said, 'There's one important thing I want to make clear. I'm hungry. So lay off my croissants.'

The door closed on the maid. Aristide came over, took a hot roll and buttered it, flicked the silver foil off the raspberry conserve, put a spoonful inside the roll, removed the cigarette from his mouth and wolfed the lot.

'I said lay off.'

He said, 'You specified croissants, which by the way, were first made in Budapest in 1686. That was the year the Turks besieged the city. They dug underground passages under the walls at night, but the bakers—naturally working at that hour —heard them, gave the alarm and Johnny Turk was thrown out. In return the bakers were given the privilege of making a special pastry in the form of the crescent moon which, I believe, still decorates the Ottoman flag. Fascinating, no?'

'Someday,' I said, 'I must buy myself a copy of *Larousse Gastronomique*.'

But I was fascinated. Not by what he had said, but by what he was doing as he spoke. I've turned plenty of rooms over in my time, and seen experts turn rooms over, but I'd never seen an expert like Aristide turn a room over. He did it without any fuss, restricting himself to the probable size of the article he was looking for. He was neat and he was fast and afterwards there wasn't going to be a sign that anything had been disturbed. He found the gun I had taken from O'Dowda and pocketed it without comment.

He disappeared into the bathroom and then came back and said, 'All right. Now the bed.'

Reluctantly, I got out. He searched pillows, sheets, mattress and the frame then replaced the stuff tidily and waved me to take up residence again, which I did. He buttered and jammed himself another roll. I said, 'Of course, you've checked the hotel safe and my car?'

'Naturally. And of course, I know you've got it—somewhere. Let us just regard you for now as the custodian. If you lose it, of course, you could be in trouble.'

The roll finished, he came back to the tray, tipped the

wrapped sugar lumps from the bowl, and said, 'Do you mind if I share your coffee? I've been driving since four o'clock this morning.'

'Ever since Guffy passed you my telephone number?'

'Yes. Your Miss Wilkins, of course. She had no option.'

'She didn't have to. She had my permission. That's why I've been expecting you—though not so soon. Perhaps now you will tell me on what score you are gunning for O'Dowda?'

He smiled. 'I understand you've finished your work for him?'

'I found the car, yes—and passed O'Dowda the location.

'O'Dowda, I gather, isn't very pleased with you.'

'News travels fast in these parts. You must have a line to Durnford.'

'Yes. He's had communication with us before—first anonymously—subsequently openly. He's not always been strictly honest about his objective. Isn't now, quite. But he's been helpful.'

He raised the sugar bowl and made a horrible sucking noise at the coffee.

I said, 'Was Durnford the only one who sent you anonymous letters?'

'So far as I know. One came to me at Interpol. Guffy had two others at Scotland Yard.'

'And naturally, even though there might not be any truth in them, the police couldn't altogether ignore them?'

He nodded, squatted on the edge of a chair, and said, 'Guffy passed his to us. The subject concerned was, in a sense, an international figure. More particularly for us, a European figure.'

'With a prototype in fiction?' Remembering Julia and the way she had behaved about Otto, I didn't think it was a shot in the dark.

'If it was fiction. There was the Chevalier Raoul de Perrault's *Contes du Temps*.'

'Or Giles de Retz, the Marquis of Laval. Holinshed, I believe. My sister used to scare me with the story at bedtime.

For such a nice, gentle, green-fingered person she has a macabre taste in bedtime fairy stories.'

'All fairy stories, the best, are macabre.'

'Is this a fairy story, or fact?'

'It remains to be seen.' He stood up and looked out of the window, at the terrace below with its cropped trees and the lake beyond. 'You have an expensive taste in hotels. *De la terrasse ombragée belle vue sur le lac.*'

'Poetry?'

'No, Michelin. It goes for any hotel near water. *Repas sous l'ombrage, face au lac.*'

'You want to change the subject?'

'Not particularly.'

I said, getting out of bed and beginning to hunt for my cigarettes, 'I can understand Guffy, with murder in mind, telling me to keep an eye open if I were working for O'Dowda, but what I don't understand—from an Interpol point o view—is the interest in what may or may not have been in a submerged Mercedes?'

'No?'

'No.' I lit a cigarette, climbed back into bed and poured myself what was left of the coffee.

Aristide came back from the window. 'You have finished with the croissants?'

'Yes.'

He helped himself to one of the remaining pastries. He masticated slowly, smiling at me. Then he said, 'There are many differences between Interpol and the semi-honest little business you run.'

'Naturally. I don't get a pension at the end. That's why it's semi-honest. I have to work a handsome rake-off now and then.'

'Resist the temptation this time. Interpol is a police organization. The International Criminal Police Organization. Inevitably, it deals with more than crimes. Any international organization must occasionally accept some political influence from its members. The little parcel which—I concede you this—you have so cleverly found and so cleverly hidden, is a political matter.'

'And who are the interested parties exerting this influence?'

He cocked a sleepy eye at me and then rolled a grey lid down in a tired wink.

'That would be telling.'

'You can do better than that.'

'Not much—except that the interested governments prefer that neither Gonwalla nor O'Dowda should recover it. The interested governments could make good use of it—if they were ever forced to.'

'I'm sure. Though they would never call it blackmail.'

'In respectable hands, for respectable purposes, blackmail is a respectable weapon.'

'Put it to music and you've got a hit.'

I got out of bed.

He said, 'Where do you go from here?'

I said, 'To have a bath and a shave.' I stripped off my pyjama jacket.

He looked at my arm and said, 'You have been wounded.'

'You know what women are when they get excited.'

He said, 'You could finish up with more than a scratch. There could be a murder charge against you.'

I said, 'Even you can't say that with conviction. By the way, assuming I had the parcel, what sort of price would Interpol offer?'

'They wouldn't. Not cash.'

'They would. Tell them to forget the free pardon for murder and name a price.'

He sighed. 'I'll pass on your request. Meanwhile, I have to inform you that the parcel must be handed to us within four days.'

'Or else what?'

He grinned. 'A special disciplinary sub-committee is considering that right now. You don't mind if I finish the rest of the croissants?'

'Help yourself.'

I went into the bathroom and turned on the taps. When I came back to dress he was gone.

But that didn't mean I was going to be left unattended. The parcel had political significance. Interpol was a crime organization but—much as Aristide might hate any political pressure, which I was sure he did because he was a professional crime man—if a directive had been given then no employee could do anything else but obey it. That's where the real difference lay between Interpol and my semi-honest little business. I didn't have to obey anyone. I was my own boss. I just did what I thought was best—mostly for me.

I picked up the phone and put a call through to the Château de la Forclaz. If Durnford answered I was going to put a sugar lump in my mouth and do a little spluttering to disguise my voice. From now on, so far as I was concerned, Durnford had too many irons in the fire to be trusted. The call was answered by a girl on the château switchboard, and I asked for Miss Julia Yunge-Brown.

When she came on I said, 'This is Carver here. If you want to help me, pack a bag, get in your car and ring Talloires 88.02 from an outside phone as soon as possible. If you don't call me within the hour I shall enter a monastery. Probably La Grande Chartreuse—it's not far away. Incidentally, I had a brief meeting with Otto Libsch.'

I put the receiver down before she could say anything. Forty minutes later she rang back.

CHAPTER SEVEN

'Rack well your hero's nerves and heart,
And let your heroine take her part.'

MARY ALCOCK

I PACKED MY BAG and left it in my room. Then I went down to reception, paid my bill, said I wouldn't be in for lunch but would be back around five o'clock just to pick up my bag.

Then I took a stroll along the lakeside and up into the village. I picked up one of Aristide's men quite quickly. Not because I was all that clever, but because he had meant me to spot him. That meant there was another one around somewhere. I would be lucky if I spotted him. The only thing to do was to isolate him, and I'd already made arrangements for this.

The front man was a plumpish little number, wearing a beret, a sloppy linen suit, and had a camera slung round his neck. He worked overtime with the camera whenever I hung him up. There was probably no film in it anyway.

I took him for a stroll around, hoping I might spot the other, but I never did, and after an hour I gave up trying because it had suddenly occurred to me that it wasn't a camera at all but a walkie-talkie and he was just giving a running commentary to his chum somewhere out of sight.

About one o'clock I went back to the hotel and got the car. As I drove across the quay-side I saw the camera man sitting in a parked car by the *pissoir*. He was lucky to have got a parking space because the quay was crowded with visitors' cars. He took a nice little shot of me as I went by—f.11 at 250, with a heavy cloud overhead, what did he care?—to tell his hidden chum I was moving.

I drove along the road to Annecy for a mile and then turned left-handed up to the Annecy golf course. I parked with three or four other cars outside the little club house and went in and had lunch. Halfway through, my camera man took a table well away from me and ordered beer and a sandwich. There were only a few other people eating and they had all been there before I arrived. That meant that number two was outside somewhere by now. I took my time. Julia had a longish drive ahead of her, even in the Facel Vega, and various things to do before we met.

Finally I went downstairs, paid a green fee and hired a small bag of clubs from the professional. I was wearing a pullover and thick brown shoes so I had no changing to do, but I went into the dressing room to see a man about a poodle. There was the usual notice over the place asking you not to throw cigarette ends into it. Some wag had added underneath: *Cela les rend si vachement difficile a fumer après*.

I was more interested in a camera that was hanging from one of the coat-hooks in the changing room. I didn't examine it, but I made a note of the brown suit jacket which was also on the hook.

When I went outside there was a man tapping balls about on the putting green. He was wearing brown trousers that matched the jacket inside. His shoes were suède moccasins. Never mind, like good policemen, they were doing their best. They couldn't have anticipated golf. He was a big man, with the height, bulk and look of a de Gaulle but with a nervous, hesitant smile on his face when I nodded to him that would never have done for a man of destiny. He didn't look as though he could say '*Non*' to anyone. But appearances are deceptive— or Aristide wouldn't have chosen him. He was going to stick to me. Just for a moment I was tempted to ask him to join me, set the stakes high and hope that I'd got a pigeon. Then I thought of Julia and gave up the pleasure.

I was lucky that I was operating on familiar ground. I'd once spent a memorable month in these parts and played the course a few times. I climbed the flagpole-decorated mound to the first tee and saw that my tail was wandering across to play round after me.

I didn't hurry. I couldn't have done because it was one of those days when I was right off my game. If I'd been playing the whole course—which I wasn't going to do—something in my bones told me that I would never break a hundred. I lost a ball on the first hole, in the long grass of the right-hand slope down to the green. I sliced one out of bounds on the second, over a stone wall and trees into a bungalow garden. On the third, which was a short hole of about two hundred yards, and the farthest outward point on this section of the course, I hit a lucky screamer to within three yards of the green. I wasn't too happy about that because this was the point I had picked for operations. I didn't want par golf, I wanted manly work in the rough, so I took a seven iron and chipped the ball boldly across the green into the bushes ten yards behind it. Then I started to look for it, and couldn't find it naturally. Behind me my tail hit a bad shot halfway down the fairway, and then a few more bad ones, working to the green, and giving me time to find my ball and play out.

I stepped back from the bushes and politely waved him through. He had to come. It was a nice spot, low down and far out and not so easy to see from the clubhouse.

My tail holed out on the green, and then, with the camaraderie of an afternoon potterer, strolled across to me to help look for my ball. He came up with that nervous smile that meant nothing except that he wasn't going to lose sight of me, and I hit him, hard, with the side of my hand across his windpipe and again across the side of the neck as he choked and fell back. He went down with a rattle of irons from his bag and stayed down.

I ducked through the bushes and ran. Three hundred yards away, over a field and some small farm plots, was the road to Annecy.

The timing was beautiful. As I hit the road, a horn honked behind me and the Facel Vega came screaming down from the direction of Talloires.

A couple of miles further on, through Menthon on the road to Annecy, Julia swung hard right up the hill.

I said, 'Where are we going?'

She was driving fast, concentrating, and said without turning, 'I've got a ski-lodge near Megève. There won't be anyone there.'

'You collected all the things I wanted?'

She nodded.

I'd asked her to hire a projector and a tape recorder as she came through Annecy on her way down. She'd then gone to Talloires and picked up my bag from the hotel and the parcel from the safe at the Auberge du Père Bise.

When we hit Megève, some hours later, she stopped in the main street, near the Casino.

She said, 'There's no food in the place. You get coffee and bread. I'll do the rest.'

She was being very brisk and efficient, playing the role of assistant conspirator and enjoying it.

The shopping done, we went out of the town, along the road to Mont Arbois, past the golf course and then a mile further on she swung into a small open drive. Isolated in the middle of a small alp was a neat two-storey chalet, great stones wired to the roof, the façade polished boards, and the pink-and-grey shutters at all the windows cut with little heart-shaped openings. She parked the car round the back on bare gravel and we carried all our stuff in. There was a large main room with a tiled stove in the centre, comfortable chairs and a couple of settees, and an open stairway running up to the top floor. In a way it was not unlike Ansermoz's place.

When all our stuff was dumped in the middle of the floor, I said, 'I want a room to myself for half an hour. Okay?'

'You can take the big spare bedroom.'

I looked at her. She was worth looking at. She wore tight tartan trousers—I wouldn't know what clan, but there was a lot of red and yellow in them—a black sweater and a loose leather coat. On her head was a peaked black cap, shaped like an engine driver's. I could imagine the original photograph of it in *Vogue*.

She looked good; just the sight of her did things for me—but there was no getting away from the fact that our wavelengths were different. However, I had an idea now of the station she was more or less permanently tuned in to. As though to confirm it, she said, 'What about Otto Libsch?'

I said, 'We'll come to him in good time.'

I lugged the projector, tape recorder and the parcel up to the spare room. I took a sheet off the bed, hung it across the shuttered window and set up the projector. Then I locked the door and ran the two reels.

They were more or less what I had expected; *dramatis personae*—Panda Bubakar and, a safe bet for the other two, General Seyfu Gonwalla and Mrs. Falia Makse. It had all been shot from a hidden camera somewhere high up in the room. Either Durnford or Tich Kermode, I thought, could have been responsible for that. More probably Tich. As a display of acrobatics it had its limitations; as a fillip for a tired businessman it was just run-of-the-mill stuff, but for private showing to Gonwalla's cabinet it would have been a bomb, particularly under the seat of the Minister for Agriculture. The public image set up for Gonwalla in his country was that of the stern father-figure, determined to stamp out corruption, immorality, and all social and economic evils. Given selective showing in the General's home country, I could see that the film would lead to a speedy change of government. Which, of course, was what O'Dowda was after.

The tape recorded a conversation between the General and Mr. Alexi Kukarin. They were very friendly, referring to each other as General and Alexi, and it was all in English. And it had all been taped, I was sure, without their knowledge, otherwise the General would not have offered some of the comments he had about his government colleagues, and Alexi would not have made one or two beefs about his which would have made him very unpopular at home. The meat of the conversation, however, was that Alexi's people would be happy to supply aircraft, arms, and equipment against a guaranteed percentage—a large one, and at cheap rate—of certain minerals, ores and chemical products, simple innocuous things like cobalt, aluminium ore and uranium, which were to be produced eventually by a state-owned monopoly of mineral and mining resources now in process of being established. In addition, Alexi was insistent that no compensation should be paid to existing European concerns already operating in the country. Straight appropriation was the ticket. The General stuck at this one a bit, but Alexi insisted—pointing out that the country had suffered decades of colonial exploitation, and there was no need to be soft-hearted. The General in the end agreed.

I must say that, from the tapes, their characters came over well. Alexi—for all his charm and occasional jokes—had been given a brief and when it came to facts he was diamond-edged. The General was a nice enough chap outside of a bedroom, but he was a bit fuzzy around the edges, wanting things explained more than once. He had to have a big streak of simplicity in him, otherwise he would never have fallen for the invitation to use the Château de la Forclaz. O'Dowda, I knew, had made it open house for visiting members of the government for years and it hadn't occurred to the General to question the propriety of going on using it, as he had no doubt often done in the past when he felt the need for peace and quiet and the stimulating company of old friends like Panda and Mrs. Makse. We all of us live and learn. It's a question of the proportion between the two. The General was miles away from ever breaking even.

I dismantled everything, and then packed the film and tape away in the parcel.

Downstairs the stove was alight, the room warm, and bottles and glasses had appeared on a side table. I could hear Julia moving about in the kitchen. I rummaged a desk, found paper and string and rewrapped the parcel. One thing was certain, I didn't want to have it around this place longer than I could help. I addressed it and then poked my head in the kitchen.

She was doing something at the side of the sink with meat. I said, 'Can I borrow your car? I want to go down to Megève to the post office.'

She looked at her watch. 'It'll be shut.'

I said, 'There are ways round that.'

There was. I went back along the road to the golf course and then turned into the drive of the Hotel Mont d'Arbois. It was pretty deserted because it was almost the end of the season.

I handed the parcel, and a hundred-franc note, to the clerk at the desk and asked him to post it for me. He said it wouldn't go out until the next morning. I said that that was fine, asked if they'd had a good season, was told that it had been so-so, and went.

Going into the chalet it was a nice feeling to think the parcel was well out of my hands. It was nice, too, to see Julia.

She'd changed into the dress she had been wearing in my office the first time we had met; it could have been design or accident. Anyway, just watching her move in it was enough to soothe away the strain of the last few days. I said what would she have and she said a gin-and-Campari with a big slice of lemon and a lot of ice, and it was all there on the table. I poured a stiff whisky for myself. She squatted on the settee, drew her legs up, and took the drink with a polite little nod of her head. Something from the kitchen smelled good.

I said, 'You cook as well?'

'*Cordon bleu.*'

I said, 'You know why croissants are called croissants?'

'No.'

'Good.'

I stretched out in an armchair and lit a cigarette, sipped my drink and felt the first caress of whisky go lovingly down. All was well with the world, almost.

Almost, because she was giving me her dark-eyed gipsy stare, and I wasn't sure where to begin. Semi-honest, Aristide had called my business. He was right. Well why not, I thought, just for once, just for the hell of it, try straightforward honesty?

Why not? It could pay off. It would hurt, of course, but I already had a four-thousand dollar purse to ease the pain. I decided to give it serious thought, later.

I said, 'Can you listen as well as I hope you cook?'

'You're nervous about something,' she said.

'Naturally. I'm considering being entirely honest. That's strange ground for me.'

'Take it a step at a time. It won't spoil what I'm cooking.'

I did. She listened well. Summarized it went like this.

1. I had been employed by O'Dowda to trace his Mercedes. In the course of my investigations I had learnt that a parcel—of importance to O'Dowda—was hidden in the car. O'Dowda had told me that the parcel contained Japanese Bank Bonds. I did not believe this.

2. While tracing the car it had become clear that two other parties were interested in finding it and obtaining the parcel it contained. They were, in order of activity: Najib and Jimbo Alakwe, working under the orders of General Seyfu Gonwalla, head of an African state; and Interpol.

3. I had found the car and taken the parcel, which contained certain film and a tape recording. (I didn't mention Otto or the Tony interlude.)

4. The film was a record, taken without their knowledge, of the sexual activities of General Gonwalla, Miss Panda Bubakar and a Mrs. Falia Makse at the Château de la Forclaz.

5. The tape was a record, made without their knowledge, of a conversation between General Gonwalla and an Alexi Kukarin in which an exchange of arms, aircraft and equipment was agreed against a major proportion of the state's production of minerals, etc., in Gonwalla's country.

6. Clearly, the film and tape records had been secretly organized by O'Dowda for use in the General's country to stimulate the overthrow of his government and thus

186

ensure the grant of a monopoly of mineral and mining rights promised O'Dowda by the previous government.

7. The Alakwe brothers wanted the tape and film in order to destroy it. O'Dowda wanted it to ensure his monopoly being granted. Interpol wanted it so that they could pass it to the custody of an interested government or governments. What the government(s) would do with it was pure guesswork, but clearly they weren't going to destroy it and so keep General Gonwalla in power, otherwise there would have been a link-up already between Interpol and the Alakwe brothers. Equally clearly they weren't going to hand it over to O'Dowda, otherwise Interpol would have linked up with me. Probably then there intention was to let Gonwalla know that they had it, and could at any time they wished release it to his governmental opponents, but wouldn't do so as long as Gonwalla made concessions either political or economic to the interested government(s), and none to Kukarin's government.

At this stage, I said, 'You get that?'

She said, 'Yes. But I'm surprised that Interpol would do a thing like that.'

I said, 'Governments are outside morality. What is devaluation but defaulting on your creditors? Governments can short-change but not individuals. To go on to the most important point—'

8. Following the question of morality—I had the vital parcel. I ran a small semi-honest business, patronized mostly by clients who were non-starters in the Halo Stakes. Some of them were bad payers. It had become my habit, in selected cases, to supplement clients' fees by imposing substantial rake-offs for myself where possible. The money escaped tax, and I flattered myself that I spent it wisely and not all on myself and, let's face it, a fair amount of it did eventually go to the government in

the orm of Betting Tax. The real problem of the moment was—what should I do with the parcel? I could sell it at a good price to either O'Dowda or General Gonwalla. Or, I might sell it to Interpol, though they would never match the price of the others. Or I could destroy it.

'And what,' Julia asked, 'do you intend to do with it?'
'It's a testing question, isn't it?'
'Is it?'
'For me, yes. What would you do?'
'Put it on the stove right away.'
'Crisp, positive. If I had it here I might consider it. But it's in safe keeping.'
'That doesn't surprise me. It stops you doing anything impulsive like burning it here and now.'
'Bright girl.'
'Did you enjoy the film?'
I didn't like the way she said it.
I said, 'I've seen better. However, let's come to another point, which is more of a domestic matter. Interpol have another interest in all this—apart from the parcel. Somebody has been writing them anonymous letters about your stepfather.'
'It certainly wasn't me.'
'No, I didn't have you lined up for that. But would you have any idea what the letters might be about?'
She didn't answer, but I was sure that she did have an idea. Before the silence could become embarrassing, I went on, 'All right. Let's approach it another way. You've been wanting to talk about it for a long time. If I'd been on the ball I might have got it from you the first time you came to see me. In a way I'm glad I didn't because it could have complicated things then. Why didn't you tell me right away that Otto Libsch had once been second chauffeur at the château?'
'I didn't see that it was going to help.' She was ready enough with that one, but it was unconvincing.

'Look,' I said, 'I'm on your side. Just give a little. Okay, knowing about Otto at that time wouldn't have helped me much in the job I had to do. Oh, I can guess how he was linked up with Max. Zelia was the lonely type. Otto drove her around. They talked. She liked him. It was part of his form to have people like him. Maybe he took her to a discothèque or something in Geneva, gave her a pleasant time, and then eventually she met Max, and she kept the whole thing secret because it was her first big romance and that was the way she saw it. Something like that?'

'Yes, I suppose so.'

'Well, if so—there would have been no harm in telling me about it in Turin. But you didn't. And I know why.'

'Why?'

'Because you had a different interest in Otto. Right?'

She gave me a long look and then gently nodded her head.

'Good. You had another interest in him, but you weren't sure how to handle it. Not even sure you could tell me about it because you still weren't trusting me. You thought, maybe still think, that any private or confidential information I get I immediately look over to see where their might be a profit in it for me.'

'That's not true!'

'No?'

'No!' Her indignation sounded real and that pleased me. 'In that case, let's have it now. What had Otto got to do with the way your mother died?'

She put her cigarette down slowly and then stood up and came and picked up my empty glass and went to fill it, her back to me. It was a nice back, nice legs, and I liked the way that her dark hair fell about the nape of her neck.

'Slowly, in your own words,' I said, to help her.

Back to me, she began to talk.

'It was over two years ago. We were all at the château. My mother told me she was leaving O'Dowda. She was in love with someone else.'

'Who?'

She turned. 'She didn't say. Wouldn't say. I think, maybe, even then, she was scared to. She said we would know very soon. She was leaving first thing in the morning, and Otto was going to drive her to Geneva. This was late at night. I went to bed, and I never saw her again.'

'Why not?'

She came back and put the glass in front of me.

'I was told by my stepfather at noon the next day that she had been drowned in Lake Léman. He said that she had got up early, called for Otto to drive her down to the lake—we kept a couple of speedboats there—and she had gone out with Kermode and the boat had capsized.'

'Was it a likely story?'

'She loved boats and she loved speed. And she liked going out early. Any other morning it was something that could easily have been true. But not that morning. That morning she was due to go off for good with this other man.'

'And her body was never recovered?'

'No. But that happens sometimes in the lake. It's very deep.'

'I see. And Otto swore at the enquiry that he drove her down and saw her go aboard with Kermode?'

'Yes.'

'And Kermode told his story. Speed too high, tight curve, capsize, gallant effort to save her and so on?'

'Yes.'

'And you—and Zelia—have had your suspicions of O'Dowda ever since?'

'I think he had her killed.'

'And what about the man she was going away with? Did he ever show?'

'No.'

'And you've no idea who it was?'

'No.' She went and sat down, curling her legs up under her.

'I imagine that Otto left your stepfather's service soon after?'

'Yes.'

I said, 'You like me to tell you who the man was—the man your mother was going away with?'

'How can you possibly know?'

'Some of it's crystal-ball stuff, I'll admit. But not much. It was Durnford ——'

'That's impossible!'

'No, it isn't. We're talking about love, and loves comes up with some odd combinations at times. It was Durnford. He's the one who has been writing anonymous letters. His hatred of O'Dowda isn't the ordinary comfortable hatred of a secretary for a millionaire employer. He's so full of hate for your stepfather that he's buzzing around like a wasp trapped against a window pane. He's doing everything he can to bitch up O'Dowda—particularly over this car business. He must have been the one who tipped the Gonwalla crowd off about the film and tape in the first place. He'd do anything to spite O'Dowda. He was going off with your mother and, somehow, O'Dowda found out, and it would suit his sense of humour to get rid of your mother and keep Durnford on, half-knowing that Durnford would guess the truth and wouldn't be able to do anything about it. That's just the situation O'Dowda likes. That's why he has that waxworks. And Durnford has been trying to get at him any way he could. He's worked the ends against the middle so much now that he's got himself tied in a real Turk's Head—and if he's not careful Kermode will take him for a ride when O'Dowda's tired of the whole thing.'

'Durnford . . . I can't believe it.'

'I can. And I can believe something else. If your stepfather murdered your mother there isn't anything you or anyone else can do about it. Otto's dead, and can't give evidence of perjury. Kermode's alive and won't give evidence. She went to the lake, like they said. It can't be disproved. And that's not just my opinion. I've an idea that Interpol feel that way. So my advice to you is to forget it. You got money of your own?'

'Yes.'

'Then follow Zelia's example. Just get out on your own. Feeling as you do, you can't go on living under his roof.'

'That's just what I've done.'

'Done?'

'Yes. I'd have done it before, but this Zelia thing came up. But when you telephoned me yesterday I was packing to leave. This chalet belongs to me. I was coming up here anyway for a few days to settle things in my mind.'

'Did you tell O'Dowda you were leaving him?'

'Yes, in a letter which I left with Durnford . . . Durnford. I can't believe it.'

'I'll bet on it. Did you mention anything of your reason in the letter?'

'No. But he won't have difficulty reading between the lines. And I don't care a damn if he does.'

She stood up, smoothing the dress wrinkles over her thighs.

'Life's complicated,' I said. 'For the most part I like it that way. All this parcel business and then your mother. . . . Whew, what a tangle. Sometimes a return to simple things is therapeutic. I'll pick the parcel up first thing in the morning and destroy it.'

She smiled for the first time, holding out her hands to the heat of the stove.

'You will?'

'I'll go and get it now if you like.'

'No, the morning will do. I'm not having the meal spoiled.'

She moved towards the kitchen door, then half-turned, her face serious again.

'You really think it's hopeless to do anything about . . . well, about my mother?'

'O'Dowda's a millionaire. He knows how to be careful. He can buy and sell, not only people, but truth. My advice is to forget it all. If he did it, it's written in the book against him and one day the charge will come home to roost. But there's nothing you can do.'

She nodded and went into the kitchen.

It was a good meal. We had *tranches de mouton* done in brandy and served with a *purée* of spinach, and then spent a pleasant evening together.

When we went up to bed, she stopped at her door and she said, 'You really are going to get that parcel and destroy it, aren't you?'

'First thing in the morning.'

She moved close to me and put her arms around my neck. I had to do something with my arms so I put them around her. She kissed me, and a little carillon of bells began to tinkle at the back of my skull. She drew back and looked into my eyes.

I said, 'What's that for?'

She smiled. 'To say I'm sorry for having been mixed up about you. You're not a bit like you want people to think you are.'

She kissed me again and then I held her away from me.

I said, 'You've no idea what I'm like, given the right stimulus. And it's working now.' I reached round her, opened her door, kissed her, fought against the one thing I had in mind, won, and gently armed her into the room. I pulled the door shut and, from the outside, said, 'Lock it. Sometimes I walk in my sleep.'

I waited until I heard the key turn. Then I went into my own room, telling myself that just for once I would do things in their right order. I wanted that parcel out of the way, destroyed, first. I knew me too well. I could have gone into the room with her, and had second thoughts about the parcel in the morning. After all, it was worth a hell of a lot of money, and money is real, so many other things fade and wither.

Before I undressed, I got out my four thousand dollars and hid the notes spread flat under the linoleum. If I were going to do the proper thing and all was to be right between us I knew that I would be back here soon. And if things didn't go right, well, it would still be here. After all, every winning fighter is entitled to his fairly won purse money.

I was down at the Hotel Mont Arbois by eight o'clock the next morning to get my parcel before it was collected by the mail. I was too late. The post had gone. Well, I should just

193

have to collect it at Evian—where I had posted it to myself *poste restante*. I drove slowly in the Facel Vega, wondering why I was throwing away the chance to collect a few more easy thousands for myself. So far as I could see it wasn't going to do me any good. I couldn't even detect the slightest beginning of any spiritual change in myself. Why was I doing it? Clearly, just to get a good standing in Julia's eyes. Some day, I thought, I might find myself in circumstances where I could do something out of pure principle, and no strings attached. It would be interesting to see how I felt then.

I parked the car round the back and hurried into the kitchen, looking forward to coffee and eggs and bacon. There was a good smell of coffee from the pot on the stove, but no sign of breakfast or Julia. I went up to her bedroom. The bed was made, but all her clothes and her suitcase had gone. In my room the bed had been made up.

I went down to the big main room, puzzled. On the table where the drinks were an envelope was propped against one of the bottles. I tore it open.

It was from Panda Bubakar.

Honey-boy,
    We've borrowed your Miss Julia for an indefinite period. Don't fuss, we'll take good care of her. Tell her pappa that he can have her back just as soon as you return you-know-what. Ritzy pyjamas you wear.
                                A hatful of kisses. Yum-yum!
                                    Panda.

I went into the kitchen and poured myself some coffee and sat on the table, thinking.

I had an idea that all this had stemmed from Durnford trying to free himself from the Turk's Head he'd got tangled in. He was prepared now to do anything to muck O'Dowda up and wasn't giving a thought to any consequences. If he couldn't get the parcel from me he was prepared to help Najib to get it. Anything so long as O'Dowda didn't get it.

I called the Château de la Forclaz and got him.

I told him where I was and went on, 'Did you know Miss Julia was going to be here?'

'Yes. Before she left she asked me to forward any mail to her there.'

'And you told Najib where he could find her?'

'What I do is my own business.'

'Well, all I can say is don't go out in any speedboat with Tich Kermode. You've made a real old muck of things. Where's O'Dowda?'

'He's back here and he wants to see you.'

'I'll bet he does. Tell him I'll be along pretty soon. Has he read Julia's letter?'

'What letter?'

'The one in which she says she's finished with him.'

After a pause, he said, 'Yes.'

'Pity.'

I rang off.

O'Dowda, knowing now that Julia had cut adrift from him, wasn't likely to consider that Najib and company had any great bargaining pawn in her. O'Dowda wanted that parcel badly. He wouldn't care a damn what happened to Julia— and plenty could happen to her because Najib was playing for high stakes on the General's behalf.

I fried myself an egg and did some more thinking. It didn't get me anywhere. Then I went up and packed my things, including the ritzy pyjamas. I had a fair idea why Panda and Najib had not waited for me to come back from the hotel. They weren't interested in talking to me. They would go straight to O'Dowda himself.

Only one thing was clear to me. I had the parcel, and I didn't intend that any harm should come to Julia. That meant that I would have to hand it over to Najib. O'Dowda wasn't going to like that, and neither was Aristide. Both of them would do all they could to stop me. For the time being I decided that it would be best to leave the parcel sitting waiting for me at the Evian post office until I had got things straightened out.

I locked up the chalet and drove off in the Facel Vega. It was a good thing that I hadn't got the parcel with me. Just this side of Cluses, I was flagged down by a couple of police types on motor cycles. They were very polite, checked my papers, and then went over the car inch by inch. Disappointed, they asked me where I was going. I wasn't quite sure, but to keep them happy I said the Château de la Forclaz. They waved me on with a couple of Gallic flourishes and sat on my tail for the next ten miles. But they must have been busy on the radio because, as I came down to Thonon on the side of the lake, a couple of fresh motor-cycle types appeared, slowed me down, took up station one at bow and one at stern, and escorted me into the town and on to the Quai de Rives where they pulled up. Aristide was waiting in a shabby old blue saloon.

He got out, dismissed the police, and came back to me and invited me across the road for a drink. He ordered a Pernod for himself, and a beer for me and gave me a warm smile. The cornflower in his buttonhole was faded and he had cut himself in a different place on his chin shaving.

'Nice job you did at the golf course,' he said.

'I thought it was neat.'

'You have girls all over France you can call on for help?'

'Quite a few—but I'm not giving away any addresses. I'm not in a giving-away mood.'

'Pity. You spent last night with this Miss Julia Yunge-Brown?'

'Yes. She's a *cordon bleu* cook, and we had *tranches de mouton* with brandy. I don't know how she cooked it, but it took about two hours.'

He nodded. 'Could have been *a la Poitevine*. Should have had garlic with it. If only a touch.'

'It did.'

'Where is she now?'

'I don't know. I went for a stroll before breakfast and when I got back she had gone. A friend of ours left this note.'

I handed him Panda's note. He studied it without emotion

and then put it in his pocket. 'What is so special about the pyjamas?'

'The design is made up of the flags of all nations.'

'Julia picked up the parcel for you, of course? I should have thought about the Auberge du Père Bise. And now you have safely disposed of it?'

'Yes.'

'Good. I would not want to think that anyone else could get their hands on it. That would be unfortunate for you.'

'Naturally, until I can hand it over in exchange for Julia.'

He shook his head.

'You are taking far too chivalrous a view.'

'If I didn't she could end up floating in a lake. General Gonwalla, fond though he may be of girls, isn't all that soft-hearted. He wants to keep his power seat warm, so he won't mind who he shoves out into the cold.'

'Power, politics—they are the bane of my life. It is nice to concentrate on simple things like murder, theft, forgery. Unfortunately one cannot always choose. I have the strictest instructions to obtain the parcel. Following your request, my organization have agreed to make a payment for it.' He sighed. 'Until now, I thought that it would be a simple little matter of bargaining between the two of us. You would not have got the price Gonwalla or O'Dowda might have paid, but since your heart is in the right place I know you would have fore-gone the extra profit in order to do me a favour. Now it is very much complicated by this kidnapping—and becomes very difficult for you.'

'You think so?'

'I know so, and so do you. I must have the parcel for my employers. They insist, ruthlessly. Gonwalla may be ruthless and O'Dowda, too, but theirs is a personal form of ruthless-ness. It does not approach the ruthlessness of an amorphous organization like a government or group of governments using a perfectly legitimate international organization. No individual would be personally responsible for the girl's death —not that we shan't try to find her and release her, of course—

because it would be a bureaucratic necessity. It is very sad, is it not?' He drained his Pernod and called for another.

'You expect me to hand the parcel over and let what may happen happen to Julia?'

'That's what I've been saying.'

'You know that I won't bloody well do that!'

'I know that you will try to find a way around it.'

'What way?'

'That is up to you. I have no objection to anything you do, so long as I get the parcel. If I don't get it, you know, of course, what will happen to you?'

'Go ahead. Frighten me.'

'It will be out of my hands, of course. Happily another department will deal with it, so I shall have no guilt feelings. But you will be eliminated—out of pure bureaucratic pique, of course. I don't suggest that they will do it in any sadistic way, or make it particularly lingering. They will do it quickly and it will look like an accident. You are not naïve enough to think I'm being flippant about this?'

I wasn't. He was pressuring me, but behind the pressure was a fact, a simple, frightening fact. They would do just as he was promising. As a bureaucratic necessity. I would have to go. It was a straightforward situation. I had the parcel. If I gave it to Najib in return for Julia—then I would go. If I gave it to O'Dowda (which I couldn't see myself doing)— then it was ditto, with the addition of Julia. And if I gave it to Aristide, which I could do by motoring a few miles up the lakeside, then Julia would go because Gonwalla would have to make someone pay for the trouble that lay ahead of him. All I had to do was to find some way of getting my hands on Julia, freeing her, and then handing the parcel over to Aristide. That was all. Simple. I ordered myself a Pernod. Beer was too insipid in the circumstances.

Aristide watched me in silence. I downed the Pernod much too fast and stood up.

'I will have to think about this.'

'Naturally. You have my telephone number. Just call me.'

'And what,' I asked, 'are you doing about the other aspect of this O'Dowda affair?'

He shrugged his shoulders. 'That is a simple matter of murder. I have had instructions to leave it in abeyance until this far more important matter is settled. You are, I imagine, going to the château?'

'Yes.'

'Then please don't mention to O'Dowda our interest in this affair. That is between us.'

'Of course, I wouldn't do anything to embarrass you.'

He grinned. 'That is the correct attitude.'

It would have been nice to sock him on the nose before leaving. But it wouldn't have done any good. He had nothing to do with it. He was just a cipher. He took his pay and went through the prescribed motions and when he went home at night everything dropped from him, leaving him stainless. Just wipe the knife down with a wet rag and you couldn't tell that it had been used. As long as the correct official form had been made out, endorsed by the right department, and neatly filed in the correct cabinet, then there was nothing to worry about.

I drove along the lake as far as Evian, and then I phoned the château and got hold of Durnford. I asked if O'Dowda was around. He wasn't. He had gone to Geneva for the day. I told Durnford I was coming along to see him.

The last person I wanted to run into at the moment was O'Dowda.

I parked on the gravel outside the château, went in and across the big marbled floor to Durnford's office. He was sitting in a swivel chair, staring at a green filing cabinet, smoking, and, from the ash scattered down his waistcoat front, he'd been in that position for a long time. He just cocked his head at me as I came in and then went on staring.

I sat down and lit a cigarette. There was a photograph behind the desk of O'Dowda on the shores of some loch holding up a pike that must have gone all of thirty pounds.

I said, 'This is purely private talk between us. We won't go into the muck-up you've made of things. We'll just stick to some straight answers—from you. Okay?'

He nodded and then reached down and produced a glass from an open desk drawer at his side. He took a generous swig, blinked his eyes at the filing cabinet and put the glass back.

'How long have you been on that?'

'Since lunchtime.'

'Then just knock it off until we've finished our business. First of all—have you had any communication from Najib Alakwe today?'

'No.'

'Did you know that he's grabbed Julia—and she isn't coming back until I hand over the parcel from the car?'

'No.' He didn't seem much interested. Well, whisky can blunt the susceptibilities of the best of us.

'When you've wanted to get in touch with Najib in the past, how have you done it?'

He said, 'That's my business.'

I said, 'It's my business now. I want to know and I'm in the mood where I don't mind beating up a man some years older than myself. So give.'

He considered it for a while, then turned and fished in another drawer and passed a card across to me. I looked at it and wondered how many different kinds Najib had. It was the usual Mr. Najib Alakwe, Esquire, of the import, export and specialities line, but this time there was an address in Geneva. I had to turn it over. You never knew what gem the Alakwe brothers were coming up with. I wasn't disappointed. The motto read: *A bon entendeur il ne faut que demi parole*. Well, I was hoping to have more than half a word with Najib—and soon.

Without looking at me, he said, 'All you had to do was to let me have the parcel, or destroy it.'

I said, 'I was going to destroy it—but you spoilt that. Things are a bit more complicated now.'

He shook his head. 'You would have kept it. Made money from it. I know you.'

'That's what I thought myself—but it didn't work out that way.' I stood up. 'You want some advice?'

'Not particularly.' He sounded completely apathetic, not the crisp number I had first known.

'Pack up and get out of here, get a long way away from O'Dowda. You were going to do it once with her and he bitched you. You should have done it on your own after that.'

He looked up suddenly, his eyes blinking.

'How did you know that?'

'It was a guess—until this moment.'

'He murdered her.'

'I'm inclined to agree. But there's nothing you can do about it. After what you've done, and when he learns the full story, you need to be thinking about your own skin.'

He said, 'I think I may kill him.'

I said, 'I wish I could think that was a firm promise. But when the whisky is finished your only concern will be how to get rid of a hangover.'

'Tich Kermode did it. He's an evil bastard—worse than O'Dowda. They get drunk sometimes, those two. Shut themselves up in that bloody great waxworks room with all the people O'Dowda hated. You can hear them laughing and pounding around. I kept it from the girls for years and years . . . but they knew in the end. . . That's why they've left him.'

I made for the door. Then, a thought occurring to me, I said, 'Have you got a gun?'

'Gun?'

Why do drunks always have to give off echoes?

'Yes, a gun. It could be that I might need one—and for sure you won't.'

I think he fancied that I might be going to use it on O'Dowda because he co-operated by opening another drawer and tossing a gun to me. It's not an action I like. Guns are full of gremlins. I looked at it and said, 'What the hell's this?'

'It's all I've got,' he said, as he handed over to me a box of ammunition.

It was a .22 compressed-air pistol, powered by a Sparklet compressed air tube which gave about forty shots at somewhere around a muzzle velocity of four hundred feet per second. It could be nasty and looked like the real thing. I'd used one in Miggs's shooting range before. I hoped that it would be good enough to impress Najib and make him hand over Julia.

I went back to the car and sent up a fine shower of gravel going down the long drive. I wanted to be clear of the place before O'Dowda got back.

It was dark as I rode into Geneva. The address I had was in a cul-de-sac just off the Rue des Vollandes and not far from the Gare des Eaux-Vives. It was a top-floor flat and had a blue door painted with diagonal yellow stripes and when I thumbed the bell-push chimes inside played a simple melody that was vaguely familiar.

As I stood there trying to remember what it was, the door opened and Najib appeared. He'd gone back to his old style of dressing, ginger shoes, cream linen suit, red shirt and a yellow tie with garlands of multi-coloured roses trailing over it. It was a bit of a shock but I kept the air pistol firmly pointing at him.

'I'd like to come in,' I said.

The brown face beamed, the smudge nose crinkled, and the whiter shade of white teeth flashed.

'Certainly, Mr. Carver. Damn glad to see you again. Welcome to not so humble abode.'

I said, 'You lead the way and cut out the music-hall patter.'

He went ahead of me down a softly carpeted hallway into a large sitting room. Not so humble it was. The furniture was all upholstered in black velvet, the carpet was pearly grey with great whorls of red in it. The curtains were green and the walls were covered with a paper that imitated great chunks of granite with thick white plaster marks in the joins. There was a sideboard nearly six feet long, covered with bottles and the things that go with them, a long table untidy with magazines, the covers of which were showing a lot of female flesh, and the place reeked of Turkish tobacco.

Najib turned, waved a hand around, and said, 'You like? No? Tastes differ. Some people say, just like a whore's parlour. Personally I have found many such parlours very comfortable and entertaining. What is your favourite tipple sir?'

'My favourite tipple,' I said, 'is a large whisky and soda which I'll fix myself in case you have any poison around. Personally I'm hoping that it's not a drink I shall have to linger over because I want my business cleared up smartly. Also, please cut out all the babu talk. You're probably a D.Litt. and, no doubt, could start at Chaucer while I pegged off at Shakespeare and beat me handsomely through to T. S. Eliot. So let's stick to a reasonable syntax, Najib, eh?'

He gave me that big, wide-open smile, and said, 'Actually, it's B.Sc.(Econ.) but I have not neglected the arts. Also, we should get the names right. I am disappointed that you have such a bad memory for faces. I am Mr. Jimbo Alakwe, Esquire.'

I was so surprised that he went and fixed my drink for me while I got over it. When I had recovered and the drink was in my hand, I said, 'What the hell are you doing here?'

'Temporary posting. Najib has a lot on his hands. Also, remember I now work for Mr. O'Dowda so have to be on the spot.'

'You don't mean he actually took you on?'

'Why not? He doesn't trust me, but he likes to know where I am. Also, if he gets false information from me about affairs in my country, he probably guesses it is false and can make something from it. Wrong information can be as revealing as correct information. Mr. O'Dowda is prepared to pay for both. Needless to say, my loyalty, my true loyalty, is to my country. I am inordinately proud of that. One of the things, I feel, which prevent you from becoming a success is that you have no loyalty to anyone but yourself. That can only lead to limited profits. What is your asking price for the parcel?' He held up a hand and went on quickly, 'Naturally the girl will be returned as well, but I realize that you will want something for yourself. But not as much, of course, as though we didn't have the girl.'

I said, 'No money passes. And no parcel passes. I want the girl.'

'I think,' said Jimbo, 'we had better discuss this situation a little more fully.'

'Let us do that,' I said, and sat down on a soft-sprung chair.

Jimbo reached for a cigarette box. As he opened the lid it began to play a tune. He grinned at me.

'*Au clair de la lune*. The toilet container in this place plays *Sur le pont d'Avignon*. This is really Panda's flat. You like her?'

'She's a great girl. Good swimmer, too. I'd like to know how she and Najib knew I was at Ansermoz's chalet, by the way.'

'It was very simple. They lost you so they made a phone call to the house. You answered the phone. Remember—you said to the woman caller that Max was in Cannes. So they knew you were there. After that they kept an eye on you from a safe distance.' He smiled. 'A man travelling fast, dreaming of profit, should look behind him occasionally.'

I said. 'You ought to print that on one of your cards.'

'Maybe.'

I stood up. 'All right, let's have a look round. You go ahead and don't make any sudden movements.'

He showed me round the flat. It was furnished throughout in Panda taste and it wasn't difficult to guess that she used the place for her professional entertaining. The whole place was probably wired for sound and film. One thing it didn't have, however, was any sign of Julia.

I took Jimbo back into the sitting room and he sat down and helped himself to another musical cigarette and waved his hand at the drinks for me to help myself.

Bottle in hand, I said, 'All right—she's not here. Where is she?'

He polished his ebony chin with the tips of his fingers and

said, 'If I knew I wouldn't tell you, but the sad fact is that I don't know.'

'Why sad?'

'Because it shows that Najib, in a most unbrotherly way, doesn't altogether trust me. I have no means either of communicating with him. He phones me when he needs me. So please don't bother to exert yourself with any physical measures to make me talk. I have nothing to say. That is the most honest statement I have made for some weeks.'

I wondered. Then I decided to give him the benefit of the doubt. He realized it and gave me a sympathetic nod of his head.

'I should say, however, Mr. Carver, that I am authorized to discuss details for a satisfactory exchange. What price were you thinking of?'

'I wasn't. I don't intend to do any deal.'

'Unchivalrous. She is a very beautiful girl, and—a little bird says—has some tenderness for you. Just think—for a parcel which is of no importance to you intrinsically you can earn yourself, say, a thousand guineas and her release. She will be delighted and, no doubt, eventually show her gratitude in the one way which constantly occupies men's minds. I am assuming, of course, that you still have the parcel and that it is in a safe place?'

I said, 'You can assume that. But you're not getting the parcel. Nobody's getting it.'

He shook his head. 'Not us, not Mr. O'Dowda, or Interpol?' He gave me a big beaming smile of disbelief. 'You are, as they say, on the horns of a dilemma. A most unusual one, too, because this beast has three horns. I am sad for you. It is a predicament I should not like to be in myself. As I say, she is a very beautiful young woman. What you call, I think, the Celtic type. . . . No, no, perhaps Romany would be the word.'

He was right, of course. Not only about her physical type, but about my dilemma. At that moment I did not know which way to turn, what to do or where to go. Just for a moment I did reconsider using force on him in the hope that he might know more than he professed, but it was only for a moment. I could have taken him, but I didn't think he would speak before he passed out. Jimbo was a resolute type, inordinately proud of his loyalty.

I finished my drink and made for the door.

'Just sit there,' I said.

He nodded.

I went down the hallway and out. As I closed the door of the flat the solution to one question, at least, came to me. I realized that the tune the doorbell had played was 'Happy Birthday to You'.

A few minutes later, as I was about to get into the Facel Vega parked in the cul-de-sac outside the flat, Tich Kermode clubbed me over the back of the head and O'Dowda grabbed me like a sack of potatoes before I could hit the pavement. I passed out without protest.

CHAPTER EIGHT

'No human being, however great, or powerful,
was ever so free as a fish.'

JOHN RUSKIN

IT WAS A ROLLS-ROYCE. Kermode was driving and I sat in the
back with O'Dowda. I felt in my pocket for the gun that I had
borrowed from Durnford. It was gone. When O'Dowda saw
that I had surfaced he handed me a flask without a word, I
drank, then shivered, and blinked my eyes at the road un-
winding before the headlights. We were climbing steeply
through pine woods. Probably, I thought, the road back to
the château.

Kermode had his chauffer's cap pitched at a jaunty angle
and was whistling gently to himself, happy at the thought of
a good time ahead. O'Dowda was wearing a knickerbocker
suit of hairy Harris tweed. There was a big bruise on his right
temple.

Nobody spoke for a long time. Then, staring straight ahead
of him, O'Dowda said, 'You're a bastard.'

It wasn't a good conversational opener, so I ignored it.

He said, 'You're a bastard. So is Durnford, but he's a
drunken bastard. If it's of any interest to you, I've sacked him.'

'After twisting his arm to say where I was?'

'Both arms,' said Kermode over his shoulder.

The two of them had a merry chuckle over that.

I didn't relish the thought of the next few hours. O'Dowda
wanted the parcel and he wasn't, I was sure, contemplating
any kind of a deal—even if I'd been in a position to offer one.

He said, 'I hate time-wasting. Someone always has to pay
for that, boyo.'

I yawned, closed my eyes, and leaned back against the
genuine pigskin.

O'Dowda said, 'What makes you think you can sleep?'

I said, 'Try and stop me.' I slumped lower down and gave a drowsy grunt.

Kermode said, 'He should be fun, sir.'

O'Dowda said, 'Yes. Worth waiting for.'

From the corner of a half-opened eye I saw him pull out a cigar and light up. Despite the throb in my head, I went to sleep.

I woke as we turned into the driveway of the château.

O'Dowda said, 'Feel better?'

'Thanks.'

'Good. I want you in fighting trim. And this time I'm not taking bets.'

We went up the mile-long drive but we didn't go to the château. We turned off, down a side road, and climbed for about half a mile and then pulled up. Kermode dowsed the lights. Outside I got a glimpse of an expanse of water stretching away, steely blue under the moonlight. It looked like a lake, and that brought unpleasant memories.

Standing at the side of the lake was a small cottage with a boat-house attached to it. They took me across to it and into the large main room.

'My workroom,' said Kermode.

There was a long bench down one side of the room, an open fireplace at the far end and on a little plinth in the middle stood an unclothed life-size wax figure without a head.

'When it's finished,' said O'Dowda, 'it's going to be you. We'll use the suit you're wearing now, so just take it off.' He looked at Kermode. 'Turn up the heating, Kermode, so that he doesn't get cold.'

Kermode moved around the room, turning on three or four electric heaters. O'Dowda lit another cigar and went to a cabinet and poured himself a brandy.

'There's one for you,' he said, 'when you've got the suit off.'

I stripped my suit off. What else could I do? If I had refused they would have enjoyed doing it for me.

O'Dowda—going to get me a brandy—said to Kermode, 'Do we want his shoes?'

Kermode shook his head. 'Too scruffy.'

O'Dowda handed me my brandy.

He said, 'Don't be too long drinking it. We want to tie your hands behind your back.'

I said, 'Have you figured out a place for me in the rogues' gallery?'

'Not yet,' said O'Dowda.

'Do me a favour and keep me well away from the policeman. I'm allergic to them.'

'So you should be. I suppose Interpol have been telling you that you have to hand the parcel over to them, or else?'

'Something like that.'

'Powerful things, governments,' said O'Dowda. 'I should know, I practically own a couple. I also have two Interpol men on my payroll. By the way, as of this date, you are no longer on my payroll. What is more, I don't intend to pay you a penny of what I owe you for your work so far unless you hand over the parcel to me.'

'Why not? You employed me to trace the car for you. I did just that.'

'You did far more than just that. You walked off with my property.'

While we were talking Kermode was busying himself at a large cupboard. So far as I could make out he was sorting out a collection of fishing rods.

I said, 'Have you had any communication from Najib lately?'

He nodded, blinked his small blue eyes at me through his cigar smoke, and said, 'A phone call. To save unnecessary beating about the bush, boyo, let me say I am well aware of the whole position. Najib wants the parcel in return for Julia. Interpol want it from you—or else. And I mean to have it. Tricky. For you. You have my sympathy but nothing else. Oh, and there is the other thing, too. This nonsense about my late wife. That's pure poppycock. Just the kind of thing Julia would dream up and that a crazy fool like Durnford would jump at. Mind you, I knew he was having an affair with my wife just before her unfortunate accident, but it didn't worry me. I was going to divorce her anyway. I'd already instructed my solicitors to prepare a petition. One of life's little accidents saved me the cost of their fees. Tie his hands, Kermode.'

Kermode came over, politely waited for me to finish the last of the brandy, and then tied my hands behind me at the wrists tightly with thin cord.

Thinking it might interest me, he said, 'It's a piece of Corolene Dacron braided spinning line.'

'It cuts like hell,' I said.

'It's meant to.'

I looked at O'Dowda who was helping himself to another brandy.

'If I hand the parcel over to you—you know what will happen to Julia?'

'As the night follows the day. General Gonwalla can be a very mean-minded man.'

'And you don't care a damn?'

'She's not my true daughter, and anyway she has now formally severed all relationship with me. I have no responsibility for her. That's not to say that she isn't a nice-looking girl and it will be a sad thing. I wouldn't be surprised if you hadn't a soft spot for her. All this puts you in an awkward situation, but it is of no interest to me. Just hand the parcel to me, however, and I'll try and make Gonwalla see sense—though I can't guarantee anything.'

'If I do, then Interpol will rub me out.'

'Yes, I think they would do that. That's why I'm sure that I shall have to use some method to make you tell me where the parcel is. I couldn't expect you to do so willingly.'

Kermode looked towards O'Dowda. 'What do you think, sir. Let it get a bit lighter?'

O'Dowda nodded. 'I think so. Won't be as much fun then as a big sea-trout in the dark, but we mustn't expect too much. What rod do you think?'

'Salmon?'

'We'll try the A. H. E. Wood.' He turned to me. 'Of course you could save yourself all this by just telling me where the parcel is.'

'I destroyed it.'

He grinned. 'Not you, boyo. If you gave me an affidavit signed by St. Peter I wouldn't believe that one.'

'What about St. Patrick?'

'Less so. Think I don't know the Irish? No, you've got it somewhere safe and I'm having it. Come to think of it, I'd rather force it from you. You need some of the spunk taken out of you. I wouldn't say that your manner towards a man of my standing is deferential enough. And even if I did, there's a well-developed sadistic streak in me that says go ahead and have fun. God, it's hot in here.'

He stripped off his Harris tweed jacket. Over by the cupboard Kermode was fixing up the salmon rod with a reel. I had a fair idea of what they might be going to do, but I couldn't believe it. I tried to remember what I could about the breaking strain of lines, and then I recalled reading somewhere that a good rod and line had stopped a really strong swimmer dead after he'd done about thirty yards. I stopped thinking about it. O'Dowda was right. It was hot in the room. The lake would make an unpleasant contrast in temperature.

Then I thought about the parcel. What the hell was I to do? The whole thing had me properly confused. Give it to O'Dowda and lose Julia? Give it to Najib and save Julia—but put myself in the soup? Give it to Interpol and save myself and lose Julia, and then have Najib and O'Dowda gunning for me out of sheer political and economic spite? If there'd been time of course I could have written to some lonely hearts column and got advice. 'In the circumstances I think this is a problem where you must squarely face your own conscience. . . .' Trouble was there was no sign of my conscience being around at this moment. It was that kind of conscience, never there when you really wanted it.

I sat and sweated. O'Dowda had a little snooze. Kermode—

he was the type—kept busy, tinkering away at some metal-work job at a bench down the far end of the room. Now and again he went to the window and looked out to see how the light was coming along.

After a couple of hours he came over to me and strapped a leather dog-collar affair around my neck. There was a steel ring fitted into it just under my chin and attached to the ring was a three-yard length of line.

'It's a wire gimp,' he said. 'So you can't bite through. Some big pike have been known to—but you've got to have real teeth for a job like that.' Then he looked at O'Dowda and, believe it or not, there was a touch of gentleness on his craggy, monkey face. 'Pity to wake him. He needs his sleep, does the boss. Drives himself hard. Always on the go. Don't pay any attention to that sadistic talk. Heart of a lamb he's got really. If you just coughed up now, he'd call it a day. Probably hand you a bonus on your pay. What do you say?'

I said, 'He looks far too much overweight. The exercise will do him good—or give him a stroke. Want me to tell you which I'm cheering for?'

He went and woke O'Dowda, shaking him gently by the shoulder, and then holding his jacket for him.

And that was the beginning of the entertainment. They led me through a side door, Kermode carrying their equipment, into the boathouse.

We got into a rowing boat and Kermode took the oars and we pulled out on to the lake. It was a beautiful morning; no sun yet, but the hint of it, and the sky pearly grey with a rosy flush in the East. Not a cloud in the sky and a few late stars still flickering in protest against the coming day. Some duck got up from the weed beds near the boat-house.

'Pochards and a few garganey,' said O'Dowda. 'We tried to keep goldeneye here, but they wouldn't stay.' As he spoke he leaned forward making the end of the reel line fast to the loose end of the wire gimp.

'Make sure the knot's good,' I said.

'Don't worry, boyo,' he said warmly, 'I've had my tackle

broken but I've never lost a fish yet through a sloppy knot. All you have to do when you've had enough is just to shout. Don't leave it too long so that you're too weak to shout.'

I drove upwards with my right knee, trying to get him in the face before he could fix the knot, but he was too quick for me. One of his big hands grabbed my leg and held it. From behind me Kermode leaned forward and hauled me back, and O'Dowda straddled my legs and finished tying the knot.

From that position they didn't take any more chances with me. They took off my shoes and I was lifted and flung overboard.

I went under, and I thought I would go out with the sudden shock of the cold; and while I was still under I felt the strain come firmly on the collar round my neck. When I came up the boat was twenty yards away. O'Dowda was standing up, two-handing the salmon rod, and taking the strain nicely on me. Kermode was at the oars, not rowing, just holding the boat evenly.

I trod water and felt my shirt and shorts ballooning around me. The cold began to cut into me. O'Dowda increased the pressure through the line and my head came forward until my face was underwater. I was forced to kick out with my legs and swim towards the boat to get my face up into the air. I heard the reel take up the slack, and the pressure came on again as I stopped swimming. Again my face was dragged under. This time, I turned in the water, and kicked away strongly from the direction of the boat, knowing that the pull of the line would at least keep my head back and my face clear of the water. It did, and damned nearly choked me. I swam against it for as long as I could, and then the line pressure stopped me, rolled me over and I went down about two feet. If I'd been a salmon I would have come up in a great silver, curving leap, hoping to catch O'Dowda unawares and break line or rod tip. I came up like a sack of wet horse-hair, gasping and choking for breath, to hear O'Dowda shout, 'Come on, boyo, put some life into it. I've known a two-pound tench do better.'

I tried again. Not to please him, but in the hope of reaching the bank about fifty yards away. I swam towards the boat but at an oblique angle, hoping to gain a little ground towards shallow water. If I could once get my feet down and stand, I might have enough strength in my shoulder and neck muscles to hold them until I could turn round a couple of times, winding the line around my body and getting a grasp of it with my free fingers.

Kermode called, 'Watch him, sir. He's making for the weeds. Ah, he's a cunning one.'

The boat altered position and my face went under as O'Dowda tightened the line. I fought against it, jack-knifing my legs forward to bring my head up and then leaning back against the pressure of the line, taking the full power on my neck. O'Dowda held me like it for a few moments. I saw the arc of the rod bend more and I couldn't fight the power of the line and split bamboo rod. My face went under again and I had to kick forward fast to take off the full power of the line strain to get my mouth above water. I gulped in air, but before I'd had my fill, the boat moved away from me and the strain came in again. For five minutes O'Dowda played me, letting me have just enough air and respite to keep me going, but all the while I was getting weaker and more desperate, knowing that I was slowly being drowned. O'Dowda could have made a fast job of it, but he was taking his time. Now and again as I got my head up I saw them in the boat, and heard them laughing. I made a last kicking thrust for shallow water, but I was stopped dead. Then the strain went off and I was allowed to breathe.

O'Dowda shouted, 'Well, where is it?'

He had me. There wasn't any question about it. Another five minutes of this and I wouldn't care what happened to me. But at that moment I was just conscious enough to care about the future. Quite frankly I didn't want to die, and I wasn't in any mood to make sacrifices for anybody. I wanted to stay alive. It's a powerful instinct and there's no arguing with it.

I opened my mouth to shout, but Kermode gave a couple

of strokes on the oars and O'Dowda put more strain on the line and my face was under again. For a moment or two I blanked out from intelligent thought, just sinking into blackness, and stupidly telling myself that it was enough to put a man off fishing for life. . . .

They must have seen I was all in and ready to talk, because the strain went off the line. I surfaced slowly and lay in the water on my back, facing the gold and silver morning sky, seeing a flight of starlings skeined right across it. I lay there gulping in the lovely air.

The strain was right off the line now and I heard the boat coming towards me, the reel singing as O'Dowda took up slack line.

O'Dowda's voice called, 'Ready to talk?'

I rolled over and faced them. The boat was about four yards away. I trod water feebly and nodded my head.

O'Dowda said, 'Good. Where is it?'

'I'll have to go and get it. I posted it to myself,' I said.

'How long will that take?'

'Not long. It's *poste restante* at——'

Several things happened then to make me break off. There was the sound of a shot, O'Dowda ducked, raising the tip of the rod, and the strain came sharply back on to the line, choking the rest of my words silent.

Feebly I kicked to take the strain off. There was another shot from somewhere to my left. I slewed my head round to see three figures standing on the far bank. One of them plunged into the water and headed for me. At the same time one of the others raised a hand and I heard another shot. O'Dowda and Kermode went down flat in the boat and the strain was off me completely.

I made a few weak, token kicks towards whoever was coming out to me.

A few seconds later a familiar voice said, 'Hold on, honey-chile, while I get the hook out of your mouth. Yum-yum, fish for supper.'

It was, bless her black little heart, Panda Bubakar, heading

215

for me at speed, a grin all over her face, her white teeth flashing, and, held between them, a knife.

She came threshing up to me, grabbed the wire gimp, worked her hand up to the line and slashed it with the knife. Then she turned me over on my back, grabbed the slack of my shirt and began to tow me ashore, while the two on the bank cracked off an occasional shot to keep O'Dowda and Kermode low in the boat.

When we reached the bank Panda pulled me out and helped me to my feet and went round behind to cut my hands free.

'Brother,' she said, 'have you got a thing for water! Your old lady must have been a mermaid.'

Standing higher up the bank were Najib and Jimbo Alakwe, both with guns in their hands. Najib, neat and tidy in a dark grey suit, beaming at me; and Jimbo in red jeans and a loose yellow sweat shirt with a man's head printed on it in black, a shaggy-headed, craggy-faced man with the word *Beethoven* under it. He beamed at me, too, but only briefly, turning away to give the row boat another shot.

My hands free, Panda gave me a wet smack on the bottom and said, 'Start running, handsome. Mamma show the way.'

She moved off up the bank. I followed, stumbling along, clumsy from loss of circulation, but now with enough interest in life to give more than a dull data-recording glance at her long brown, heavy-breasted figure clad only in briefs and brassière. At the top of the bank she stooped and jerked up a track suit and kept running.

'Be with you soonest,' said Jimbo as we went by.

'Sooner,' said Najib, and, nodding at me, added, 'Good morning, Mr. Carver.'

Panda took me through the trees, along a small path and finally out on to the open space behind the cottage. Parked short of the Rolls-Royce was their Thunderbird.

At the car she jerked the rear door open and reached inside for a couple of rugs.

'Come on, honey,' she said. 'Get that wet stuff off and wrap up in these. And, boy,' she warned, 'no tricks. No jerking any torch out of your pants and slugging me. Jeese, was that something disappointing to a girl for a man to produce.'

She half-turned from me and began to slip out of her pants and bra' and then slid into her track suit. I stripped, too, and wrapped myself in the blankets and she bundled me into the car just as Najib and Jimbo appeared, running.

As they went by the Rolls, Jimbo put a shot in each of the back tyres.

Five seconds later we were streaking down the château drive towards the main road and my teeth were chattering in my head like an electric typewriter going at speed.

Najib, next to Jimbo, who was driving, handed a flask back to Panda.

With a wink, she said, 'Ladies first—which almost means me.' She took a good swig and then handed the flask over.

I took a deep pull, and she said, 'Keep sucking, baby. We'll soon have you in a nice hot bath and Mamma will give you a friction rub afterwards. Whoof! Whoof!' She put her long arm around my shoulder and gave me a great she-bear hug.

Driving, Jimbo said, 'That millionaire man sure has a thing about fishing. Only time I ever did it was with hand grenades in the river at home. Remember that, Najib?'

If Najib did, he didn't consider it worth recording. He turned back to me and said, 'Did you tell them anything?'

I said, 'Another two seconds and I would have done. I wouldn't have believed water could be so cold.'

'Healthy, though,' said Panda. 'Early morning swim, wham, gets the old corpuscles stirring and ready for mischief.'

She leaned forward and tucked the blankets round my legs. She found her cigarettes and lit one for me, sticking it into my mouth and giving me a fat, almost motherly kiss on the cheek.

'Nice. Yum-yum,' she said, and to Najib added, 'Can I have him after you've finished?'

Najib said, 'Panda, for God's sake, throttle down.'

'She always like this?' I asked.

'Even in her sleep,' said Jimbo and chuckled to himself.

217

'I sure am,' said Panda unabashed. 'I've got over five hundred witnesses that'll testify.'

And from there, right to Geneva and Jimbo's flat she kept it up, ignored by the two in front. Her talk didn't trouble me too much. I had a lot to think about. But I had to fight off her long arms and hands occasionally as she checked now and then to see that I was comfortable inside the blankets and nicely warming up.

Nobody paid any attention to me as I went through the lobby to the lifts wrapped in blankets. Geneva is a cosmopolitan city. If a Zulu in war paint walked down the street everyone would know that he was just over to a conference hoping to get economic aid.

Panda ran me a bath, suggested we should share it, yelped like a disappointed puppy when I managed to lock her out, but was happier when I had to shout for a towel and there was no way of escaping the friction rub.

They found me a suit of Najib's, navy blue, and a white shirt and other odds and ends, but the only spare shoes were a pair of ginger suèdes.

Back in the sitting room, I said, 'Why always these suède jobs?'

'We get them wholesale from Panda,' said Jimbo. 'She has a small factory in Liechtenstein.'

Panda, coming in with coffee, said, 'Well, a girl has to do something with her profits. It's for my old age. When I retire from the entertainment business, round about eighty, I guess.'

She put the coffee tray down in front of me and the top half of her nearly fell out of the low-cut yellow dress into which she had changed.

Najib said, 'You two get off. You know where. I want to talk to Mr. Carver.'

Panda winked at me. 'You want I give her your love, honey-chile? She's a peach. I'll hand you that—but she'll never have the touch I have with a towel.'

'Out,' said Najib.

Jimbo said, 'That O'Dowda might come along here.'

'Let him,' said Najib. 'And he can bring his fishing rod, too —but it won't do him any good.'

They went and I leaned back and sipped my coffee. I was feeling all right now, physically. Mentally, I was as scrambled up as ever over the problem of the parcel, except now I was beginning to feel bloody-minded, in fact, more bloody-minded than ever, towards O'Dowda. The man didn't care a damn for anyone but himself. Julia could go, I could go, everyone could go, just so long as he got his hands on what he wanted. With me, that just strengthened the desire I had to make sure that he never did get it. Just for once somebody was going to spit in his eye.

'How did you know I was out there?' I asked Najib.

'Jimbo saw them jump you from the flat window. The Facel Vega is still down there. But that's the past. You know what you're going to do, don't you?'

He was a different man, serious, calm, no babu talk, and it was easy to see him in his real role, an army officer seconded to an Intelligence position in Gonwalla's service.

I said, 'I never did believe in that old business of which would you save when the boat sinks, your wife or your mother?'

Najib nodded. 'I thought putting Julia in danger would work with O'Dowda. He's made it clear that it doesn't. That's the kind of man he is. But you're not that kind, Julia is in danger. I'm serious about that. I don't care for the situation particularly, but I have my orders. You'll never see her again —nobody will—unless I get the parcel. Life, a life, in our country isn't very important. Never has been, so don't think that I shan't carry out the order if you refuse to hand over.'

'I've got Interpol on my back, remember.'

'I know. But you've got to take a chance on that. In fact, your Western philosophy or code demands it. You know that. Up to this moment you've been trying to find a way round it —sometimes there are ways—but not this time. So—there is nothing you can do. I'm sure that you agree with me.'

I poured myself another cup of coffee and considered it. He was right, of course. In cold blood he was nothing but right. Up there at the lake, with the good air being choked out of me, I'd been ready to give up, to forget all codes, but down here, under no physical pressure, I was thinking straight, and feeling straight. He was dead right. I just had to get Julia out of trouble and then take my own chances with Interpol. I could go to ground for three or four months and they might decide to forgive me or forget me; they might. But I didn't think it likely. The only thing that would make them change their minds would be pressure, political or public.

Although my mind was made up, I said, 'When you've got this parcel, what are the chances of Gonwalla putting pressure on whoever is using Interpol? Would he? Could he?'

Najib considered this. 'When we have the parcel and it is destroyed, then our government is safe. We have friends as well as enemies amongst the world's governments. Many of them are members of Interpol. I should say that there is a fifty-fifty chance. But to be fair—and you must have thought of this— the individual government which hopes to get this parcel through Interpol might take its own private, vindictive revenge for a failure.'

They might. But that was all part of the chance I had to take.

I said, 'All right. How do we do it? It'll take me about an hour to get the parcel.'

'You go and get it. When it's in your hands, phone here. By the time you get back I'll have Julia waiting somewhere handy and we'll do the change-over in the open, in the street outside. Satisfy you?'

I nodded, and then got up to make a note of the telephone number.

I said, 'You'll be here waiting for me to call?'

'Yes.'

'Good.'

As I went to the door, he said, 'We'll do what we can for

220

you afterwards. I'm in no position to lecture, of course—but it's difficult to resist. You've only got yourself to blame for whatever the aftermath may be. You thought you could make something for yourself out of the parcel. Human greed. It's a constant problem.'

So it might be, I thought, as I went out, but without it the world would be a very dull place. Personally, at that moment I was all in favour of dullness. At that moment I would have liked to have been away on the holiday I had promised myself, sitting dully somewhere wondering what to do and knowing that if I thought of something I would never have the energy to do it. That's what holidays were for, to smooth you down to a nice, flat dull surface which you could take back for the rest of the year's events to mark up again.

It was a beautiful morning. The road out around the lake to Evian was choked with cars—parts of it were under repair so there was single-line traffic and hold-ups at lights which did nothing to ease down my impatience. All I wanted now was to get the parcel and have Julia back.

Away to the left, when I could see it, the lake was a great sheet of blue with the Juras somewhere beyond in the haze. Right-handed, somewhere out of sight, was Mont Blanc, and not far from that was the chalet where I had spent a night with Julia . . . Najib was right. Human greed. I promised myself that if I came out of this little lot with a whole skin I would really try to do something about it. I knew I wouldn't be able to cut it out altogether, but I would try to cut it down. For me that was a big promise. Money was such a comforting thing to have. The way things were I wasn't likely to get any fees or expenses from O'Dowda for this job. Wilkins would have something to say about that.

Good old Wilkins. I wondered what she would have made of Panda. I spent the rest of the journey imagining them together. For all I knew they might hit it off.

I parked the Facel Vega and went into the post office with my English driving licence, my international driving licence, and a banker's credit card, per favour of O'Dowda (all of which had been in my case in the car) in order to identify myself. Sometimes at *poste restantes* they asked you and sometimes they didn't. They worked on some system, probably their mood of the moment.

The woman behind the guichet had a pink nose, pink lips, fluffy blue-grey hair, and big moist eyes, doe-like, and reminded me of an Angora rabbit which I had once forgotten to feed for a week so that it died and my sister had leathered me with a slipper. Sensitive green fingers she had, my sister, even at the age of fourteen, but she also had the wrists of a squash player.

I spread out my *cartes d'identités* like lettuce in front of the girl.

She wrinkled her pink nose with pleasure.

I said, 'Carver. Rex Carver. I think there's a parcel here for me.'

She picked at the corner of the banker's card and said, Carvaire . . .?'

I knew she would.

'*Oui*, Carvaire.'

She turned away to the rows of pigeon holes behind her, had a brief chat with a chum on her left, and then, starting on the lower row which ran backwards from Z, gave herself the trouble of a long ride up to C. There was a wad of stuff in it which she brought over to me.

'Carvaire?' She started to sort through it.

'That's right.'

She shuffled through the lot, and then shook her head at me.

'There is nozzings, monsieur. Caballaire, there is.'

'Carvaire,' I said. But my heart was right down in my ginger suède shoes already. Nothing she held in her hand looked the size of the parcel I had sent.

'I'm sorry, monsieur. Perhaps he comes the next collection?'

I shook my head and began to gather up the lettuce leaves.

I was about to turn away—wondering what the hell had happened, the thought flashing through my mind that maybe Aristide had been at work (he could have made a check of every *poste restante* in the East of France by now and picked it up)—when the girl said with a sudden note of recognition in her voice, 'Ah, you are Mr. Carvaire?'

'Yes.'

'Then it is explained. You are guest of Monsieur O'Dowda, no?' From the way she said it, it was clear that she knew Mr. O'Dowda. Who wouldn't in this district? He owned half a mountain not six miles away.

I nodded, not trusting myself to speak. I was way ahead of her. But there was no stopping her. A guest from the château was something to relish and hold on to for a while.

'But Mr. O'Dowda himself telephones this morning to see for parcel of his guest, Mr. Carvaire. I say, yes, is waiting, so he send his chauffeur with passport for parcel. It is not long ago. One hour, maybe. Maybe a little more. The chauffeur I know well. Is a little man, much joking and winking the eye. . . .'

I didn't wait for the full description of Kermode. I was on my way out.

I sat in the car and lit a cigarette, smoking it as though I hated it, sucking the life out of it. Not Aristide but O'Dowda had done it. O'Dowda had had more to go on. He had my suit with my passport in it. I had told him that the parcel was *poste restante*. I had told him that it wasn't far away. He could have phoned every main post office around the lake in half an hour and his name would have waived aside all question of formalities. Monsieur O'Dowda's guest? Certainly. Mr. O'Dowda's guests were always important . . . politicians, film stars, the famous . . . naturally one would send the chauffeur down with a passport for identification.

So what did I do now?

O'Dowda had the parcel. I could imagine him and Kermode, sitting up there in their wax works, laughing their heads off, and probably celebrating with a few bottles of champagne. It would be good stuff, too, as the occasion demanded. Veuve Clicquot, Brut Gold Label, 1959, probably.

I chucked the cigarette out of the car window and swore. Aloud. One word. A good, coarse, satisfying one, and it did something for me. The key log in the timber jam slipped and the run began. O'Dowda was not going to keep the parcel. If ever God had made one man who was due for a disappointment it was O'Dowda. I elected myself as the chosen instrument to bring it about. I didn't know how, but I was going to do it. There wasn't any point in thinking of the hows and whys and whats. At this moment the only sensible course was to home on the target. But before I did I had to make sure of Julia's safety.

I went into the post office to the telephones and called Najib.

When he answered, I said, 'Look, there's a little hitch over the parcel. Nothing serious, but it might be rather later in the day before I can get my hands on it. Is that all right?' I tried to keep my voice normal. It wasn't easy.

Najib said, 'Let's get one thing straight, Mr. Carver. I'm trusting you over this. But I cannot go on trusting and waiting forever. If you do not telephone saying you have the parcel by six o'clock this evening, my deduction will be that you will never have it. In that case I shall have to take other steps. Just which at the moment defeats me. But one thing is certain. If someone else gets the parcel—then you know what will happen to Miss Julia. And, Mr. Carver—I shall know very soon if anyone else has it because they will not delay in letting us know. Anymore than I should delay in letting them know that I had it. Understand?'

'Don't worry,' I said lightly. 'You'll get it.'

I rang off and went out.

It was difficult to keep my speed low going through the town. Once through, I put my foot down hard. But if I thought that speed would wipe out thought, I was disappointed. All the way I kept asking myself—how? How was I going to get the parcel? Long before I got there it became clear to me that the last thing I could do was to barge in empty-handed on O'Dowda. The man dealt in force, understood power. The only way to deal with him was from a position of strength. That was the logic. How did one translate it into practical terms?

CHAPTER NINE

'I rage, I melt, I burn . . .'
JOHN GAY

I TURNED OFF the main road into the driveway to the château, but I didn't go straight to the place. I swung off up the track to the lake.

The Rolls-Royce was standing outside the cottage on flat rear tyres. I went into the cottage, looking for something that would weigh nicely in the hand and give me a feeling of confidence. I had no luck inside. My suit was there with my passport gone, and there was a mass of fishing tackle, but I couldn't find a single sporting gun or any other weapon. The best I could do was a heavy wrench from Kermode's bench.

But outside, an idea struck me. I went over to the Rolls-Royce. In the glove compartment was the compressed-air pistol which had been taken off me when they had jumped me in Geneva. I took it and left the wrench.

I drove back almost to the main driveway and then left the car in the cover of some trees. I made the rest of the way to the château on foot, keeping well off the drive.

A big shooting brake was parked by the entrance steps. I watched the château from the cover of the trees, saw no movement, and started to work my way around the back. I wanted to be inside without anyone seeing me enter. I found a side door and enough cover from a thick thuya hedge to get me to it unseen.

I went into a wide, stone-flagged corridor. When I was halfway down it a door opened suddenly a few yards ahead of me and a man came out and dropped a suitcase on the stone floor. It was Durnford and he saw me.

I went up to him, gun in hand, and he backed into the room.

I went after him. It was a bedroom and one glance showed me that he was in the process of packing up.

'Leaving the happy home?'

'Yes.'

He hadn't been drinking. He was stone cold sober. He was more than that. He was pure ice. Gone was the nervous flicker of the eyes, gone the bad-tempered officiousness. Something had happened to change him. Normally I might have tried to find out what, but at the moment I had my own problems.

I said 'Where are they?'

He turned and began to stuff shirts and underwear into another case. Over his shoulder, he said, 'On the second floor.'

'In the waxworks?'

'Yes. Celebrating. They had a case of champagne sent up.'

'Celebrating what?'

'I don't know. And if I did, I wouldn't tell you.'

He was right back to not liking me. And not only me. At this moment he wasn't liking anybody.

I said, 'How long will they be there?'

'Until they come out.'

'If they had a case sent up it might be a long time.'

'Yes. When they decide to get drunk, they take their time. They're both Irishmen. You know how drunk an Irishman can get.'

'I know how drunk anyone can get if they really set their mind to it. You've been sacked?'

'I handed in my notice.'

'Same thing. Can I get into that room?'

'Not unless they let you in.'

'But you've got some way of communicating with them—or they with you, surely?'

'Yes.'

'Lead me to it.'

'I'm not doing anything for you. You're as bad as they are. Money, that's all you're interested in. You never stop to think about anything else but that. Just money—and to hell with

227

what happens to anyone else. People don't mean anything to you.'

I said, 'I seem to remember a coloured number called Joseph Bavana that you helped once—to something very unpleasant.'

'That wasn't me. That was O'Dowda's personal secretary carrying out orders.'

'Same thing.'

He swung round from his pile of candy-striped pants and shouted, 'It is not! He's gone! Now—this is me! A different man!'

I said, 'Work it out any way you want. I'm not going to argue. But I want to talk to them and you're going to show me how. If you don't, I'll just tell the police what I know about Bavana, and the new Durnford won't get very far. It's not something I want to do, but push me and I will.'

He looked at me in silence for a while and then he said bitterly, 'Yes, you'd do it. You'd do anything to get what you want. Just for a while I thought that you might have something that a man could respect. But I know better now. You're like them. You'd put up any front, tell any lie that would help you to get what you want.'

'It's an interesting point, but I haven't time to discuss it. Just show me how to talk to them.'

For a moment or two I thought he was going to refuse. He just stared belligerently at me, hating me, hating himself more probably, and his mind all twisted up with memories of the woman he had loved who had been drowned in the lake; a mind that had been warped and commanded by O'Dowda to the point of revolt. Beyond that in fact. At this moment he wasn't sane. He was capable of anything. If he refused to show me, I knew that I could never make him.

With a slow, cunning look, he said, 'What are you going to say to him.'

'That's my business. I've got to have a talk with him. Come on, show me how.'

He gave me a nasty little smile and said, 'You're still trying to make something for yourself, aren't you? Still after a profit —no matter who else suffers?'

'I've got things to do. For my own personal satisfaction.'

'Quite.' He snapped the word at me. Then, abruptly, he turned and walked from the room. I followed him.

We went through a rabbit warren of corridors and finally fetched up at the foot of the main staircase. He went up ahead of me and down the wide upper hallway to the tall leather-covered steel doors of the waxwork room and halted in front of them.

I said, 'Can't they be opened from this side? I'd like to go in unannounced.'

He shook his head. 'Not if they've got the trip over on the inside. And they will have. Always do when they have a drinking bout.'

He went to the side of the doors and opened a small recess let into the wall. He pulled out a microphone speaker, flicked a switch in the recess somewhere, and said, 'O'Dowda!'

The way he said it must have given him great pleasure. He put into it everything he disliked about the man and worked off just a little of the years of servitude behind him.

There was no reply.

'O'Dowda!' Louder this time, and knocking off a few more years.

This time there was a reply.

From a concealed loudspeaker over the top of the doors O'Dowda's voice boomed, 'Who the hell is that?'

'Durnford.'

'Then get the hell off my property!' O'Dowda boomed, and roared on, 'Try to steal my wife, would ya, you rabbit-eyed bastard! Get to hell with ya!'

He'd been drinking all right, not yet drunk but expansive.

I saw Durnford's face tighten as he held on to his control. He put the microphone to his mouth and said, 'Carver is here. Wants to see you. And one of these days I'll prove you murdered her, you black-hearted bog-trotter.'

'Carver!' The voice boomed, and then a great gust of

229

laughter came over the speaker. He said, 'Well now, is he? Clear off, the both of ya.'

I said to Durnford, 'All right, you've done your bit, I'll take it from here.'

He handed me the microphone, and said, 'If you're wise you'll get out of this place. He's not drunk yet but he's in a mad mood. Whatever you want from him, you'll never get it.'

'You're damned right about that, boyo,' O'Dowda roared.

'Make yourself scarce,' I said to Durnford. 'When they do open up you might find Kermode at your throat. Go on.'

He hesitated for a moment and then said, 'Even if you can, I advise you not to go in there.'

'Don't worry.'

'I'm not. If you don't want my advice, don't take it.'

He turned and went away down the gallery. I watched him go and then walked down to the head of the stairs to check that he was really gone. I went back to the microphone.

As I picked it up, O'Dowda's voice yelled, 'Are you still there, Carver?'

I said, 'Why should I not be? I'm going to take at least five thousand pounds off you.'

There was silence. There had to be. I'd mentioned money, and money to O'Dowda was important, so important that any mention of it aroused his curiosity.

'And why would you be taking five thousand pounds off me?' His voice had lost some of its kick.

'In a straight sale. That's excluding my fees, of course.'

'And what would you have for sale, boyo?' He was coming back a bit, but I knew that I had him hooked.

I said, praying it would be so, 'Don't tell me that you just collected that parcel from Evian and stuck it straight in your safe without checking it?'

There was silence, a long one, and a heavy one for me. It was the kind of thing he could have done. It was what I wanted him to have done, because it was the one thing which would give me the little edge over him that I wanted, the one thing which gave me the remotest chance of getting Julia back. The silence went on. I let it. The longer it went on the better it was for me. I let it run until I knew that I was betting on a certainty.

I said, 'Don't tell me that a careful man like you put it away without checking it?'

He tried to bluff. It was clear in his voice.

'Of course I checked it.'

I laughed. 'You're a bad liar, O'Dowda. You think I'm such a fool that I wouldn't keep one ace up my sleeve? Dealing with types like you, Najib and Interpol? And anyway, I'm like you, O'Dowda, I don't trust the mails. That parcel at Evian was a phoney. Sent there to give me a breathing space if things went wrong—which I'll admit they damned nearly did at the lake. Are you with it? Are you listening good and hard? You haven't got what you think you've got, O'Dowda. If the safe's in there, check it and see—and then we'll talk.'

I sat down on an Empire chair by the door and lit a cigarette, blew smoke, and prayed. Hard. That his safe was not in the banqueting room. If it were my bluff was called.

I sat there, pretending to myself to be cool, knowing the runners were coming up to the last fence and mine leading, knowing that anything can happen at the last fence—and usually the thing you're praying will not happen. I blew a smoke ring and watched it spin up towards the loudspeaker over the door and then fade away like a grey dream.

Suddenly the big double-doors whined and slid back on their runners. Kermode stood just inside the threshold and he was holding a gun on me.

He said, 'Come in slowly and keep your hands out in front.'

I gave him a beaming smile. Why not? I'd won the first round. I was feeling good, but being careful not to be over-confident.

I went in and he halted me. Holding the gun at my navel, he ran his hands over my pockets. Aristide wouldn't have thought much of the job he made, or Najib, I guessed. I'd got the compressed-air pistol stuck barrel first into the inside of my left ginger suède shoe and the turn-ups of the suit trousers came well down, hiding it. The pistol was ten inches long, three or four inches of barrel in my shoe and the butt just above my ankle. The only thing I had to be careful about was fast movement because it weighed just under two pounds and could be shaken loose unless I watched it. I wasn't worried. I wasn't going to make one fast movement until I reached for the gun. Kermode's hand came down my leg, over my calf and stopped short a couple of inches above the pistol. He stood back.

'Take a seat over there,' he said. He pointed through the crowd to a divan that stood just in front of the Cairo merchant or whatever who had gypped O'Dowda in a diamond deal.

I went over and sat down carefully, crossing my legs so that the inside of my left shoe was hard up against the front of the divan and out of sight.

I looked around at the wax figures and said, 'Same old crowd you've got, I see. Time you made some new enemies.'

O'Dowda was sitting at the far end of the room, just in front of the candelabra-flanked, oversized effigy of himself. He was wearing a loose oriental dressing gown for comfort, black patent leather shoes with elastic sides, and a white turtle-necked shirt. The dressing gown was black with silver peacocks on it. He was lounging comfortably in an armchair with a table at his side on which stood glasses and a champagne bottle, and a hand microphone with a flex that trailed away into a far wall recess.

He stared at me with his small blue eyes out of a very red face, and said, 'Don't worry—you'll join 'em soon, you bastard.'

I said, 'If you want to do a deal with me, you overstuffed bullfrog, just keep things polite, will you?'

I was in, and I was enjoying myself, and I was full of comforting hatred for him, a warm, intoxicating desire to see all the kick and egotism knocked out of him. I'd taken a chance so far and it had worked. It had to be my day. I had that feeling that all men know . . . that feeling that the moment you strike the twenty-foot putt you know it's going to drop, that the moment you flick the line out with a Blue Upright on the end and it settles like a fairy on the water under the alders that a three-pounder is going to bulge up to it, that the moment you swing the gun up as they come fast and oblique down wind you're going to get one with each barrel. . . . I was feeling good, optimistic, ready for anything.

O'Dowda reached for his champagne glass on the table, lowered his head and sipped, watching me over the rim. Two yards from him was another armchair and a table stacked with bottles and glasses. That's how they liked it. To sit there, drinking, steadily getting tighter and shouting comments and abuse at their guests. Fun . . . once in a while.

O'Dowda said, 'You're a fool. You think I believe that stuff about the parcel? You're bluffing. If you had the real thing you'd never poke your nose in here.'

I gave him a friendly smile. 'If you really thought I was bluffing you'd never have opened the door. You couldn't have cared less about me. I'd come in the Julia category. By the way, I've decided that I don't want anything to do with that either. Oh, I've got a weakness for pretty women, but it never goes over the five-hundred-pound mark. My price, exclusive of my fee, is five thousand pounds.'

Kermode said, 'If the parcel isn't genuine, boss, all we have to do is persuade him, like before.'

'Do that,' I said. 'But it won't get you anywhere. The parcel's with a friend in Geneva. If I don't call her within the hour, she'll just phone Interpol and tell them I'm out here. They won't waste any time getting here.'

O'Dowda said, 'Her? What woman?'

I said, impatiently, 'For God's sake what woman do you imagine? How do you think I got out here, away from Najib? Miss Panda, of course. We sort of got together, financially and otherwise, to do ourselves a bit of good.' I reached for a cigarette in my pocket, saw Kermode tighten up, reassured him with a shake of my head, lip up, and said, 'Come on— check the parcel and let's get this over.'

I was doing well. I had them. I just told myself to go easy

and not get too confident. The difficult part was still to come. I wanted the parcel brought back into this room for checking.

The champagne helped me. O'Dowda was comfortable in his chair, he was used to having servants do things for him.

He said to Kermode, 'Go and get it. But give me that gun first.'

Kermode handed him the gun. Then he went out of the room.

O'Dowda held the gun on me with one hand and drew a new bottle of champagne across the table towards him with the other. He began to fiddle with the wire around the cork, one-handed, to open it, found it awkward and gave up. Kermode could do it when he returned. Behind him the lit candles surrounding his effigy flickered and smoked a little in the draught from the open doors.

He said, 'You could have got a price from Najib.'

I said, 'Yes.'

'Or from Interpol.'

'Yes.'

'Why come to me then?'

I shrugged my shoulders. 'You're slow, boyo. Bejabbers, you're slow, slower than an old bog donkey with a load of peat.'

He didn't like it, and I was happy. I went on, 'I want to take you. I want to show you that there's somebody around who can make you look like a shagged-out carnival giant. That's what you like doing to people, isn't it? Rubbing their noses in it. Well, that goes for me, too.'

Slowly, he said, 'I'm promising myself the pleasure of killing you inch by inch one day.'

'And there's another thing,' I said, ignoring him. 'I want you to have it. The moment you have, I'm getting on to my stockbroker to buy me a fat slice of shares in United Africa Enterprises. I should make a healthy profit from that when you begin to operate the monopoly you will get when Gonwalla goes.'

For a moment he screwed up his face, as though he had a bad taste in his mouth. He said, 'You're just like all the rest.

You hate my guts because I'm a millionaire, but all the same you'd like to be one. But remember this, Carver, whatever happens—I'll get you. You'll wish that you'd never been born.'

'We'll see,' I said. 'If I make enough money I might even have my own waxworks. I can think of a lot of people I'd like to have in it.'

I looked slowly around at the assembled company. Yes, I could think of a lot of people for my own collection. I finished up with my eyes on the steel doors. Kermode had left them open. When he came back he would be sure to shut them, so that if I were bluffing I couldn't make a quick departure. I wanted to see how the doors were operated. I wondered just how fast and how accurate I could be with the compressed-air pistol. As far as I could remember from sessions with Miggs this type of pistol usually grouped at under three-quarters of an inch at twenty-five feet. It ought to do the job I had in mind.

From outside, far down the gallery, I heard the sound of footsteps on the marble. Kermode was returning.

I glanced at O'Dowda, and said, 'Remember, no bargaining. Five thousand plus my fees and expenses, and I'll need it in cash at the handover.'

He said nothing. His big head was lowered, bull-like, and, he was watching me and the door behind me. I screwed round a little to keep the door in view. Just behind me a dowager-type with a little coronet perched on straw-coloured hair stared blankly towards the big wax figure of King O'Dowda on the raised dias.

Kermode came into view in the gallery, hugging my parcel to his chest. He came through the door, went to the right of it, raised his hand and pushed one of the two white knobs that were let into the wall—one for opening and one for shutting the door. He had pressed the one nearest the door. I would have to press the one farthest from the door to open it.

The doors slid across, and Kermode came up the room, past me and heading for O'Dowda. I knew the exact moment I wanted. It would be when Kermode handed the parcel over to O'Dowda for him to open and O'Dowda handed him the gun to keep me covered. I would have to shoot fast and move fast. I dropped my right hand low, just touching the inside of my left leg, feeling gently for the wide trouser turn-up so that I could get at the pistol.

Kermode stopped at the table by O'Dowda. O'Dowda ignored him and looked at me, gun in his hand still.

He said, 'Feeling nervous, boyo? You think I don't know you? You're playing a bluff right up to the last moment, hoping to get some advantage. I could even like you for it. You've got guts, all right. You sit there, smiling, but you're sweating inside.'

I said, 'You're the one who's nervous. You know you've been out-smarted, but you don't want to face the moment. Go on, open it. I want to see your face as you do.'

O'Dowda tapped the table for Kermode to put the parcel down. As he did so, O'Dowda handed him the gun.

'Keep that Anglo-Saxon bastard covered,' he said.

He was too late. As the gun rested between their two hands, butt towards Kermode, I jerked out the pistol and began to fire as it came up from near ground level. I went for Kermode's legs, hoping to make him fall. As I pumped away I was on my feet and moving for them. My aim was something that would have made Miggs spit with contempt. I saw wood-chips fly off the far leg of the table as the slugs smacked into it, saw Kermode moving fast, swinging the gun round, and saw O'Dowda throw up a fat hand to protect his face against the flying chips, and then the god of battles—who often makes up his mind far too late to be of any help in a just cause—came up trumps for once. Still firing, I swung the pistol left to get Kermode's legs and the movement made me fire high. The lead slugs smashed into the bottles of champagne that stood on the table and they went off like bombs. Froth spouted high, spraying over O'Dowda and Kermode. Shards of glass whined through the air viciously. I saw a red streak suddenly appear down the side of Kermode's face. Despite himself, he raised his gun-hand to it and by then I was in amongst them. I grabbed at the gun, got it, and wrenched it round until he had to let go to save his arm from being broken. It came free in my hand and I kicked out at his feet and he went down, thudding into the table, sending glasses, broken bottles and parcel flying.

By the time they had sorted themselves out, I was standing ten yards back from them, pistol in my pocket, parcel in one hand, and their gun in the other.

O'Dowda, who had been knocked backwards, picked himself up and stood shaking his head and rubbing at his eyes. Kermode sat on the floor, face wincing with pain, grabbing at one of his legs—in the last second a couple of stray slugs must have got him. An ugly line of blood ran down his face from a glass cut.

Suddenly O'Dowda came out of his shock. He looked at me, his face purpling and he roared, 'You bastard! By Jasus . . .' He started to come for me, crashing through the wreckage of the table. I fired at his feet, obliquely. The bullet hit the stone floor and ricocheted away, thudding into the stomach of the policeman effigy. It tottered and then fell to the floor.

O'Dowda pulled up fast.

'You come a step further, O'Dowda,' I said, 'and I'll let you have one where the bobby just got his.'

He teetered there, mad with frustration, and it was touch and go whether he came on. Then he saw wisdom and moved back a little and looked down at Kermode.

'You useless sod. I told you to keep him covered.'

Kermode didn't say anything. Buddies they might be but he still knew when not to argue with his master.

I said, 'Don't fuss, Kermode. You can pick the pellets out with some tweezers later. Just get on your feet and sit somewhere where I can see you. And that goes for you, O'Dowda. Sit down somewhere and keep your hands in the open.'

They did it slowly, under protest, but they did it.

I stood there, watching them dispose of themselves, and I was feeling good. I had O'Dowda exactly where I wanted him. And I was human. I had to tell him so. It was a pity, but there it was. I just had to tell him. It would have been better

237

if I had been magnanimous in victory and just cleared off. I should have stuck to action and left the preaching to others.

I held up the parcel. 'You were right, O'Dowda. I was bluffing. This is the genuine article. The blue films and a nice roll of tape that's political dynamite. How do you feel, master mind? King O'Dowda outwitted by one of the palace servants. O'Dowda, with men and money at his command; O'Dowda, who, if he wants a thing a certain way, fixes it that way and no expenses spared. . . . How does it feel to sit there now, feeling the wind going out of you?'

I should have known better. It was schoolboy stuff. Gloating stuff. When you've got what you want, get out quick is the motto. I ought to have known that, but then, again, it wasn't often that I had a chance to cast myself for the role of boy David, or Jack the Giant-Killer, with a touch of Sir Galahad thrown in.

I began to back to the door, covering them.

'Know what I'm going to do with the parcel? I'm handing it over to Najib in exchange for Julia. No money, just a straight exchange. That means you'll never get a thumb in Gonwalla's pie, ever. Means, too, that I'll lose my fee from you, but it will be worth it. Oh, yes, it'll be worth it. Every time your name comes up somewhere, I'll have a little chuckle to myself. I'll think of the oversized O'Dowda that I put in the hot seat to melt down to size.'

He sat there and looked at me. He said nothing, but I knew that he was feeling a lot. Close to him Kermode, still shaken, dabbed at his face with a handkerchief. Behind them, on their tall holders the candles flickered around the giant, throned effigy of King O'Dowda, lording it over his once-rebellious subjects, over the people who had thwarted him, or tried to out-cheat him from cheating them.

Then he said, 'One of these days, I'll get you, Carver.'

I backed to the wall by the door. 'Oh no you won't. The moment I'm gone, you'll want to forget me. You'll make a good job of it, too. You'll bribe your memory to make it a blank. But every so often it will come back.'

'Get the hell out of here!' He bellowed it at me.

'Gladly, O'Dowda.'

I tucked the parcel under my gun-arm and reached behind me for the wall knobs, found them, and pressed the one to open the door.

Nothing happened.

I pressed again. Still nothing happened. I pressed the other knob in case I had got them mixed up. Nothing happened.

Stupidly, I said, 'The damned door won't open.'

O'Dowda with a flicker of new interest said, 'That's your problem, boyo.'

To Kermode, I said, 'These are the pushes, aren't they?'

O'Dowda said, 'They are.'

I tried them again. Still nothing happened.

Just then there was a crackle from the loudspeaker over the door, and Durnford's voice came booming into the room. He sounded in good spirits as he announced a servant's farewell to a well-hated master.

'Be happy in there, you bastards! I'm glad to think that I shan't see any of you again. Goodbye—and the devil take you!'

'Durnford,' I shouted.

The loudspeaker gave a click and went dead.

'How the hell could he do it?' I asked.

Kermode said, 'He's pulled the main fuses from outside.'

'The doors are inch steel. You couldn't force them, Carver. You're stuck.' O'Dowda had begun to sound happy.

'The man's mad.'

'I'm inclined to agree. What the hell does he think this will achieve? Not that I care.' O'Dowda smiled. 'I'm just content to know that you're not away yet, Carver.'

After victory never preach. I could have been out of the place if I had kept my mouth shut.

I moved away from the door, covering them.

'I'm going to be very nervous if either of you two makes a move.'

I went slowly round the room. All the windows were close-barred on the outside. The glass could have been smashed but

239

no one could ever have squeezed between the bars. Keeping the two men in view, I went up as far as the curtained throne and looked behind. There was no other door leading out of the room. I went back to the main door and sat down.

'You were doing a lot of gabbing about master minds, Carver. Let's see you tackle this one.' O'Dowda got up and began to move towards the upturned table.

'You sit tight,' I said.

'You go to hell,' he said. 'You stay up there. This is our half of the room. And I'm thirsty.'

He salvaged a bottle and a glass and poured himself some champagne and then sat on the foot of the throne under his own outsized figure.

I said, 'Kermode. Get over to one of the windows, break it and the moment you see anyone outside give them a shout.'

Kermode looked at O'Dowda.

O'Dowda said, 'Do as the master mind says.'

Kermode went over to one of the windows, jabbed a lower pane with the leg of a chair, placed the chair by the window and sat down.

O'Dowda wrapped his loose robe tighter round himself and said, pointing, 'See that smooth city type.'

He indicated an elderly, distinguished-looking man in pin-striped trousers and black coat; a man with a square, honest face and nicely greying hair.

'Floated a company with him once. He was clever. Brilliant. And he got me to the point when he thought he had me on toast to the tune of thousands. He damned near did. As near as you are at this moment to doing me. Know where he is now? Doing time—eight years—for fraud. It must be bitter for him because the fraud was mine not his. I heard that his wife committed suicide. No kids, thankfully. I don't like hurting children until they're over eighteen.' O'Dowda rose and came halfway up the room carrying a bottle and a spare glass. He put them on a chair. 'This may be a long wait. No reason why you shouldn't have a drink.'

I said, 'If you come past that chair, I'll shoot.'

240

O'Dowda said calmly, 'I know you will.'

He went back to his throne and sat down. He filled his glass, raised it to me, and said, 'It'll take some time, but eventually I'll be missed and one of the servants will be up here. We'll get out—and then I'm shouting for the police, for Interpol, the whole boiling. I'm laying charges. Assault, armed robbery, the whole book. I'll make such a fuss that Interpol will have to back out because they'll be scared of the publicity. They will forget the parcel. Even they have their limits. Yes, boyo, one way and another it's you sitting in the hot seat. Ever been in a French prison? No coddling like in ours. French are a practical people. Punishment is punishment.'

I said, 'Before that happens I'll set fire to this lot.' I tapped the parcel.

'Yes. I see you'd do that. I'll accept that. But I'd still lay the charges. Eventually, boyo, I'll have you keeping my city friend company. Pilch his name was. Eye for the women, he had, too. Not that his wife ever knew, or she might not have committed suicide.'

I said, 'What happens up here if you want someone, want to have something sent up?'

'Good question,' said O'Dowda. 'And I'll be honest with you. Nothing. This is my place. When I come up here, I make sure there's everything I want here. Only two men have permission to disturb me up here, Kermode and Durnford. They use the loudspeaker. But if we sit here long enough, Kermode will spot someone from the window.'

I stood up and walked towards the champagne.

He grinned. 'Thought you might get round to it. If I'd known I'd have had some non-vintage stuff up here for you. Veuve Clicquot is only for friends. But this time I'll overlook it. You get a wine issue in French prisons, you know. Probably only plonk. So enjoy that while it lasts.'

I went back and sat down, put the parcel on the floor between my feet, and opened the champagne one-handed, steadying the bottle between my knees.

I was in a jam. I drank some champagne and tried to think.

Lots of thoughts came, but none of them seemed to have much comfort to offer in the present situation. I was really in it, up to my neck. We might be stuck here for hours. All day, all night. They could take it in turns to cat-doze. They were two to one. Eventually they would get me. There was no question about that.

I looked at my watch. We'd already been locked in for half an hour. I was feeling hot and tempted to take another glass of champagne, but I put the temptation from me. At any time O'Dowda or Kermode might try something. I couldn't afford to be fuddled.

Maybe some such thought had occurred to O'Dowda for he raised his glass to me and beamed over the top of it.

Across the room at the windows, Kermode kept watch on the outside world. If he did see anyone he probably would not say so, not yet, because he, too, must know that the waiting game up here was the one which would pay off for O'Dowda.

I picked up the parcel and, with the gun in my other hand, went over to the windows and pushed a chair into place. To Kermode, I said, 'You get back with him.'

He quit his place without a word and went over to O'Dowda. He sat down, rolled up his trouser leg and began to examine his pellet wounds. I sat at an angle, so that I could cast an eye outside from time to time and also keep the two of them in view. Outside it was a beautiful late September day, and miles away I could just glimpse a corner of the lake and a huddle of white houses shimmering in the heat haze on the far side. It was hot in the room. I ran the back of my hand across my forehead.

O'Dowda said, 'Finding it warm, eh?'

I said, 'You don't need the heating on on a day like this.'

He shrugged his big shoulders. 'On all the time. But there's an automatic control. Constant temperature of sixty-eight. You're only feeling hot because you're worried, Carver. You don't know what to do. Things are going to be much hotter for you before we finish. Pity—because if you'd played ball with me, I could have learnt to like you and put a lot of work your way. I might even have taken you into one of my organizations and made a fortune for you. But not now . . . oh no! I'm going to see you fry. I'm going to have you regretting that you ever knew me.'

I didn't answer. I sat there, enjoying the coolish air through the broken window. But for all the draught, I was still hot.

After a while I got up and moved so that I stood above one of the grids that covered the underfloor heating. Warm air was flooding up through it. For my money, it was a damned sight more than sixty-eight in the room. Something must have gone wrong with the thermostat. I went back to the window.

It grew hotter. There wasn't any doubt about it.

O'Dowda had noticed it too. He loosened the front of his oriental gown and said, 'What's that thermometer say?' He nodded to a wall space between two windows close to me.

I got up and checked the thermometer.

'Something's wrong with your system. It's seventy-two. Where's the thermostat?'

'In the gallery outside.'

'Well, if it gets any hotter you'll have all your guests here melting on you.'

He grinned and drank another glass of champagne.

I lit a cigarette, and glanced out of the window, and was rewarded with a sunny world in which nothing stirred except a pair of blackbirds kicking up soil in a worm search on one of the garden beds.

Kermode and O'Dowda refreshed themselves with champagne, and I sat smoking, one sticky hand holding the gun across my knees, and thought about the closed steel doors. Durnford was crazy. What the hell was the point of shutting us all in here? In fact, if he'd known that it was going to help O'Dowda, then he would never have done it—because O'Dowda was the man he hated. Then, why the hell be content to go off just leaving us all locked in? It was like throwing a snowball at a tank as far as O'Dowda was concerned. He really was crazy—yet crazy or not he was basically an intelligent

243

man and intelligence did not just disappear in a mad moment of hatred. Usually it reinforced the crazy action. He didn't have a very high opinion of me—largely because he thought that I'd failed him in mucking up O'Dowda's plans. But he didn't hate me as he hated O'Dowda. He'd advised me not to come in this room and see O'Dowda.

I stood up and loosened my tie, opening the neck of my shirt. Then I walked over and had another look at the wall thermometer. It was now reading eighty. I really was worried then because something had begun to nag at me.

I looked at the copper grid in the floor by the window. There was a line of them all round the room, set about two feet back from the walls. This one was fastened to the floor by a couple of screws at each end. Hot air streamed up through the ornamented grid work, very hot air.

I looked at the thermometer again. It now read eighty-two. Ever since Durnford had closed the doors on us the temperature had started to rise. When I had first come in here the place had been at a comfortable room heat. Now it was hot enough to grow orchids.

I looked across at O'Dowda and Kermode. O'Dowda, his gown flowing open untidily, was leaning back in his chair, glass in hand, watching me, the light from the candles behind him on the raised throne burnishing the stiff stubble of his red hair.

Kermode was sitting on the edge of the throne, a small, bent-up grasshopper of a man, the side of his face caked with dried blood, his dark eyes on me, full of interest, promising himself, no doubt, some dark pleasure of revenge when the moment came.

O'Dowda, imagining I was about to say something, said, 'Not so cocky now, eh? But don't waste your breath trying to make any deal. You're here and we're here and we're going to get you. So no deals.'

He was right. I was going to speak, but not about deals.

I said, 'What's the temperature limit on this heating system?'

244

They both looked surprised at the question, then Kermode said, 'Somewhere around ninety-five.'

I said, 'It's gone up from seventy to over eighty in the last ten minutes.'

'So what? It's that bloody fool Durnford. He's locked us in and turned up the regulator,' said O'Dowda. 'The man's gutless. He doesn't like us and that's all he can think of doing. I'd have had some respect for him if he'd pulled a gun on me —even though he was talking through his hat about all that murder stuff. Sit down, boyo, and take your jacket off and finish your champagne. Might feel like a nice sleep afterwards.' He chuckled to himself.

I had it then, of course. For the last few minutes it had been at the back of my mind, but now I had it clear. Durnford was crazy, but he was no fool. And there wasn't any question of his being willing to wound and afraid to strike.

I said quickly, 'Remember the first time I was in this room, O'Dowda? I handed over a thermal bomb to you. A big overweight beast of a thing that could blow this room to bits. What did you do with it?'

He wasn't any fool either. He was with me at once.

'I gave it to Durnford to get rid of.'

'Well, my guess is that he has. Somewhere in this room. Probably, on the pipes under one of the floor grids, that bomb is sticking like a limpet waiting for the temperature to hit the right mark. Durnford has pulled a gun on you all right, and the rest of us.'

They were both on their feet.

I said, 'Kermode, go quickly round this room and see if you can spot any grid screws that have been scratched or tampered with.'

'The windows,' said O'Dowda, and now there was alarm in his voice. 'Smash 'em open, that'll bring the temperature down.'

'Only the air temperature. It won't affect the bomb. It's clamped against a pipe somewhere.'

'We can take up all the grids and turn the heat off at the individual radiators,' said O'Dowda.

He was panicking now.

I said, 'There are about two dozen in this room and we need a screwdriver. The only thing to do is to spot the grid he used. We can rip that up, maybe.'

As I spoke, Kermode was already on his way round the room, examining the grids.

I checked the grids along the window wall. None of them showed signs of having been moved. The thermometer on the wall now read eighty-five. What would he have set the temperature control at on the bomb? Ninety? Eighty-seven?

Kermode came out from behind the throne and said, 'I can't see any grid that's marked.'

'Pull 'em all up,' shouted O'Dowda. 'Come on.'

He went to the nearest grid, bent, got his huge fingers in the ornamented copper-work and pulled. The soft copper face bulged upwards, stretching under his power, but the screws at either end held. And they would hold, I knew that. He was a millionaire. Millionaires don't tolerate shoddy work. In any suburban house the screws would have come out as though they had been set in soap. Anyone who worked for him was forced to give full value for money. That was his epitaph. I couldn't bother with mine. I checked the thermometer again; it was eighty-seven. I put what might be my last bet on Durnford having plumped for ninety and headed for the door. The grids ran all around the room except across the door end. If any spot was going to be safer than another, it might be this end. Also it was well away from the windows. I didn't want momentarily to survive the blast and have a sheet of glass take my head off.

Kermode stood, lost, at the foot of the throne and shouted, 'What the hell do we do?'

I said, 'Come down here and fix yourself some cover.'

As I spoke, I toppled over a duchess and laid her lengthways as a barricade. I piled a gent in diplomatic corps dress on top of her. At least I was observing social levels.

Kermode began to move, but O'Dowda, panicking, not believing that there wasn't something that could be done, working on the old millionaire's principle of maintaining immunity from everything unpleasant, shouted, 'Give me a hand with this!'

He was tugging at another grid, the sweat lacquering his red face. Kermode hesitated, glancing towards me as I broke the social code and put a Coptic bazaar merchant on top of the diplomatic corps man.

O'Dowda roared at Kermode again and Kermode went to him. He had to, he had to bank on survival, and that meant he had to be in O'Dowda's good books. Master and man, it's a bond that lasts right up to death, when the master is a millionaire. I was glad I was my own master and man. There was no quarrel between us. I added three more bodies and then propped a tall, thin, ascetic-faced university don with a fur-tipped robe against the pile. I wondered what he'd done to annoy O'Dowda. Voted against him in convocation, maybe, when the others wanted to give him an honorary law degree in return for some new university building.

Between them, they ripped up the grid at last, buckling it back. The screws were still holding but they gained enough room to feel inside. O'Dowda bent and groped and almost immediately was up and reaching for another grid. He was a trier. With luck—and it would have to be the luck of the Irish —he might strike the right grid this time, might even get it opened up and have his hand poised, but he was running a race with ninety degrees Fahrenheit and my bet was that it was pushing the eight-nine mark already.

Gun and parcel in either hand, I settled behind my barrier and shouted, 'For God's sake be sensible. Get some cover away from the grids!'

Kermode, straining at the grid with his master, turned and looked at me. All he could see was my head behind the barricade. His eyes were full of longing, but he dared not leave his master.

Then suddenly he straightened up, taking his hands off the grid.

'KERMODE!' roared O'Dowda angrily.

'Wait a minute.'

Kermode turned and ran towards the throne. There was a strip of fine Persian carpet across the floor four yards away from the monstrous effigy of O'Dowda. He ripped it aside. There was a grid underneath it.

'I'd forgotten this one. . . .' He bent over, examining the screws. 'This one! This one!'

O'Dowda moved towards him, gown flying, knocking over a table as he went, shoving a Rajah-like figure, turbanned, white-suited, out of his way.

'The screws . . . look!' Kermode pointed.

And then they were at it, fingers gripped in the copper work, both of them putting their backs into it. The bomb had to be under there. That's where Durnford would have put it. Under the monstrous effigy, and close to where O'Dowda normally sat. If Kermode had remembered that grid at the start. . . .

I yelled, 'Give it up! Get down here!'

They took no notice of me. Big man and little man, sweating at the grid, master and man, linked by so many things in the past: loyalties, villainies, drinking bouts, fishing trips, rough houses in the old days, sophisticated manipulations as the master grew richer, and always the one thinking he was untouchable, his own law, and the other knowing himself safe in the shadow of the other's power. And they didn't listen to me. They had forgotten that I was there. You don't sit down and let unpleasant things happen to you, not an O'Dowda, you fight and you overcome. That was how it had always been and that was how it would be, had to be, or life was not worth living.

I dropped behind my barrier, snuggled in against the cold, bare wax back of the duchess and then pulled the don down on top of me.

As I did so it happened. The end of the world. There was a bang as though a jet had broken the sound barrier in the room, and everything moved. I was slammed backwards, tangled up in duchess, diplomat and don, towards the steel doors. I should have been killed. I thought I was killed, ears ringing, all breath gone from my body. The steel doors waited for me, waited for the shock-wave to slam me against them and flatten me. But the wave must have hit the doors a second ahead of my body and flung them back like untidy crumpled wings. I slid twenty yards down the gallery and lay flat, eyes closed, waiting. . . . And in the waiting I heard glass crashing, heard plaster and stone and wood falling and breaking.

I came slowly to my feet and, dazed, rubbed dust and grit from my eyes and face. On the floor at my feet was my gun and the parcel, and the severed head of the duchess with a six-inch glass splinter sticking out of her right cheek. I stepped over a red-tabbed general, half of his white moustache torn away and one glass eye shattered, and made for the door.

The room was full of smoke and dust and I could only just see the full length of it. There was no sign of O'Dowda or Kermode. But there were heads and arms and legs scattered all over the place. Most of them were wax. As I went over the threshold, staggering, not really knowing what I was doing, a gentle rain began to fall on me from the remnants of the fire sprinkler system in the roof. I went through it to the throne. The curtains and woodwork on both sides were burning away, and the robes of O'Dowda's effigy were blazing. The flames licked up around its face as it lay on the floor, one arm and one leg severed. I stood looking at it from a distance, and wondered if I were still really alive, or trapped for ever in some nightmare of death. O'Dowda was burning and melting away.

The wax of the face began to run. With the heat beating at my face, still full of stupidity from the shock-wave, I watched the great figure slowly melting before me, melting down to size, melting down to less than size. The sprinkler rain fell on my bare head, streaking down my dirty cheeks like tear-runnels, and the blaze burned fiercely at my skin so that I slowly began to step back, my eyes on O'Dowda's wax face. As the features ran away into shapelessness, I watched in horror at the thing that came swelling up through the wax into the flickering flame-light. Slowly, like a film developing, another face surfaced, grimacing up at me through the running, bubbling wax,

249

another face, fleshless, eye-sockets first dark, then filled by the fire and alive with hissing little flames. A mouth grinned, tight, and then slowly fell open as the jaw broke away and slid to the floor with burning wax spurting little red and yellow tongues from it.

Behind me, miles away it seemed, I heard voices shouting, heard a great stir of life, bells, sirens, and the clatter of feet.

I staggered to a far wall, bent over and vomited, knowing that the horror was going to be with me on many a night . . . the sight of a small, fragile skull slowly coming back into the light as O'Dowda's face melted away.

As I straightened up, I saw the real O'Dowda. When the bomb had exploded Kermode must have been shielding him. He had been slammed away across the room to hit the window wall like a two-hundredweight sack of corn. He lay huddled against the wall and floor angle, naked from the waist up, his head cocked horribly to one side and his one remaining leg twisted back up under his body. In the fingers of his right hand, outflung, was still held a large, jagged piece of the copper grid-work.

I went back, out of the room, leaving the fire flaring away around the throne. I picked up the parcel, nearly falling from giddiness as I did so, and then staggered away down the corridor, tucking the parcel into the waistband of my trousers and buttoning my jacket-front over it.

Sitting in a red velvet chair at the head of the stairs was Durnford, smoking, quiet, composed. He looked at me, nodded, as though congratulating himself on a neat piece of arrangement. O'Dowda and Kermode killed—main targets; Carver, shaken, contrite—minor target; and he, himself, not caring what happened now, because no one could ever take away from him the savour of the last hour, content to wait, no man able to touch him.

He said mildly, 'I phoned the fire brigade. They're arriving now.'

I said, throat dry, words coming like the dry rustle of old reeds, 'I don't feel in the mood for company.'

He pointed to a side door beyond his chair. 'Go through there. Down the stairs at the end and you'll find the garage.' Then, as I braced myself for the move, he said, 'How was he at the end?'

I said, 'I thought it was panic, but it wasn't. He just knew, as always, that nothing could ever beat him. He missed out by about five seconds.' Then I went to the door and, my hand on it, added, 'When the police get here they won't let you into that room. If you want to make your farewell, do it now.'

'To him?'

'No, to her. She's on the throne, waiting for you.'

He looked at me, not understanding for a moment, and then he got up slowly and began to move away, up the gallery towards the smoke-veiled and water-sprayed room. I found my way down to the garage and out across the grounds, knowing that I had been lucky. The exception. I had got away with something that belonged to O'Dowda. That was a record. Even the things he owned but no longer wanted, he kept. Just as he had kept her, locked up in himself. . . .

CHAPTER TEN

'Kissing don't last: cookery do!'

GEORGE MEREDITH

THE FACEL VEGA was still where I had left it. I crawled into it like a hermit crab going back to its shell and drove off. A fire tender nearly put me into the bushes before I reached the main gates. Nobody can accuse a French *pompier* of not driving with panache. A police car nearly did the same for me as I turned into the main road. Somebody shouted at me through an open window. I didn't stop. It could have been Aristide Marchissy la Dole.

I went down to the lake and along to Geneva, and I kept seeing that melting wax face, bubbling and seething, and the horror coming up through it. I was going to have bad dreams for a long time unless I got away and grabbed my long-promised holiday.

I stopped at a call box and rang through to Najib.

I said, 'I've got the parcel for you. How long will it take you to get Julia?'

'No damned time at all.'

'I'll meet you outside the west end of the Cathedrale de Saint Pierre in half an hour. Okay?'

'We'll be there, and as a bonus you'll also get two thousand pounds.'

'You're slipping,' I said. 'The Alakwe brothers always pay in guineas.'

'Guineas,' he said.

I drove to the cathedral and waited.

They made it in twenty minutes, so they must have been holding Julia in Geneva somewhere.

They came trooping across to me in a merry family party, the Alakwe brothers, Miss Panda Bubakar and Julia.

I stood by the car and waited for them.

Jimbo patted Julia on the shoulder and pushed her gently towards me. He was wearing a green corduroy jacket, black trousers, a yellow shirt and a red tie with a great leaping salmon on it. He couldn't have known that the salmon touch was the reason for my frown.

He said anxiously, 'You tell him, missee, we treat you with every respect and courtesy.'

Julia came into the crook of my arm. She didn't have to tell me anything. It was all in her face.

I handed the parcel to Najib. He fingered it, and I knew he was itching to open and check it.

'Go on,' I said. 'It won't offend me.'

'I trust you,' he said.

Panda semaphored her teeth and eyes at me and said, 'You never gave me a chance. Everything I had I was ready to trust you with. Don't forget, lover-boy, when she throws you back in the pond you come swimming to Mamma. Whoof! Whoof!' She did a high kick, pirouetted, and tossed me a fat envelope.

'American dollars,' said Najib. 'All you do now is avoid the arm of the law.'

I shook my head. I said, 'You can twist it a bit for a while, but never avoid it.'

We drove off, heading for Bonneville and then the road to Megeve.

She said nothing for a long while.

I said eventually, 'Where do you want to stop and do the shopping?'

'Anywhere. You sold the parcel to them?'

'No—it was a straight exchange for you. I didn't ask for any money. But when it was offered I thought I had earned a bonus.'

I went on and told her all that had happened since I had last seen her. Before I had finished her hand was out just touching me on the arm, and when I had finished she said, 'But what happens about you and Interpol now?'

I said, 'I don't know and I don't care. I'm just not going to think about it. What are you planning to cook for dinner?'

We had *poulet sauté aux olives de Provence*. While she was making it I had a bath and changed and laid out my ritzy pyjamas, and then I came down and sat and drank and got up each time she called from the kitchen for her glass to be refilled and it was on the second refill that her arms went round my neck and her lips found mine.

'I'm a shy girl, really,' she said. 'I always need time.'

'Don't rush anything.'

The *poulet* was delicious.

As she disappeared to make the second course, the telephone rang.

It was Aristide.

He said, 'I thought I should find you there. You have company?'

I said, 'She's just served me with *poulet sauté aux olives de Provence*.'

He said, 'Did she serve the chicken on top of the hot sauce, or pour it over the bird?'

'On top.'

'Treasure her.'

'For the time that is left to me, I shall.'

'Ah yes, it is of that which I wish to speak. You had much trouble with O'Dowda, of course?'

'Of course.'

'The whole room was gutted, including many valuable paintings. However, enough was left to establish the secondary matter of murder. My people are pleased about that.'

'I am so happy that they are.'

'They were disappointed about the parcel, though.'

'Naturally.'

'Until I explained that you were, in fact, making an heroic effort to recover it for us, and that it was not your fault that the flames consumed it. On your behalf—and you will understand that I can think of no one else for whom I should do such a thing, and not a very strong reason why I should do it for you, except that, of course, I have a sentiment for you which, illogical though it be, I am forced to acknowledge, since I feel —and you will bear with me in this——'

'I can bear with you, Aristide, but somewhere I have lost myself in your sentence.'

'*Enfin*, I have persuaded them to abandon any drastic action. You were trying to get the parcel for us, you failed. Disobedience is punishable, but not failure. So you should be happy now, yes?'

'Very.'

'Good. But also you must not go unscathed.'

'It's a good word.'

'Najib drew a large sum of American dollars today, we are informed by his bank. I presume they are in your possession?'

'You speak officially or privately?'

'Both. Interpol have a charitable fund with which they do much good. Often it receives anonymous contributions. May we expect another soon?'

'I will send the money to you.'

'I am delighted. Money is always to be treated seriously, and talking of money, I would advise you, if you can bring yourself to it, to marry this Miss Julia. She will undoubtedly inherit much wealth from O'Dowda. She will have you, and you will have her and her money, and I shall never be bothered with you again. We shall all be happy.'

'Except Miss Julia,' I said. 'If you keep me on the line after she brings in the *omelette soufflée aux liqueurs*, which she is now making.'

He gave a deep sigh, and said. 'In the village of Inxent in northern France there is an inn where they make it perfectly. If she does not bring it to the table frothing and on the point of spilling over the dish, do not marry her.'

It came to the table, as he had said it should, filling the room with the aroma of fresh eggs, sizzling butter and the warm, heartening smell of liqueurs.

There were many times in the next two weeks when I knew that I would marry her, and then there were days when I wasn't sure, and in the end I agreed with Meredith, *Kissing don't last: cookery do!* But who wants to spend his life just eating?

So, in the end I retrieved my four thousand dollars from under the linoleum and went back into the big swim, wondering how long it would take to get my fees and expenses from O'Dowda's executors, and hoping that Panda was nowhere around. But Wilkins was, and no smile or warm word did I get from her until she came into the office one morning to find an electric typewriter waiting for her.

She beamed, and then almost immediately frowned.

'Why did you buy a German machine? British makes are just as good. Not that I've got anything personally against the Germans but one really should support . . .'

I shut my office door on her. You can't win.